T0095082

The Silent War

The Silent War

Wayne Patrick

iUniverse, Inc.
Bloomington

The Silent War

iUniverse books may be ordered through booksellers or by contacting:

iUniverse
1663 Liberty Drive
Bloomington, IN 47403
www.iuniverse.com
1-800-Authors (1-800-288-4677)

ISBN: 978-1-4620-3559-5 (sc)
ISBN: 978-1-4620-3560-1 (hc)
ISBN: 978-1-4620-3561-8 (ebk)

Library of Congress Control Number: 2011911150

Printed in the United States of America

iUniverse rev. date: 10/20/2011

This first walk on the wild side is dedicated to my son, Trevor, who swindled me into a Byron-provoked-Mary Shelley-like competition to create, and to my wife, Ellen, who encouraged my efforts and consequently endured four years of sleepless nights never forsaking our love.

PART 1

WARNING SHOTS

"True—nervous—very, very dreadfully nervous I had been
and am; but why will you say that I am mad? The disease
has sharpened my senses—not destroyed—not dulled them.
Above all was the sense of hearing acute.
I heard all things in the heaven and in the earth. I heard
many things in hell. How, then, am I mad? Hearken!
And observe how healthily—how calmly I can tell you the
whole story."

The Tell-Tale Heart—Edgar Allan Poe, 1843

CHAPTER 1

THE SPARK

"How could you ask me if I enjoyed the party? You know I only go to these parties of yours because it could mean more money for you," Mary McShane said to her husband with a smile, while driving in the fast lane of the freeway. She almost always drove in the fast lane, even on a night like tonight when there were no other cars on the road. "Your boss loves me, you know. He told me so." She enjoyed serving her wit with a facetious bite.

"I don't know about that, Babe," her husband, John, said from the passenger seat, his words a bit slurred from one too many glasses of Christmas cheer. "But even though you weren't drinking tonight, you sure looked like you had fun."

Mary laughed. "How would you know, looking out from the bottom of a Stoli bottle?" She turned her head toward John to glimpse his reaction to the clever comeback. Her long, auburn-dyed hair slipped off the left shoulder of her white silk blouse and dangled in front of the steering wheel. She loved to make him laugh, and in this, she excelled.

The smile she anticipated was missing. It seemed to have been snatched in an instant by fear, as his face lit up like a holiday tree on fire. Her eyes widened seeing the look of horror stamped into his handsome face, his mouth wide open. Her smile vanished.

Throwing his hands out toward her, he shouted, "Look out!"

Mary caught a glimpse of two bright lights shaking violently, getting much too big and way too fast.

Oh, my God! Where the hell did you come from?

With a crack like a lightning strike, the head-on crash echoed into the December night. It knitted together an old clunker of a pickup with the McShane Pontiac Grand Am using crushed and pleated sheet metal stitches.

An air bag deployed with a wallop, instantly mashing Mary's nose and snapping her head backward into the headrest. Stars replaced the headlights. Blackness blotted out vision.

Her body jerked forward with agonizing tension across her chest in a successful yet painful restraint. The left side of her neck and her right ribs burned in pain.

A fierce jolt of pain shook her entire body, as the collapsing front end of the car assaulted passenger space with vengeance and a roar, obliterating all other noise including the stereo. Mary's legs snapped in agony under the intense pressure of the conquering floorboard. The steering wheel, in spite of the air bag, punched her chest so hard she lost her breath.

She wanted to faint, expected it at any moment, but somehow remained on the edge of consciousness. She felt sick and drained at once. She screamed inwardly, endured the torture, and wished to be knocked out cold.

And then the violence stopped. In the relative stillness, pain took over, growing stronger.

Mary felt wedged. Unable to move, her chin slumped to her chest, her forehead resting on what she assumed was the steering wheel. She sat in total submission. That's when the tears came. Only tears. Unrestrained crying was impossible because she could barely breathe. Her senses tried to cope, but the sting of affliction bullied them into regression, an escape. For what seemed like eternity, Mary drifted into a silent world without substance.

She inched back to reality with the sound of faint ticking noises, and then the stereo. Incredibly, it still worked. Strange how those ticking noises came before the much louder stereo.

Then, she began to feel again. Not overpowering pain as before but the minute sensation of something dripping. Blood. She felt it trickling from her face onto her white silk blouse and down her chest. She realized she was breathing, not through her clogged nose, but through her mouth, in short, rapid gasps. Her chest was unable to fully expand. Even though her eyes were closed, she knew what it was. *My nose is broken.* Just like she knew blood was dripping down her crushed legs and the sensation she felt was not a swarm of insects assaulting her shins and rushing to her feet.

Her attention snapped to John. Is he okay? Oh, God, what happened to him? She refused to believe the bad thoughts to which her mind ran. He was hurt. But he couldn't be. *Not my Johnny.* No. He promised he'd always be there. She needed to see him, to find out how he was, but she couldn't move her head. The effort sent a new surge of pain into the back of her head. If anything . . .

"John?" she whispered in a gurgling and muffled voice. She waited then tried again, this time a little louder.

Why is he not answering?

She knew why, deep inside, but refused to believe. He didn't respond.

The sound of a desperate baby crying for its mother could not have elicited a fraction of the powerful emotions of sorrow and urgency that Mary experienced in thinking what this horrible accident had taken from her. The thought of loosing John forever was no less crushing than the thought of never seeing her son Charles again. The poignant yearning in her heart for the two great loves of her life forced her to fight against the pain.

The hand of God molded a twisted and doubtful future through this head-on collision, and she felt this thought reflected in the twisted features of her dejected face. Tears welled in her eyes and ran down her puffy cheeks to join the blood flowing from her battered and broken nose.

"John? Can you . . . hear me?"

Only the stereo made any sound.

She had to know. Amid all the pain and suffering, she dug deep inside to find the strength to open her eyes. That was a start. They were sticky, almost glued shut. The movement of her eyelids hurt. Nothing like the pain in her legs, but pain nonetheless. She willed them open and prayed desperately that she might see her husband alive, at least like she was; clinging to life, determined to survive, working to beat the odds.

The effort paid no reward. All she saw was the dark, deflated airbag.

If she could have clenched her broken fingers, or stomped her shattered legs, she would have, to emphasize the sudden rage that now filled her spirit. All she wanted was to see him. *Is this too much to ask?* In denial, her wrath eclipsed her pain and this horror she was forced to endure.

Damn this accident, and whoever caused it. When I get through this, I will find out who did this and I will have my revenge. God help me.

She began shaking. Uncontrollably. In anger, or pain, or shock, she wasn't sure, but Mary wallowed in misery, while her relaxing eyelids slowly descended. And with their closing, she imagined that she stood at the edge of a small stream between life and death, and watched while it grew, until it became a bloated expanse so wide the banks on the far side blurred from her view.

* * *

From the time the call came into the firehouse, it took twenty long minutes for the ladder truck to arrive at the accident scene. A plume of drifting steam directed by a cool, light breeze flowed from the accident across the slow lane to the west. It became disoriented and chaotic with the wind blown by this first emergency vehicle's arrival.

The driver, Kip, as apparatus operator and second in command to the captain, parked his rig at an angle near the crash to block all lanes of southbound traffic for scene safety. He turned off the sirens but left his emergency lights pulsing into the darkness. Distant wails announced more emergency vehicles on the way.

Kip surveyed the accident scene. Dissolved safety glass salted and dirt and gravel peppered mechanical gravy composed of a mixture of oil, gas, and radiator fluid. The accident gods would be pleased with this newest gourmet contrivance. This exotic mixture, together with plastic debris, seasoned a desolate stretch of the Estrella Freeway west of Surprise, Arizona, which the rubbernecking northbound drivers failed to savor.

"It's game time, Captain," Kip said. He got out, leaving the task force commander in the cab to direct police cruiser arrivals to drop flares and close down the freeway at the nearest exit.

With twenty years of heavy rescue experience, Kip quickly assessed the scene and ordered critically needed resources by radio. Two firemen under his direct command frantically pulled enough hose to reach around both vehicles and loaded the line with water. One stood ready at the hose while the other pulled the pin on a dry-chem extinguisher.

Within a minute of arrival, Kip and the captain checked the victims involved and formed a game plan to prioritize and extricate them. The male driver of the pickup and the male occupant in the passenger seat of the Grand Am were already dead. The female driver in the Pontiac was unconscious and slumped behind the wheel, in critical condition but still alive. Her eyes revealed unequal pupils, a sign of major head injury. The crushed metal encasing her body and the steering wheel wedged into her chest indicated other major trauma that would need to be further appraised. The focus was on her in the race for life.

"This one's number one, Cap. She'll need the Jaws," Kip said, and ran to his rig.

The captain shouted orders to new arrivals. He informed paramedics of the status and location of Number One. Still more firemen assembled needed equipment at the driver-side door and around each vehicle, chocking wheels for stability and safety.

Kip cut his way through metal to remove the driver door. Paramedics worked on the patient from the rear seat, all the while being serenaded by Blue Oyster Cult's song, *The Reaper*, on the stereo. Kip thought it fitting, but annoying. It segued into Ozzy Osbourn's, *Mr. Crowley*, which continued to play until another fireman cut the battery cables, reducing the risk of an electrical fire.

Kip hydraulically pried the driver's seat away from the steering wheel in the Pontiac as fast as he could without subjecting anyone to additional hazards. The paramedics took immediate steps to control bleeding and stabilize the woman's neck.

The job ended ten minutes later as the patient was removed from the Pontiac, her neck C-spined. She was secured to back boards and strapped to a gurney with an IV started before she was loaded into the waiting ambulance.

Fifteen minutes later, while other firemen retrieved equipment and cleaned up the scene, Kip threw his helmet onto the bench seat of his rig next to a paramedic filling out a medical form in the passenger seat. The coiled radio wire in the cab stretched outside through the passenger door where the captain was deep in conversation.

"Didn't even get to ask her what day it was," Kip said. "She never came around." Kip's white, reflective safety stripes blazed in the glow of headlights from the engine company truck as he began removing his fifty-pound, full turnout fireman's coat. The smell of spent diesel fuel filled the air.

"Well, Kip," the paramedic said, not bothering to look up from his clipboard, "don't feel so bad. She won't be talking to anybody. Captain here," he looked over at Kip while pointing with his pen at the commander, "is in touch with the ambulance driver. Says the woman died on the way."

"Oh, shit. That sucks." Kip threw his coat on top of his hat.

The paramedic slid further away from the increasing pile on the seat.

"At least none of them were crispy critters this time," Kip said, and then smirked at his own gallows humor. The paramedic flashed a knowing smile. Kip was always amazed at how stress created such a strange brand of humor among his comrades in the fire department.

"What was her name? You know?" Kip asked.

"Ah, Mary . . . Mary McShane," the balding paramedic said. "The passenger was her husband, John. They were probably on their way home from a Christmas party. Had to toss gifts from the back seat to access her."

Kip shook his head.

"The other driver had no ID. The truck is registered to Pablo Morales . . . expired, of course. May or may not be him. I'm thinking he's illegal. They never carry ID, only large amounts of cash, had almost four hundred bucks on him. Probably not a drug runner, not enough cash. Money's probably the remains of pay day minus the cost of getting drunk."

"Fucking idiot, if you ask me," Kip said. "Crossed the median drunk as a skunk. Cops think he was doing about a hundred when they hit."

"Yeah?" The paramedic said. "Well, I'm just glad I never have to be the one who calls to tell the family members the good news."

CHAPTER 2

THE WORD

Charlie McShane isolated himself in his dead parent's living room, a brooding angry victim. He sat on the floor with his back propped against the base of the fabric sofa among all the clutter and boxes from his move avoiding work and his friends, Ben and Becka. He contemplated the cruel random circumstances that masqueraded in the guise of an accident, which authored the murder of his beloved mother and father at the hands of a drunk undocumented Mexican driver as they headed home from a holiday party. The asshole—driving under the influence according to the state police and driving while Mexican INS agents submitted—lost control at one hundred, crossed the median, and met John and Mary McShane head-on in a mangled, two-vehicle wreck.

Charlie dwelt on these events in the swirling heated waters of his mind and bitter thoughts, like bubbles, rose from the depths. They grew larger, more numerous, and threatened boiling hate. In his simmering temperament, where no whistle or alarm would become audible to anyone, the physical exertion involved in moving back into his parents' house to save money exceeded his ability. The move became another vulgar victim abuse. Manual labor of any kind, for any purpose, became a distant thought lost in the far galaxy of his embroiled attentions. Three pickup truck loads of all Charlie's worldly possessions were moved from his apartment back into his old house without any help from Charlie.

A voice that Charlie perceived as distant and muffled disturbed his thoughts. "Where do ya want this box, Charlie?"

Charlie judged the sounds to be an unwanted interruption, a slight outside disturbance to the more important concerns within his mind, unworthy of acknowledgement. The question would remain unanswered. In Charlie's inner world of distorted painful reality, verbalization was hard to achieve and concentration should not be hindered. The sound of a box dropping to the floor near Charlie's feet in response to perceived rudeness did not move him to speak.

Instead, he continued to surf through his web of memories and past events, as though selecting video images on YouTube in the advanced-hate search preference. He attempted to gain some insight, to rationalize the misery and contemplate certain recollections that, when compared to his current circumstances, might help him deal with the traumatic, life altering circumstances.

Charlie's exploration paused at the World Trade Center disaster, a day, in his opinion, worthy of comparison to what he now felt. The shocking news of the terrorist attack affected him in a similar fashion. The terrorists had a goal in view resulting in the destruction, but the seemingly accidental occurrence of an uncontrollable event caused trepidation on a grand scale that day. Fear, easy to perceive but difficult to define, took root in Charlie on the way to school and it compared reasonably to the fear he felt now in a life without parents.

He had many unanswered questions then—as today—that created anxiety and frustration in his mind. Drifting apprehension blossomed to loathing for the terrorists while at school. Hate swelled heavily in his mind as the days passed and grew like the trailing black smoke that stretched for miles from the Towers as they burned. The fear and depression of losing his parents resulted in hate for the cause of it.

His feelings after 9/11 were unfocused and the intensity diluted; it happened far away in New York City and the terrorists were either already dead or located far away. Inaccessibility. The hate, he reasoned, lost potency because he could do nothing about what had occurred. In the end, only frustration remained.

The current situation with the murder of his parents, though, was personal and not far away. The Mexican terrorist, as Charlie came to regard the driver, killed them right on the 303 Loop. Charlie considered the so-called accident a personal attack by Mexicans, an act of war by a martyr that he could not and would not accept lying down. Something needed to be done.

After considerable thought, he decided to rise to the challenge thrown down at his feet by the asshole Mexicans. He would go to war in response to the terrorist attack as the United States had done.

THUMP!

"That's the last box, Charlie," Ben said, dropping the final box from Charlie's move on the floor near the front door, the only space left to fit the last carton. As luck would have it, there was nothing breakable inside. Ben took off his hat to mop his face on his shirtsleeve. "Da job of puttin' this shit away is all yours buddy." Ben turned and went back outside.

An icy quiver rose to the back of Charlie's neck when he considered how much more intense his hatred had become due to personal involvement. Waves of black clouds fueled thoughts of impending conflict and hostile premonitions. His heart quickened with each crashing wave in consideration for what should be done about the travesty in his mind, but the adrenalin rush, he felt sure, was unnoticeable to the outside world. Only the slight quiver he felt of his left cheek betrayed his outrage and the looming counter attack he began to plan for the future.

Turning his stare from the repair-spackled wall across the room, he focused his dark attention to follow Ben through the screened door into the bright, glorious day outdoors.

Outside, on this first day of the year, the weather assumed the role of paradise found, the reason why residents and visitors alike enjoyed being in the Arizona desert. A slight breeze blew and kept the normal, brown-haze pollution in the air at bay; deep blue skies were streaked only by white, puffy contrails of jets headed to California. Asthmatics breathed easier, and the surrounding mountains, seemed clear, majestic confirmations that nature's vacuum system was indeed working.

The usual college-bowl games were being contested and broadcast on the airwaves. Over-zealous revelers endured hangovers from the night before. The majority of the employed population relaxed on the last day of the three-day holiday weekend; New Year's fell on a Monday and gave all the more reason to celebrate—another perfect day in paradise that felt like a Sunday.

According to an unwritten rule, if someone has a day off from work, it should automatically be a good day, almost an enjoyment obligation day, at least better than a workday. But rules have exceptions and in the suburb of Phoenix, in the City of Glendale, Charlie McShane illustrated the exception.

Charlie's parents lived in a middle-class neighborhood built sixteen years ago by a national builder that cut corners whenever possible to save money in the cookie-cutter-style development. The subdivision was built on flat farmland, devoid of trees, and unless the new-home buyer paid extra for landscaping, houses were undressed displaying naked dirt. Years later, the aging neighborhood was still clothed in unremarkable scenery; green lawns peppered with weeds, queen-palm trees nearing the end of their life cycle, and overgrown flowering shrubs dotted the community. In some instances, established lawns became neglected disgraces due to the lack of a homeowner association to enforce proper care. In other cases, careless homeowners, or those that over-stepped their budget to buy a house in the first place, caused the blight. Many of the stucco exteriors were in need of paint.

The McShanes left the New York metropolitan area during the junk bond induced economic recession of the late eighties and moved into the brand new neighborhood to begin establishing roots in the transient population of melting-pot desert dwellers. They represented one of the lower middle class families in the need-to-repaint-but-could-not-afford-to demographic of the neighborhood. The southwestern flair architecture delivered a typical three bedroom, two bath, ranch style prevalent in the southwest.

The originally new and isolated neighborhood experienced encroachment over the years, as the subdivision became a permanent but tired looking sector of Glendale. The house in which Charlie moved back into had been refinanced twice over the years to afford short vacations and average furniture that littered the rooms. The never-get-ahead lifestyle forced John McShane to be generally challenged financially, and not a handyman in particular, as evidenced by obvious patchwork that speckled the dingy knock-down-texture walls like acne on a teenager's face.

In this older house of neglect where Charlie sat silently perplexed, exhausted, and feeling not up to task, boxes were piled and stacked everywhere possible, clothes lay over chairs, and furniture moved out of place. Running on reserves and isolated from reality, he exhibited minimal energy and physically could barely move a finger; eyes rarely blinked.

"Where's Becka?" Ben asked.

Charlie blinked his eyes in response and resumed his stare across the cluttered room to refocus on the wall's pimple repair in silence.

Ben shook his head and yelled, "Becka, where are ya?"

"I'm in the kitchen, Ben, drinking water. Want some?" Becka's silky voice sounded in reply from the other room.

"Sure," Ben said, and made his way around boxes and clutter toward the kitchen.

Charlie, after this most recent interruption, imagined himself a contestant on a game show where the prize of a lifetime would be awarded if he could utter one little word—right now. He feared losing because he could not *say* one word. Concern plagued him as he worked against the clock in his imaginary game. Time and again he tried to speak but failed, only incoherent groans escaped his throat. His desire to speak just one word mounted.

With his defenses overstrained and collapsing in rebellion, the loss of his parents sapped his ability to struggle to his feet. It was as though he were a cow suffering mad cow disease and each attempt to stand ended with limbs outstretched lying flat on its stomach. The levee of his defensive mechanisms was about to breach in similar fashion to the New Orleans disaster caused by Hurricane Katrina. He had concern for the devastation and the massive clean up ahead. *Who will take the blame? How can I escape this nightmarish storm? Where is FEMA when you need them?*

He realized that this turning point crisis in his imagined mad-cow-diseased life came with high frustration levels from too much input; unwanted data flooded his conscience mind and physical being all at once making the sifting process difficult, near impossible.

This furious persecution, this tsunami out of a calm sea, arrived that fateful Saturday night two weeks ago, the sixteenth of December, in the form of a knock on the door.

Charlie remembered being in his meager apartment with his girlfriend and fiancée Becka, enjoying a newly released DVD and her company lying on the couch with his head in her lap and a bowl of popcorn on the table. She was stroking her fingers through his hair, a simple act of love he cherished because it reminded him of how he was comforted by his mother as a child. His routinely boring but acceptable life was dotted with these moments of happiness with Becka and the occasional movie his meager finances could afford.

That was when the big wave hit.

The knock on the door announced an officer and chaplain from the Glendale police department who stood solemn-faced carrying the burden of horrible news. Charlie distinctly recalled the officer removing his hat before he began speaking. Vehicular manslaughter they called it perpetrated by a drunk driver. The name of the other driver in the police report was missing because there was no identification found on the body of the man driving the truck. A Mexican man registered the pickup, but the officers on the scene could not be sure who the driver was so they left most of the spaces for vehicle #1 blank until further investigation could be made. The Glendale officer had no doubt that the driver was an illegal Mexican.

They seemed sterile despite all their efforts at comfort.

The weight of a thousand pillars of granite came crashing down and Charlie collapsed to his knees under the weight. His blurry watery eyes blinked fiercely to hold back the tears while Becka held him in her arms. Charlie rolled his head back and forth and groaned as a feverish, delirious child smitten by disease in some third world African country. Becka rocked his limp body as his emotions plummeted with each descending tear.

Although his metabolism seemed to have been dramatically accelerated by the news, he could not move. All the energy was directed toward crying. Denial was not an option, but through the tears he attempted to make sense of what he found to be a dead end. Sickening and frustrating chaos churned within and he didn't know what to think or even how. All he sought to accomplish became compromised by tears and moaning. The chaplain's prayers and words of consolation had no effect. After some brief instructions, the Glendale officials left Charlie to Becka's care.

The event devastated him, an only child. Shock ensued as though an electric current had passed through him causing a full-body nerve response. Lines of communication snapped.

The psychological repairmen sent to restore communication worked hard, but inferior craftsmanship and lack of proper tools took its toll as enormous problems began to unfold. Days elapsed before the communication lines between Charlie and the outside world were reconnected. He thought they were never repaired to previous standards.

Calling Ben Marshall, his long time friend, for help constituted the last real act of meaningful communication.

Ben helped to bridge the communication gap. Ben knew that Charlie might not function well alone because Charlie's parents contributed to Charlie's life in a big way, and because help, in the form of relatives, would not be forthcoming. The nearest relatives lived on the east coast and were estranged.

Charlie and his family never talked about them, as if they were embarrassing pirates plundering waking thoughts about their existence. Arizona may as well have been another planet. Ben stepped in to aid his faltering buddy. Becka Grubb, Charlie's first and only girlfriend, also helped. Without them, he would not have been able to manage the last two weeks, but their involvement served only to delay the inevitable meltdown.

*　　*　　*

Ben Marshall was a big man—some would say fat—but he carried the weight well and kept his body clean and neat. He was balding, a little odd for a young man of twenty-two years. His cheeks were clean-shaven, except for whiskers accumulated into long side burns, hair that should have been on top of his head. He sported blue jeans, Vans, a white T-shirt, and a ridiculous, multi-colored, straw hat. Ben's head was always covered to hide the lack of hair painfully obvious without. He was not fashion conscious except when it came to tattoos. Both arms were covered.

Becka, a tall, thin, and attractive woman like Cameron Diaz, but far less expensive, stood by the sink with her water bottle in hand when Ben arrived in the kitchen. The fair-haired beauty dressed in shorts to show off sexy legs and flat-heeled sandals adorned her feet. A T-shirt in Sedona red advertised the new Arizona Diamondbacks Baseball Team colors.

She held out the water bottle to Ben. "Hope you don't mind. I have the kooties."

"No, as long as it's wet," said Ben, grabbing the bottle. He finished what was left and put the bottle on the kitchen counter.

"Ya know," he said, in a low tone of voice so Charlie in the living room wouldn't hear, "Charlie's still not doin' well. I think he's gettin' worse. I'm concerned about 'em. I know all he's been through da last couple of weeks, but he's changed, and not in a good way. God knows he's always been a moody, quiet guy, but this silent treatment lately . . . maybe he needs to see somebody, ya know, like a shrink, get his head back together."

"I've tried talking to him, Ben. When he does respond to me, he seems scared and angry. I guess he's afraid and pissed about living without his mom and dad," Becka said, twisting her engagement ring in a circle on her left ring finger. "He says he's going to take care of things, but you and I both know he really can't, not now anyway. I think he just needs more time."

She began refilling the water bottle.

"Yeah, I hope he can. Da sooner da better," Ben said. "Well, ya ready to take off? There's somethin' I want to do today, like relax on my day off. Watch some football in my overstuffed chair. I'm hungry, too. Or do ya want to stay and help Charlie put things away? He can take ya home later if ya want to stay."

"I'll stay," Becka said. She finished filling the water bottle and screwed on the lid. "Maybe we'll head out for something to eat as a break later and he can take me home on the way back. Thanks, Ben, for all your help. I know Charlie would say so if he was feeling better, so I'll say it for him."

She hugged Ben's great girth with considerable effort.

"You want more?" she offered, holding the water bottle out to Ben after the hug.

Ben grabbed the bottle, unscrewed the cap, and took one more draught. "One more for da road, eh," he said, with a smile and chuckle.

Ben and Becka directed Charlie through the various responsibilities that death involved; the calls to make; the search for records and important papers found; insurance agent and lawyer contacted; funeral and burial arrangements prepared; reports and papers all filled out and submitted, in triplicate. They handled everything the last two weeks threw at their unfortunate friend, but Charlie continued to unravel and fell deeper into the abyss of hatred in spite of the effort.

Ben headed toward the living room followed by Becka where they found Charlie still staring at the wall.

*   *   *

Charlie's ship docked, with acute awareness, at the angry pier where withdrawal became an outward appearance but revenge waited to spring to action.

He intended to discover the one word he could utter to win the game-show prize. His last ounce of sanity spent to buy just one word. As a bull ready to charge, he displayed a piercing stare out of the top of his eye-sockets, head lowered, and if he had hoofs they would have been pounding the dirt. The game clock ticked time away. Pressure mounted. The difficulty he experienced to decide on *one word* was bizarre.

The conclusion from all his comparisons indicated that Mexicans clearly needed to be punished, to put an end to their destructive pain causing behavior.

As a child, when Charlie was emotionally hurt, he released anger upon the Power Ranger and Teenage Mutant Ninja Turtle action figures he played with, causing physical abuse inflicted by virtue of dismemberments, fire, and knives, when evil triumphed over good. He realized joy from these acts of violence when he watched the faces bubble away in black liquid plastic held to matches, or when knife inflicted deep scars were slashed into body parts.

He learned to play this way in private and not get caught doing so by his parents, so the destructive habit continued unchecked. If questions arose about toy disappearances, he would lie and say they were borrowed or lost to avoid a reprimand or punishment.

It was all just a game, play time he told himself, causing no harm to anyone. It was fun. He related well to the destructive next-door neighbor kid in the animated movie *Toy Story*. His action figures were continually discarded in secret and new replacements always seemed to appear.

The nature of the word I'm searching for to win the game show prize will be decidedly evil.

At least, he knew that—influenced by all the simmering, silent hatred within. With sudden success the word came to his mind in a rush right there on the tip of his tongue. His chest filled with air to expel it, lips began to form the word, and finally—

"Charlie, Ben is leaving now."

Ben and Becka came into the living room and made their way through the clutter to where Charlie sat. They looked at him sitting on the floor as they stood.

Charlie again had no reply to the interruption of thought. He became pissed off as the word retreated into the recesses of his mind like a frightened rabbit the moment Becka started to speak. Air exhaled out of his chest accompanied by a sigh.

"Yeah, Charlie, I'm goin'. Ya gonna be okay?"

Charlie broke his stare and looked up at Ben. Unable to speak, he lifted his right thumb giving the sign of false enthusiasm. He labored under the shadow of a great threatening and unknown future.

"Good. I'll see ya later man. Hope ya feel better. I'll call ya," Ben said, to Charlie. Then to Becka, "I'll see ya later, too." Ben turned to leave.

"Bye Ben," Becka called out, as he closed the front door and left.

Becka moved a box making room to sit on the floor next to Charlie. Both sat in silence as Ben's car started up and drove down the street.

Smiling, she reached for Charlie's hand. He had returned to the forward bull stare. She turned his head with her hand on his chin until their eyes met.

He was tired, but at that moment there was the sudden rush of something remembered.

"Do you want to lay down here on the floor with me and take a nap, Charlie?" she asked, still smiling.

"*Retaliation,*" Charlie muttered, almost out of breath.

"What?" Becka asked. "What did you say?"

From his leaning position against the couch he asked, "Now where's my prize?" He then rolled over and hit the floor as if an unstable sack of potatoes.

She gently shook his arm, but Charlie didn't respond.

She lay down beside him nudging her body next to his.

CHAPTER 3

THE BREAKUP

Becka woke in the early evening before Charlie and went to the kitchen to make dinner out of what she could find that was not spoiled in the refrigerator. Two weeks had passed since anyone cooked in the kitchen. She decided on eggs, bacon, and home fried potatoes. The eggs were still within the freshness date, the bacon was a new, unopened package, and the potatoes had sprouts but were okay to use. The meal was simple and easy. All the dinner items were frozen anyway; a real dinner was out of the question. She tossed out some moldy leftovers she found. She was sure Charlie wouldn't care if he ate breakfast items for dinner tonight. She didn't mind. She made coffee first, and because the milk had spoiled, she drank it black. She was cutting up potatoes when her cell phone rang.

She picked the phone from her purse and flipped it open. "Hello?"

"Hi, Becka. It's me," Sue Grubb said.

"Hi, Mom."

"I called to see how things were going. Will you be home for dinner tonight?"

"No, I won't. I'm making dinner at Charlie's. I'll eat with him tonight. I don't think he's up to making anything for himself."

"So, how's he doing?"

"Right now he's sleeping. He's had another rough day. Thank God it was a holiday today. I'll try to get him ready for tomorrow. You know, he goes back to work for the first time since . . . since his parents died."

"All right dear, but don't stay too late. You have work tomorrow, too."

"I won't. Love you, Mom. I'll see you later. Okay? Bye."

She flipped the phone shut and put it back in her purse.

She went back to cutting potatoes.

"I smell coffee," Charlie said, entering the kitchen. "The phone woke me. Who called?"

She turned attention from the stove to face Charlie and smiled. "It was my mom. She wanted to know how you were doing and if I was coming home for dinner."

"So, what did you tell her?"

"That you were sleeping and I was making your dinner as a surprise. Coffee's made but the milk went bad. You'll have to drink it black. Maybe later we can go shopping for some things you need. You hungry?"

"Yeah," Charlie said, reaching for a coffee cup from the cabinet. He poured a cup, stirred in sugar, and sat at the kitchen table.

"We'll eat in about a half hour," Becka explained. "It's really nice to have most everything you need here at the house," she continued, trying to make Charlie feel a little better about being back in his parents' house, rather than staying in his tiny, cramped apartment.

She always tried her best to make him feel better, to look at the bright side of things. A self-proclaimed optimist, she could not stand to see anyone unhappy, especially Charlie. Becka told Charlie shortly after they learned the bad news that at least his parents didn't suffer. Conversation back then was rough. Today, things have not changed much. She was challenged and frustrated daily with the situation for the last two weeks.

"I guess," Charlie said. "Everything but parents."

"Oh, come on Honey. I know you miss your parents. It's only natural. But things will get better for you soon. You'll see," she said, almost apologetically.

He had no comment. He sipped his coffee and stared into the cup.

Charlie possessed a strong, square jaw and a brilliant smile that Becka loved when he saw fit to use it. The five thousand dollar sacrifice his parents had made for braces to straighten his teeth made him attractive to strangers and endeared him to friends. He had medium length dark hair, no facial growth beyond a few days, and steady hazel eyes. She knew he kept himself in great physical shape by adhering faithfully to a rigorous exercise regiment of running and weight training.

Charlie's superb body condition was in sharp contrast to his cigarette smoking habit. Becka remembered that his father had not understood how someone so concerned about health would smoke, and, whenever possible, teased his son in public when the cigarettes made an appearance. Charlie's parents didn't smoke.

The habit came from peer pressure in high school—principally Ben—but he didn't pick up Ben's lack of exercise habits. Ben had never played sports nor did Charlie, but at six-foot-two and 190 pounds, the high school coaches always drooled at the potential that lay dormant in him. Becka learned of the issues Charlie had with authority figures in school and the social pressure sports presented. His rebelliousness was one reason she loved him for the last five years.

She knew Charlie liked the way he felt about himself after exercise. It was the only thing he did, other than sex, that would excite him, get endorphins flowing. She witnessed Charlie in front of the mirror eying cuts in his muscles and knew that exercise gave him a feeling of accomplishment he could obtain from little else in his life.

Exercise was something he had done alone, with nobody else to slow him down or cramp his progress she was informed.

Charlie, labeled a "loner" by most who knew him, performed the solitary role to perfection. The less he socialized, the more time he had for exercise. She saw that his circle of friends was always small and was glad to be a part of it. Since high school graduation, the circle had become even smaller.

Becka directed the conversation toward this attraction to exercise. She wanted to stay away from anything Charlie could twist into negative thoughts. Lately, she felt like she walked on eggshells when talking to him.

"When do you think you'll start working out again, Charlie?" asked Becka, aware he had not exercised since the horrible visit from the police.

"I don't know, Becka," Charlie said, visibly uneasy. "It's hard for me to breathe lately, let alone get the energy to work out. I know I should, but I can't. I don't feel much like doing anything. I feel . . . like . . ."

"Sleeping?" Becka offered, trying to finish a hard sentence for Charlie. She knew emotions were hard for him to verbalize. She placed the cut potatoes in the oiled pan and began heating them on the stove.

"No, not necessarily sleeping. I go to sleep tired and I wake up the same way . . . tired. No, it's more like . . . where are my cigarettes?"

"Probably in the living room," Becka suggested.

Becka busied herself at the stove while she waited for Charlie to return to the kitchen. She thought that, maybe by then, he would figure out what he wanted to say.

He returned with a lit smoke, his pack, and a lighter. Another coffee cup became a make shift ash tray. Up until now, this *was* a smokeless house. He sat quietly for a while indulging his habit watching Becka cook.

Becka turned from the stove and prompted Charlie, "So, it's like finding cigarettes?" she said, sporting a smile and a giggle.

"Real fucking funny, Becka," Charlie said, not amused.

"You don't have to get ugly about it. I'm just trying to get you to laugh. Do you want to talk about it or not?"

"Not." He paused, "Well . . . maybe. I don't know. I'm so confused . . . and scared."

"Scared? Afraid to work out? Why?"

"I'm not talking about working out. I can't do that now, feeling the way I do. I've lost my motivation and I think I'm loosing my mind, too. No, I'm sort of scared because I think I've reached a point where I can't take anymore. For the last two weeks, I feel like I'm driving down a mountain road and the brakes are gone. I'm tryin' to slow down, slow things down, but I can't . . . 'cause the brakes are gone. At the speed I'm going, I can't control the car anymore. My heart is in my throat. I keep pumping the brakes, but . . . I think I'm going to crash," he said, visibly agitated. He took a drag from his cigarette and that seemed to have a calming effect on him.

"I don't know what to do about it, about anything," he finally finished.

"Wow, Charlie, I'm so sorry. I had no idea things were that way. I've never been in your situation, so I can't tell you what to do. I just thought maybe working out would help."

She wanted to give him a kiss, show him her love and support, but she didn't want the potatoes to burn and he wasn't making himself very approachable. She turned back to the stove and began flipping the food. Facing the stove she said, "Maybe you should talk to Ben about it."

"Ben wouldn't know what to do about it either. I'm all alone in this."

"What about a doctor, you know, psychiatrist? People sometimes see them when they're going through grief. The police officers left a card of a doctor for you to call. Remember?"

"What's a psychiatrist gonna do? I'm on my own in this. Anyway, they only ask endless questions, make you spill your guts, take your money, and run. They never have real help to offer. They prey on people in bad situations . . . make 'em poorer. I don't need a shrink. What I need is a gun with one bullet to the head—put me out of misery." He motioned with his hand, in gun form, and put his finger to his temple.

Becka saw his gesture out of the corner of her eye, pushed the potatoes off the hot burner, left the spatula in the pan, and went to Charlie. He was sitting parallel and away from the table, facing the stove, using the make shift ashtray to end the life of his cigarette.

"Don't talk that way," she said, standing in front of him. She hugged his head between her breasts. "I don't want to hear that again." She considered the gun ploy an exaggeration to obtain attention and thought humor, referring to the car analogy Charlie used, would lighten him up. "Maybe you could drag your feet to stop . . . like the Flintstones," she said, with a desperate laugh to get Charlie to smile. She began stroking his hair trying to console him. The plan backfired.

Charlie slapped her hand away and pushed her with force toward the stove changing his mood in a snap.

"I don't need your humor or pity right now Becka. It's not fucking funny! Just shut up and finish dinner!" he demanded.

She tried to help the only way she knew, by using laughter. It always worked for her in times of trouble, but this nasty behavior and unjust verbal attack hurt her feelings. She felt the need to defend herself.

"I wasn't trying to—"

"Shut up!" he said with force. "I know what you're tryin' to do. Your tryin' to blame me for something I didn't do . . . for everything that's happened. It's all my fault, right? Well, I don't care what you have to say about anything. You can take your mightier-than-thou attitude and your I've-got-all-the-answers bullshit and shove it up your ass! Sideways!"

"Are you finished?" Becka asked, sharply.

"No, I'm not finished, you argumentative bitch," Charlie said, and raised his voice in lowered patience. "Just shut the fuck up! If there's a problem here, it's all *your* fault! And it looks damn well to me like we have a problem! Don't it?" Charlie was now shouting everything he said.

"I—"

"Shut up!" he bellowed. "So, you want to add not listening to your list of aggravating bullshit? If I want your opinion, I'll give it to you. You miserable excuse for a—"

"I don't have to stand here and listen to you—"

"Shut up!"

" . . . belittle me when I'm trying to—"

"Shut—"

" . . . help you!"

"Up!"

"Fine! Make your own damn dinner then! I've had it with you, Charlie!" She grabbed her purse and started to walk out of the kitchen.

"Go ahead and leave, you bitch! You never could take criticism well!" Charlie yelled, throwing his arm in a broad-stroke, sweeping motion toward the living room.

Becka stopped at the threshold of the living room.

"Stop it, Charlie. You don't know what you're saying." She began to weep. "I thought you were scared," her voice began to quiver as she twisted her ring.

"Yeah, I'm scared all right, scared of spending another minute with you!" He screamed, and with a grunt threw his coffee cup across the kitchen. It broke against the wall just to the side of Becka as she ducked out of the way and left an indentation in the wood molding. A piece of the ceramic cup bounced off her shoulder. Others fell to the floor and scattered in a shower.

"Oh, Charlie . . ." Becka said, through anguished tears.

She turned and weaved her way through the gauntlet of Charlie's boxes to the front door.

Charlie got up and walked to the entryway where the cup left its mark.

"Don't let the door hit your fat ass on the way out!" he called after her.

Becka opened the door and before walking out she turned and gave him one last pleading stare. She wiped her flushed wet cheek with the palm of her hand.

"Go," Charlie said, in a normal tone of voice.

"Don't do this, Charlie."

He turned and went back into the kitchen abruptly flinging his hand up in the air to officially end the conversation.

She closed the door and left thinking this was a terrible way to start the new year.

*   *   *

Back in the kitchen, Charlie sat in the chair and took a few deep breaths to calm down. He had read somewhere that deep breathing would help reduce excitement and his condition was severely excited. His heart pounded inside his chest as if he just finished jogging around the block. He fired up another cigarette to help the process along.

Near the end of his cigarette, he felt calmer and gained enough wits about him to notice the stove burner was still cooking air. He got up and turned it off, like he turned off his relationship with Becka and said aloud, "Women, bah. They're always trouble sooner or later."

It was then he noticed a scrap of paper held to the refrigerator by a magnetized, miniature coo-coo-clock. His mother's writing was on the paper and it peaked his interest. He removed the paper and read a quote from Gandhi: "We must be the change we wish to see in the world."

Charlie stood for a while considering this profound quote his mother had written. It was as if she left this note for him to find, communication from her grave. A change was indeed needed in his life and the word *retaliation* came to his mind again and again as a repeating mantra. He found refuge in it, an idea that needed to be actualized for change.

CHAPTER 4

THE CALL

Twenty minutes after the argument with Becka and another calming cigarette break, Charlie sat at the kitchen table, his sagging head supported by both hands at the temples. He stared straight down to the flat surface with distorted vision caused by stretching skin around his eyes. He saw double as he tried to focus on a spot and discovered it was a crumb. He flexed the muscles around his eyes in a temporary squint to correct his vision and blew the crumb out of sight.

The smell of half-cooked, home-fried potatoes lingered in the room and tortured his stomach. He was hungry, but his desire to do nothing conquered his penchant for food.

He also pondered the idea of putting some of his possessions away, but for like reasons decided to remain immobile. The argument with Becka took all of his energy. He was spent.

Second thoughts about the argument with Becka filled his mind. He could certainly use her help right now to unpack. He briefly entertained the possibility of calling her, but then he'd have to apologize, and that would be too difficult to seriously contemplate. He'd rather stick needles in his eyes.

The work would have to wait until tomorrow morning. Maybe he'd get up a little earlier for work and tackle the job then. His attention focused on the time he would have to set the clock to get up for work, adding the extra time to find toiletries and the clothes he would wear.

While contemplating this notion, he became increasingly aware of the ticking sound of the miniature, battery-operated replica of the German coo-coo-clock held to the refrigerator by magnets. The small trinket, bought for his parents by friends that went to Germany on vacation years ago, seemed to increase in volume of its own accord. Louder and louder it sounded. He had difficulty imagining this tiny clock could make such a thunderous noise, and his head began to ring from the sound. So he moved his hands from his temples to cover his ears in an attempt to stop the racket. He squeezed his eyes shut, clenched his jaw, and pealed apart lips revealing his perfect teeth.

Still, the din became louder.

At the moment when he thought he would have to leave the room or destroy the fucking clock, the ticking stopped. Silence pervaded the kitchen, but Charlie's ears still rang from the uproar. Shortly, even that sound fell silent. He opened his eyes in the complete silence, and resumed staring at the tabletop.

Something was wrong. He sat up straight and leaned his head to one side banging with the heel of his right hand. Maybe something would come tumbling out and solve his problems. The silence continued.

He reached for his pack of cigarettes and began to fish one out. "God knows I need a smoke right now," he said to himself.

Suddenly, the phone rang shattering the silence. The alarm sounded louder than the bells in the chapel that deafened Quasimodo in *The Hunchback of Notre Dame*. Already on edge, Charlie's hands shook. His entire existence shook as the sound vibrated body and spirit. His shoulders rose with a jerk as though someone threw ice water on his back. The pack of cigarettes fell first to his thigh, then to the floor.

Charlie jumped up from the chair that slid back a few feet across the smooth floor surface. The sound had to stop immediately. He whirled around and in two steps found the phone on the counter as it rang again. He picked up the cordless phone with his right hand, his left clenched in a fist. He frantically read the caller identification squinting in a scowl. It read "RESTRICTED." He leaned against the counter as he pressed the talk button; his pinpoint pupils stared down to the floor.

"Yeah, what?" He said, annoyed.

"Charles?" A familiar voice came to Charlie through the telephone speaker.

He looked up at the wall. His pupils became much bigger, eyes widened, and goose-skin popped up all over his body. A chill sprinted down his spine.

"Charles, is that you? This is your mother speaking," the familiar voice on the phone said.

His mouth drooped open; he blinked in incomprehension. The focus of his eyes began to dart around the room. He held his breath.

"Charles, answer me," the high-pitched female voice commanded.

Charlie said cautiously as he exhaled and swallowed, "Mom?" His emotions raced: Suspicion, disbelief, excitement. He knew the voice on the other end of the telephone line extremely well. "Is it really you?" he asked, after a second pause.

"Yes, Charles. Now that I have finally got your attention, we need to talk. Are you listening?"

"Yes, Mom."

"Good. First of all, it is great to hear your voice again, Dear. Your father and I know you have been going through some rather rough times since our . . . departure, but things are going to change now. Do you understand me, Charles?"

His parents always addressed him by his given name, not by that vulgar nickname, Charlie.

"Things are gonna change. Yes, Mom," Charlie said, mechanically.

"Going, Charles, going to change," she said, instructionally.

"Yes, Mom, going."

"That is better. You need to pronounce your words properly. You were brought up to speak properly.

"As I was saying, you will *feel* better, and you will *be* better, as soon as you begin to follow our instructions. Your father and I have plans for you, Charles.

"The first thing you need to do is to get your things ready for tomorrow, tonight. You know, you are not a morning person. Take care of your clothes and toiletries tonight. If you wait until tomorrow, setting the clock earlier, you will sleep in and then be late for work. Do it tonight."

"But, Mom, how are y—"

"Next, you need to get rid of that girlfriend of yours. She will only be a distraction to you and your recovery. She is not good for you—not for now, maybe not ever. Do not go back to her."

"Becka?"

"Third, you will pull yourself together and conduct yourself in the expected manner of a McShane. Stop feeling sorry for yourself. You are a man now. It is time to grow up. Understand me?" She said, in well-bred tones.

"Yes, Mom." Charlie said, following orders.

"You have work tomorrow. We do not want *them* to see any change in you. You have to pretend as if nothing has happened. Can you do that?"

"Yes, Mom. Who are *they*?" He asked, thoughtfully.

"Our enemies, Charles. *They* are all around, everywhere, at work, in the stores, on the streets. *They* are waiting for you to make a mistake, and if you do, *they* will spin into action, persecute and blame you. *They* will make your life a living hell, Charles. Believe me, you will not want that. So, always be on the lookout, from now on."

"Okay."

"Now," she went on, "I am sure you will appreciate what I am about to tell you, since we can talk again."

"Yes, Mom." Charlie said, obediently. He continued in wonderment and asked inquisitively, "How you doing this? I mean you and Dad are . . . dead. Aren't you, Mom?"

"Never mind that now, Charles, and stop interrupting. You can hear me, can you not?"

"Yes, I can hear you," he said, disappointed that an explanation would not be given.

"Then just listen and do what your parents tell you to do for once in your life. You do not wish to waste this final opportunity to make your parents proud of you, do you?" She didn't wait for a reply. "I have not come all this way to have you ignore me like you did with college. You remember what happened with college?"

Charlie remembered: He did practically nothing for the first two semesters and finally quit school. It was a very contentious period in his life, but followed a pattern of struggle and surrender established in early childhood.

He went to juvenile birthday parties only to be the first to leave—the event being too socially demanding. He begged to attend karate classes only to quit before reaching the next belt level—being punched in the stomach by a girl and doubling over crying was an embarrassment. Baseball, football, competitive bicycling, musical instruments, all disciplines desperately needed by Charlie to satisfy a fleeting desire, became a glimmer of hope that dissolved into an unattainable accomplishment. The process wound up encouraging defeat throughout his youth.

Charlie ascended toward adulthood with deficient values regarding self-control and the ability to finish projects. He refused submitting to authority, except for his parents, and the negative reinforcement of triumphant quitting, coupled with misdirected tough love, created so much stress in success that it was a wonder he finished high school. Graduation held little merit.

"You wasted our money and your time, Charles," she said. "Look at what that accomplished: Nothing!

"It is time for you to change your life. You read what Gandhi said. I tell you, Charles, we have big plans for you. Plans that come right from the top. There is more at stake here than just *our* expectations. You understand what I mean when I say 'right from the top?'"

"A higher authority?"

"Yes. That is correct. There is a problem that needs to be solved."

"A problem?" Charlie asked, cocking his head. He went to sit in the chair in the middle of the kitchen floor.

"Yes, and the solution will dovetail perfectly with what you were thinking earlier. The process will help you grow up and finally accomplish something meaningful in your life. This will be your chance to succeed, attain a worthy goal, a deserved reward with which both you and I will be proud."

Charlie tried to recall what she was referring to, about his thinking, while she continued.

"But I do not wish to go into detail over the phone. Someone could be listening, bugging the line, tapping our conversation. This is highly confidential work you understand. Covert. Nobody is to know anything about what I will say to you. Your father and I are unanimous about this. So, again, I say, be on your guard."

"Be on my guard," Charlie repeated almost in a trance, as his uneasy, shifting eyes looked around the room.

"I am taking this opportunity to talk to you, against all odds, because *you* have been chosen. You will be the main cog in the wheels of something bigger than yourself. You need to be ready and willing to work, to accomplish the goals we set before you. You will work efficiently, quietly, and, most of all, secretly. The work is important to society and to you. You must promise to do what we tell you without question."

"Okay."

"It shall not interfere with anything we have ever taught you. So do not be concerned in that regard. With this guarantee on our part, Charles, can you promise you will do as told?"

"Yes, Mom, I promise."

"Good. You have made your parents very happy."

Charlie began to feel better about his situation. He felt the start of a smile curling the corners of his mouth.

"Now, Charles, in the future, you will be contacted every so often with some essential word or phrase that will enlighten you, give you guidance. One little word or a phrase that will provide explicit direction which you must take to advance you toward accomplishment, just as you did earlier."

"What earlier word are you talking about?"

"You know what you said, Charles. You know it. Do not interrupt me. We have very little time left. Just one little word will give you a hint of what is to be done, and you will advance toward grandeur. You, my son, will reap the reward, the renown, the honor. Your father and I will be content to work through you, in the shadows, behind the scenes. And remember, Charles, you are loved very much."

The line went dead from the other end. Charlie sat in astonishment and listened to the phone's silence. There was no noise coming through, not even the sound of an open circuit or dial tone. It was as if he had never pushed the talk button in the first place. Only the loud ticking of the small clock persisted in his ears.

In spite of not being able to say how much he loved them, or of not being able to say a simple good-bye, he felt comforted and rewarded for the first time in weeks—more energy for the first time in a long time. The call renewed his spirit, the engine of his heart, and his hope and joy in life. Everlasting bonds to his lost parents burst with uncontained exhilaration like fireworks in the night sky.

And the word his mother had referred to during the phone call came to mind . . . *retaliation*. The word brought thoughts of sinister accomplishment, a change of mind, and a smile of approval with renewed determination as he put down the phone.

CHAPTER 5

THE POOL HALL

On January twelfth, eleven days following the telephone conversation with his mother, Charlie sat on the sofa in his living room after a stressful workday sipping a Coke. The TV was on, but he was lost in thought. He remained intensely preoccupied reflecting whenever possible on what his mother had said, rehashing various frustrating aspects of their discourse. This Friday, being no different than the past few days, he again considered what kind of work she had planned for him, but could not figure anything in particular except that it had something to do with *retaliation*. What bothered him most was not being able to call her, to talk at length, ask questions, satisfy his inquisitive mind.

Charlie also wondered how she accomplished that communication. He questioned his own account concerning certain aspects of her death. *Was it truly her voice on the phone? Did she really die? Maybe the call was a dream? Maybe the police made a mistake?*

But the voice he listened to and heard all his life sounded like no other. No one he knew spoke the way she did either. That would rule out impersonation. *Who would imitate her, of all people, and why?*

When he attended the funeral of his parents five days after the car crash, he hadn't actually *seen* their bodies being cremated. Even at the wake, the caskets were closed, viewing impossible. Maybe they survived and other bodies were burned in the crematory.

He reasoned that the call wasn't a dream. Memory provided a clear and unbroken sequence of events before and after the phone rang. He was awake. The conversation happened. Charlie didn't know how, but the voice was hers.

The police might have made a mistake, but his parents never returned home. Playing a sadistic joke was beyond both the police and his mother and father.

Each session of reflection convinced Charlie the call was real, as if a daily Al Franken confirmation in front of the mirror—courtesy of *Saturday Night Live*—was necessary for a grounding reality check.

The telephone rang.

His heart rate quickened with anticipation even as the first sound began. He desperately wanted to talk to his mother again. He considered the questions he would ask and how the conversation would flow. He jumped from the sofa and ran to the kitchen to answer the phone. This ardent, even zealous, sprint to answer the phone whenever it rang had become a ritual. Finally, he'd receive some answers.

Overwhelming disappointment blanketed him again when he saw with the caller ID that it was not from his mother but from Becka. This disappointment even happened a few days ago when the insurance agent phoned to inform Charlie that the two hundred fifty thousand dollar death benefit, covering his father's demise, had been dropped off at the lawyer's office.

Charlie let the answering machine take the call.

"Hello, Charlie? Charlie, if you're there, please pick up. Charlie, I miss you. We need to talk. Charlie?" There was a brief pause. "See, he won't answer m—"

The message from Becka ended abruptly.

Charlie heard Becka's message from the master bedroom answering machine while still in the kitchen. On his way to the bedroom to deal with the message, he thought how hard it had become to follow his mother's direction concerning Becka. He wanted to concentrate on his life, prepare for the big plans ahead, follow his mother's bidding, and exclude Becka's companionship from his life.

On the other hand, Becka was persistent and beautiful. He considered his love for her and the engagement ring he recently bought to seal their commitment of a life together. It cost him over a month's wages to buy. Hell, he still made payments on it.

The day he surprised her with it gave him a wonderful memory that never failed to bring a smile to his face. He placed it on a hot dog among the chopped onions so that only the diamond showed with the gold band covered between the bun and the meat. Becka was hungry though and didn't notice it as she ate. If not for Charlie stopping her just in time, she would have consumed it or broke a tooth trying. The proposal came amidst hysterical laughing while slipping the mustard encrusted promise on her finger.

These conflicting thoughts confused Charlie as he made his way to the bedroom.

Arriving at the machine, he pushed the message playback button.

"You have five new calls," the automated answering machine voice announced. "First message, 9:06 A.M."

"Charlie? It's Becka." Charlie pushed the erase button cutting the message short.

"Message erased. Next message, 11:22 A.M."

"Char—" Becka's message again cut short by the push of a button.

Nearly every day since the breakup, there were multiple messages left on the answering machine from Becka. Charlie erased them all, some without listening, like the character Peter Gibbons deleted bothersome messages from his boss, Lumbergh, in the comedy film *Office Space*.

"Fuckin' A, man," Charlie said mimicking, Lawrence, the next-door neighbor character as the last message was expunged.

On a few occasions, Becka unexpectedly showed up at the front door ringing the bell. He did not answer each time he looked through the peephole and saw who it was. He hoped she would get the message the easy way, the coward's way. So far, it wasn't working.

Charlie felt a small twinge of pain with each avoidance because one part of his mind still wanted and needed her; another part suspected his resolve would dissolve like a Creamsicle on a hot summer day, the minute he began talking to her. How easy it would be to allow Becka back into his life—to help him, care for him, make love to him.

Charlie found though that as time elapsed without Becka in his face every day, it was easier to follow his mother's directive. He found the ability to cope with his situation alone and enjoyed that Becka no longer occupied valuable time. He didn't need to constantly express or explain himself. His emotions were safe. He needed to be serious to follow his mother's instructions and began to see some wisdom in this pursuit now that her constant and annoying laughing and joking was eliminated from his life.

Charlie eventually employed reason to help stiffen his backbone and compared Becka to the use of a cane or crutch to nurse an ankle injury. You use it until one day you find walking without it entirely possible.

He was back in control of his own life; limping a little at times, yes, but definitely able to manage. His mother was right. Becka was no longer necessary. She would impede his recovery.

Back on the sofa, Charlie's thoughts reverted to his mother again. As the days wore on, he became more skeptical. An infinitesimal gray area of doubt grew after a week without contact. Shouldn't she have called again by now? He fretted until he made a deal with himself that if she called one more time then all doubt would vanish. His remotely skeptical mind was forced to wait. He'd be happy to remove all doubt from his mind with the very next call. After all, he leaned heavily toward belief anyway.

He wanted to talk to her again more than anything at this time in his life of grief and despair. Guidance and comfort: That's what he needed. He gravely missed her influence even though at times he didn't agree with the direction given. One of the hardest things to come to terms with was admitting that she was right, especially when solid advice offered wasn't followed. It seemed he never learned until it was too late. Experience was a tough teacher for Charlie. He decided to follow her instructions this time and finally make her proud of him.

So, he waited.

He inspected his track record thus far in his ability to follow her instruction. He dealt with the immediate chore to unpack nearly all of his belongings following the call. It kept him busy and occupied. He found his necessities for work and toiletries first, as instructed, so he wouldn't have to adjust the alarm clock. He went to work, on time, and avoided any lengthy discussion with fellow employees about his parents, except to say when asked that he had everything under control. He confided in no one and worked hard to maintain an ordinary disposition. This part of her instruction was relatively easy to heed.

The hardest part of the directives to obey concerned the 'watch for enemies' admonishment. He fully intended to keep a close watch, but had trouble identifying who the enemies were. His fellow employees were not enemies; at least he found no reason to suspect them. It was hard to see enemies while driving his pickup truck or the courier van at work. In the office, everything seemed normal, same as before. He considered the characteristics he should be looking for, but he could not grasp the concept. He had made no enemies, not for a long time, not since high school. He wished his mother would call to further explain this directive and determined this to be one of the first questions he would ask the next time she called.

He maintained his distance and became more aware of his surroundings. This comprised the best he could do for now. His fellow employees always seemed to find him to be reserved anyway, a bit more aloofness could not hurt. For Charlie, social contact was stressful at best and the less contact, the less influence anxiety had upon him. This was one area where he thought his mother seemed overly cautious.

Then he began to dwell heavily on that fucking Mexican who caused all this grief. The son-of-a-bitch was lucky he died in the crash. In frustration, he again brought up the comparison in his mind, like he did when he moved into his parent's house, regarding those 9/11 terrorists that crashed the jets into the World Trade Center towers. They were hated and despised by Americans, just like this idiot Mexican was hated by Charlie, but they were already dead. Who could the country hang, electrocute, jail? Who could the law exact justice upon? His mind went around and around in frustration to the point of being dizzy.

Hostile bubbles resumed boiling inside Charlie's mind and soon a perfect white-hot hate swelled as vast and molten as the sun, but there was no outlet to release this rage. Every man with justified anger should be able to take the rage concentrated at a person and redirect it to any other person to achieve a conduit for the liberation of hate, or any other worthwhile goal. Hate, like anger, is a healthy emotion when justified and shouldn't be forgotten but nurtured, not a passion out of control but maintained and properly focused, so that its full power can be brought to bear, not as a heavy burden, but as a purposeful weapon ultimately used to exact justice.

Fury will motivate people to unprecedented achievement. Charlie had only to look to history to prove this point with Hitler and Stalin. Even President Bush demonstrated this principle, Charlie reasoned, when invading Iraq in response to the terrorist's attack on the World Trade Center. Justified anger must be allowed to flourish. Hatred for one must be satisfied even though the person or persons responsible for the inspiration and fervor is not accessible.

The phone rang again. Charlie at once popped up from the sofa and ran to the kitchen. It was Ben.

Charlie answered, "Hey, Ben, what's up?"

"Hi, Charlie. What are ya doin'?"

"I just got home from work a little while ago. I'm sitting here thinking about my mom, you know, going over things in my mind."

"Ya okay?"

"Fine."

"I called to see if ya want to play some pool tonight at the Copper Cue."

"I don't know, Ben. Maybe some other night."

"Come on Charlie, it'll be good for ya. Take your mind off things, a distraction for a while. We'll have some fun. You'll see. Just you and me."

Charlie knew Ben enjoyed both pool and beer. This was always Ben's idea of a perfect night out. Charlie thought it was okay, but Ben was his friend and he considered making the sacrifice. Ben would guzzle twelve beers—Charlie would have two. Ben would win twelve games—Charlie would win two. Ben put a great deal more effort into his favorite pastime and it showed.

Charlie considered beer just a drink. Over indulgence happened only once in his life, when he was sixteen. Ben said that he was green about alcohol then and needled Charlie saying that he was a young sapling, didn't know his limits. Sickness followed. The loss of memory, embarrassment, and hangover all ensured that it was the first and only experience for him. The lesson though, represented one time in his life when Charlie did not give up and surrender to the rigors of an embarrassment and stop drinking alcohol altogether.

The social pressures of his tiny click forbade this learned tendency.

Ben considered beer a gift from God. He only got started drinking at a six-pack. Until about a year ago, Ben was a beer counter. According to Ben, you achieved a badge of courage exceeding twelve beers, at eighteen, virtual stardom. This affinity to beer was credible reason for Ben's large and bloated appearance. Charlie always wondered why Ben was never arrested for driving under the influence.

"Okay, Ben, but I want to drive and make sure it's only you, nobody else. Okay?" Charlie said remembering times past when he endured arduous social pressure, more pool playing, and drinking than he felt necessary.

"Sure, man. Let's meet there at 7:30. Okay?"

"See you at 7:30. Right."

The Copper Cue was a six-mile drive for Charlie. The pool hall/bar was located in a strip mall with plenty of parking, in a good neighborhood, and offered a relaxed atmosphere with a genteel clientele. Charlie had been there a few times, but not recently and never without Ben.

Driving to the Copper Cue, Charlie began to experience some subtle changes, slight deviations from the norm, like a grisly silent shadow passing over him in the night. The manifestation appeared as brighter colors of the traffic control lights at intersections. They seemed luminescent. Oncoming headlights cast bright shafts that stabbed his eyes, and he began to squint to reduce the discomfort. He wished that he had his sunglasses, but he didn't think he'd need them at night.

At the same time, he was intrigued with the colors as they became more luminescent and seemed to take notice of the brilliance more so now than ever before. The spectrum of things he saw, especially the traffic lights and reflective signs, were made much clearer to him, but coincidentally, something was missing. The lights looked flatter, as if he looked at a painting of lights instead of a three-dimensional object. Vibrant sign iridescence, especially red, gripped him causing Charlie to drift in the lanes during the drive as he turned his head to observe them in passing. His sense of sight at once pleased and overwhelmed.

Charlie saw Ben's car in the parking lot and parked next to it. When he got out of his pickup truck, he stood outside the Copper Cue for a while observing the neon signs in the windows and lights of the parking lot. Everything grabbed his attention, but he was unable to focus interest on anything specific in particular. He enjoyed all the extrasensory data that was flooding into his mind. His senses were working at a higher level, and he paused to take it all in. Time passed without notice while Charlie stood gazing in the parking lot.

Eventually, he remembered the meeting with Ben and forced himself to walk to the door of the pool hall. He entered the Copper Cue's front door and stopped only a few feet inside. An old Rolling Stone song, *Brown Sugar*, was pounding so loud that he stopped to consider asking the manager to turn the music down, but he was again struck by the colors inside the pool hall. They captured his greedy attention. Meanwhile, his sensitive hearing soon grew accustomed to Jagger's crooning. The green of the illuminated pool tables resonated and gave extreme pleasure to his enhanced sight. He observed, closely, as the hues flickered throughout the pool hall.

The bar was located to the immediate right of the entrance across from the bathrooms. Charlie stood in the middle of the entrance within feet of the front door almost blocking any other customers from entering. He stared around the room in amazement. It was as if he were a child at an amusement park for the very first time. The bartender stared at Charlie from behind the bar and seemed to be evaluating and scrutinizing the newest customer to walk into the pool hall.

"Can I help you?" the bartender asked.

Charlie saw the bartender out of the corner of his eye. He didn't want to break his visual stimulation or make eye contact so he said, while still looking at the pool tables, "I'm looking for a friend I'm meeting here."

"Do you want a drink?" the bartender asked, as he put his hands up on the bar in a sort of defensive posture. Charlie noticed him and thought that the guy's face was set in a what-the-hell-are-you-doing look, like a dog owner that caught Fido in the flowerbed.

"No." Charlie said. His attention still occupied elsewhere.

Charlie stood, for what seemed like seconds to observe the colors and listen to the music, but after a minute, the bartender, looking increasingly annoyed, walked from behind the bar to stand face to face in front of Charlie.

"Look buddy, are you coming in to look for your friend or not? Or are you going to block the door?"

Charlie said nothing in response, but moved his head to one side to avoid the blocked view.

"Are you high on drugs?" the forty-something bartender asked looking old enough to be Charlie's father.

Just then, Ben came over to where the two faced off, reached his stout arm between the two men, and grabbed Charlie's arm pulling him aside.

"Hey, Charlie. You're late, man. It's almost eight o'clock. Where ya been?" He continued pulling Charlie away from the doorway toward the pool tables.

"Your friend here high on something?" the bartender asked again as they were leaving.

"No, mind your own business," Ben said, as he walked away with Charlie in tow.

"I have a right to keep certain people out of my bar," the bartender called after them.

Charlie glanced back to see him resuming his station behind the bar among all the colorful bottles and lights. The guy seemed to have lost interest now that they left the front door area.

They walked to the middle pool table in the third row back where balls were scattered about the surface. For the last half hour, Ben probably practiced while waiting for Charlie. There was a small raised café table and stool arrangement located nearby where two beer bottles already stood—one empty and one half full. A lit cigarette burned in an ashtray and the ascending ribbon of smoke contributed to the layered haze that diffused light around the room. The smell of burnt tobacco and stale beer permeated the air.

When they arrived, Charlie took Ben's cigarette and lit one of his own with jittery hands. He threw his pack next to the beers. Charlie drew a long drag off his cigarette and sat on one of the stools.

"So, Charlie, how ya doin'?" Ben asked. He took a seat on the opposite stool and picked up his cigarette.

"Okay, I guess, but man . . . I've got to say, they're playing the music kind of loud tonight. Don't you think?"

"Not especially so. Sounds good to me," Ben said. "You want a beer?"

"Yeah," Charlie said. But before he could get off his stool, Ben was already up and on his way to the bar. Ben could move his bulk fast when he wanted.

While waiting for Ben to return, Charlie stared at the vibrant green felt of the pool table. He took a drag on his cigarette. Damn, the pool hall was loud. Every sound about the room, each clinking bottle, laugh, and crashing ball registered and reverberated in his mind. The cacophony of sound and the mesmerizing colors put him in a trance. It felt like Ben had just left when he arrived with two more beers sliding one in front of Charlie.

"I got ya a light beer," Ben said, "knowin' how concerned ya are about calories."

Charlie, still in his trance, hardly noticed Ben back on the stool.

"Least ya can say is 'thank you,'" Ben said.

Charlie snapped out of his world of wonder and said, "Thanks Ben. How much do I owe you?"

"You're welcome. You get da next round."

"Okay. So what are we playing, eight ball?"

"Yeah. Go get a cue. I'll rack 'em up," Ben said rising from his stool and using the ashtray to crush out his cigarette.

While Ben set the table, Charlie went to the rack and settled on a wooden cue that had a dent on the shaft where the cue slides along the fingers. All the others were warped, had a felt tip missing, or some other problem worse than the one he selected. This shit cue selection problem always rose like a clogged toilet and contributed to Charlie's inferior play while Ben brought his own two-piece, titanium, Sportcraft cue. The pool playing deck was stacked against him from the get-go. Ben played all the time, Charlie hardly ever.

The balls were racked and Charlie got ready to break. He reached for the chalk but knocked it on the floor. Bending over he dropped his cue. When he finally got both items in hand, he had trouble chalking the cue tip.

Ben witnessed this display of clumsiness and asked, "Ya all right there, Charlie?"

"Yeah, Ben. Just a small muscular coordination problem, I'll get it right soon enough," Charlie said. He slammed the chalk on the pool table in an overly secure way making a snapping sound. He finally eyed his break shot, chalked cue in hand.

"Charlie? Ya seem a little off tonight," Ben said, as he watched Charlie position the cue ball on the table.

Charlie ignored Ben's comment. His break shot miscued sending the cue ball spinning off to the right side of the racked balls. Ben caught the errant ball, before it ruined the rack or went in a pocket. He sent it back down the table.

"Try again," Ben suggested.

"Sorry. It must be this shitty cue," Charlie muttered. Feeling a little tense he paused. "You know Ben, I *have* been feeling a little strange. I seem a bit . . . off in some things . . . like coordination," he stood up from the table, "but in other things, I feel really good. Like I can see the lights and signs in this place real clear, and the colors are much brighter. And the music is really loud. My senses seem to be working fine . . . better than fine. I don't know . . . it's strange." Charlie sighed and lowered his head looking down at the pool table.

"You want to sit down for a while, Charlie?" Ben asked.

"No. It's just hard to explain how I feel right now, that's all," Charlie said, repositioning the cue ball again. He concentrated hard to properly strike the white ball. When he finally took his shot, the racked balls scattered about the table. Nothing went in.

"Table's open," Charlie announced, as he returned to his stool. He lit another cigarette and drank some beer.

"Ya think you're comin' down with somethin'? Ya know, like da flu or what?" Ben asked, and moved around the table to calculate his first shot.

"No. I don't know what. But something isn't right . . . in my head . . . I think. It's nothing to be concerned about though. I'm sure I'll feel better in a while. I'm not hurting or anything like that. Maybe after I finish this," he said, holding up his beer. He drank a little more.

"So, what's up with you and Becka? I heard ya had a fight," Ben remarked, then took his first shot. The ten ball went in the side pocket.

"Yeah, we did," Charlie replied. "Things don't look too good for us right now." He watched Ben walk around the table to size up his next shot.

"What happened?" Ben asked, then in a nice smooth stroke sent the thirteen into the corner pocket, clean.

"I don't know . . . she thought everything was a joke," said Charlie, sharply. "She pissed me off, alright? So I threw her out of the house. It happened the night you moved me in. I was so fucking mad, I broke a nice coffee cup in the process."

"Too bad about the coffee cup," Ben said with a laugh and his belly jiggled. He walked around the pool table looking at his next shot. "Just kiddin'. I sort of like her though. Ya think you'll be gettin' back together with her?"

"No. I don't want to. Not now anyway."

"She really pissed ya off good, huh?" Ben asked chalking his cue.

"Well, I actually feel better since she's been gone. She's been holding me back. I mean … my recovery …" Charlie began to concentrate on the word recovery. The sound repeated in his mind like an echo in a cave as he thought about what his recovery entailed, following his mother's instructions, making her proud. He stopped talking to ponder the word.

Ben walked to the café table as Charlie stared into space. Ben drained half of his beer. "Your recovery?" Ben asked.

Charlie finally said, "I'm doing better now, without her." He took another sip of his beer.

Ben went back to the pool table, "Fifteen ball in the side," he said tapping the side pocket with his hand. Even though they played friendly pool games, questionable shots were called and his next attempt was a relatively hard bank shot. He made it.

"Nice shot, Ben," Charlie said, in true admiration. *Here we go again, I watch Ben play pool all night and then go home a loser. It's another wonderful night in Charlie's world.* He put his beer back on the table.

"Thanks," Ben said, walking to the café table again. He drank more of his beer then changing the subject he said, "So, ya should have come over last week to watch da game." He referred to the pro football playoffs that were on television last Saturday. He called to invite Charlie over the phone, but the invitation was declined.

Ben continued, "Ya stay home way too much, Charlie. Joe and Tony came over with da girls. We had pizza, beer, fun. You remember what fun is like, don't ya? You should have come over."

"Thanks for inviting me, Ben, but I'd just as soon stay home, watch TV, play video games. I had a lot of work to do around the house, too, you know, just moving in and everything. Beside, you should know me by now. I don't like crowds."

"Yeah, I know, ya like bein' by yourself. I have to ask though. I feel it's my duty to include ya in on every party at least. You're my buddy. Right?" Ben grabbed Charlie by the neck and shoulder and vigorously shook him.

Ben drank some more of his beer and went back to the pool table considering the ball arrangement.

Someone at the adjacent table yelled in excitement after they made an impossible shot on the eight ball to win the game. Charlie cringed in response to the extra noise.

"You're right," Charlie said. "We're good friends. Truthfully, you're my only buddy, Ben. I value our relationship. So I ah . . . need to ask you something." He paused to consider a question for Ben. A need to confide in someone suddenly urged Charlie to ask advice on the delicate subject of "the call." He hoped talking to Ben would give another perspective to consider.

"Yeah?" Ben said. He looked pleased with himself chalking the cue.

"Ben?" Charlie said, waiting for Ben's attention before he began. When Ben looked up from the pool table, he continued in a diffident manner, "Can I be straight with you? I mean I have something to tell you. I need to talk to someone about what happened to me recently. I've been going over it and over it in my mind and . . . I'd like your opinion. Please don't tell anyone about what I'm going to tell you. Okay? It's private. Keep it under your hat, no pun intended." Ben was wearing a baseball cap tonight.

"Sure man. What's on your mind?"

"I . . . I got a call. I got a phone call from my . . . about two weeks ago and, well . . . the call was f-from . . . my . . . m-my mom." Charlie felt flushed as he spoke. He was glad to finally verbalize his revelation, but it carried an underlying embarrassment. He stood from his perch on the stool, nervous.

Ben walked to where Charlie stood by the table. Both picked up their beers in unison; Ben finished his; Charlie had another mouthful. Their eyes met in searching silence. Charlie noticed his friend's eyes were bright white, almost glowing.

"Your mom?" Ben asked, coolly.

"Yeah, Ben. It's been bothering me ever since."

"Wait a minute, Charlie," Ben said. He held up his hand in a stop sign motion. "Hold that thought. I need another beer."

He leaned his cue against the pool table and left for the bar.

Charlie drank more of his beer and thought about Ben's initial reaction. He could tell Ben was surprised and confused at once by the frown that formed on Ben's normally jovial, rounded face. He didn't laugh, so he must have been taking it seriously. Charlie assumed that Ben took the time to go to the bar so he could formulate an opinion or advice. He looked forward to what Ben had to say.

Then he thought of what he had just done. Immediately, he felt warm, the kind of heat generated by guilt, and started to sweat. He considered the promise that he made to his mother about keeping silent which he just violated and looked around the pool hall as if to find help. He wished someone could transport him out of the pool hall before Ben came back.

What kind of trouble did I just get myself into?

Suddenly, the green pool table glow was no longer a comfort. Nervousness flourished unchecked and darting eyes searched for solace across the room. When Ben returned with his beer, Charlie could only see cheerless glowing eyes representing misfortune and anxiety.

"So now, what's this about your mother callin' ya?" Ben asked, with a serious look on his face.

Charlie snapped out of his fearful trance when Ben sat across from him, but Ben's undivided attention disturbed his concentration so he looked down to collect his thoughts and broke the silence.

"Well, it happened just after I kicked out Becka," Charlie finally began, looking up at Ben after finding no way to avoid the question. "I was sitting in the kitchen at the table, when all of a sudden the clock started ticking real loud. Then there was complete silence. I remember my ears ringing, and then . . . then the phone rang, real loud. It scared the shit out of me; it was so loud. When I answered it . . . it was my mom."

Ben's eyes never wavered from Charlie. He shook his head and asked, "How did ya know it was her? What did she say?"

"I knew it was her, Ben. It was her voice. I've been thinking about this since it happened. Who else could it be? Don't you think I would know my own mother's voice?"

"Well?"

"She said she was happy to hear my voice. Said both her and my dad have plans for me. That I should get my shit together and grow up!"

"No way," Ben said, slightly amused.

"It happened just like I told you."

"Yeah, right. You were probably dreamin'."

"It wasn't a dream. I talked to her."

"If ya weren't dreamin' maybe ya were hallucinatin' . . . one way or another, Charlie, it wasn't your mom. She's dead."

"Don't you believe in life after death, Ben?"

"Yeah, but callin' on da phone . . . it just don't happen."

"Well, I believe it. You can think what you want, but I know it was my mom. I started feeling better while I was talking to her. She told me I would. She also told me to drop Becka, that she wasn't good for me and you know, Ben, she's right."

"Ya broke up with Becka 'cause your mother, who died almost a month ago, told ya to?" Ben chugged more of his beer then shook his head, sniggering.

"No, I broke up with her before the call. I happen to agree with my mom that Becka is going to be problem for me, in the future. I've been waiting for her to call back but—"

"But what, Charlie, she hasn't? Well, I wonder why?" he said, looking annoyed.

"Look, Ben, forget I said anything," Charlie said. "I see that I've made a mistake talking to you about it. I'm sorry I brought it up. I thought you were my friend, that you, of all people, would understand."

"I'm sorry, Charlie," Ben said. He paused and sighed, "It's hard for me to believe. Ya want me to be honest don't ya? Maybe you're just too depressed. Maybe this is a reaction in your mind to depression. I don't know. Maybe your mind is playin' a trick on ya."

Ben seemed to run out of words to console his friend. He stood up, ambled to the pool table, picked up his cue, and took his next shot. He missed.

Charlie and Ben played pool for another two hours. Their conversation, among other topics, covered Charlie's windfall from the insurance company that he placed in the care of the attorney for investment until probate was over.

"The lawyer called the other day to tell me that probate should last for six months to a year since my father died in testate," Charlie informed.

"What's in testate?" Ben asked.

"I don't know. Something about legal stuff with the house. All I know is that I wanted the lawyer to take care of things for a while. The guy advised me that the money should go into a savings account. I can use it when I need cash, but I can't get wild because some of the money will go to pay debts that my parents owe."

"Sounds complicated."

"It is. That's why people need lawyers."

Charlie and Ben agreed to a conservative plan that provided the house to be paid off if there were enough funds to do so, with no rash spending for quite some time. Charlie did not want to make any major decisions. Financially, Charlie's life would not change dramatically. There were enough changes in his life already.

Brief reports on work followed and how most aspects of life without parents were being handled.

Then Charlie explained how he felt about the Mexican responsible for the tragedy. How he would like to beat the shit out of him, even kill him, if he were still alive. "I'm frustrated . . . the fucker's already dead," Charlie confided.

As he shared his thoughts during this part of their conversation, Charlie became animated and hateful. The standard Mexican-invasion-of-the-country discussion ensued, as it had many times before, and included border issues, businesses that employed illegal immigrants, and ended with ideas on what should be done to stop the invasion. Here, Charlie's ideas to fix the problem were all extremely violent in nature. Ben, knowing previous discussions to be just venting, took a more calm but supportive role in the analysis.

They parted ways in the parking lot, each driving home alone. On the way home, Charlie was still fascinated by the colors and lights, but the novelty wore off as he became more accustomed to this new visual experience. On the whole, it was the best night he had had in a long time. He would come to a realization that it was the last time he would enjoy playing pool with Ben.

*   *   *

Charlie parked his Toyota pickup in the garage of his parent's house and closed the garage door with the remote. Getting out of his vehicle, he heard the telephone ringing in the kitchen. It was as loud to him as if it were ringing on the garage wall. He opened the kitchen door and flipped on the light. He found the phone and checked caller ID. It read RESTRICTED. He felt a smile breach his face as he eagerly pushed the talk button with excitement.

"Hello," Charlie said, leaning against the kitchen counter.

"Charles. This is your father," a voice said, over the phone.

"Dad! Hi. How are you?" Charlie said. He began to formulate the questions he would ask after weeks of preparation in his mind.

"Frankly, Charles, the fact is, you've overstepped your bounds tonight, and, in the process, have made your mother and I extremely angry." There was unmistakable contempt in the voice.

"Me dad? What did I do?" Surprise and a weak disappointment began to build in Charlie.

"You've disobeyed our wishes. You've provoked our anger by breaking your promise to keep *secret* all that your mother discussed with you when you last talked to her."

Foreboding swarmed over Charlie like ants protecting their mound as he considered his earlier conversation with Ben. He tried, as in years past when called to the carpet, to reason his way into justification for his actions.

"But, Ben is my best friend Dad and—"

"Silence!" his father's voice boomed, over the phone.

Aghast, Charlie's mouth dropped open as he assumed the submissive bad child role.

"We're intensely disappointed with your actions! You don't seem to understand the gravity of the situation! We will not accept this behavior from you. You must be corrected!"

"Corrected?"

"Yes, corrected! A lesson must be taught, here and now, that you will not soon forget! I am sorry, son, but this is for your own good."

Charlie listened to a brief silence on the phone. Then, suddenly, a WAIL! A dreadful sound, drawn out and shrill, resonated not only from the phone but also from inside Charlie's head. He dropped the phone, but the din continued. Charlie's pupils rolled up under his eyelids stricken with horror. The wail seemed to last forever as he squeezed his eyes shut, covered his ears with his hands, and bent over in agony. The pain was more than he could endure.

Conveyed to a dark tunnel by the noise and only capable of seeing a pinpoint of light at the end, his body seemed to float in space. Then something shook him violently. Finally, he could remember nothing more as the pinpoint of light winked out.

Charlie opened his eyes, narrow crusty slits, and the kitchen ceiling came into view allowing additional light from the overhead fixture to be squeezed into his vision. He had passed out next to the kitchen table chair, wooden rungs, like prison bars, looming to his left. Darkness dominated the outside window view, as his head spun and ached. The pit of his stomach felt queasy.

He moved his head slightly right to view the vibrant, bright blue, digital stove clock. The numbers kept slipping off to the right of his vision and his eyes moved constantly with them only to refocus back to the original spot again. The experience made him nauseous. His temples drummed with his heartbeat as the numbers grew larger and smaller with each surge of blood. After considerable effort, he read the time. It was 1:13. Even reading the clock was far too great an effort. Abdominal-muscle spasms forced his eyes closed. He swallowed and drifted painfully back to the darkness.

CHAPTER 6

THE REPORT

Ben Marshall lived in a three-year-old apartment complex off of the 101 Loop in Glendale. Ben, his girlfriend and fiancée, Tammy Heart, and another rent paying roommate occupied a three-bedroom apartment on the second floor. Two years ago, Ben, Charlie, and another male friend originally leased the apartment, but Charlie moved out after one year, when Tammy moved in. Charlie had told Ben that he needed more time alone and felt that a good opportunity had presented itself with Tammy's addition, allowing Charlie to move out. The even exchange of roommates did not stress Ben financially, so Ben agreed to dissolve their contractual arrangement and let Charlie move into his own apartment.

Ben and Tammy both worked. They could afford the rent on their own now, but they saved the extra rent money for the future.

Their marriage, however, was a distant proposition with no set date. Ben didn't like to commit to anything, but to keep peace and harmony, he agreed to an engagement. He figured he'd test the water with his engagement toe. Unless it became too scalding hot to stand, he would eventually grow more serious and tie the knot. Tammy and

Becka discussed the possibility of having a double marriage ceremony, to which Ben and Charlie agreed if the details could be worked out.

At eight thirty Saturday morning, Ben sat in his bathrobe drinking coffee, smoking a cigarette, and watching Cartoon Network on cable TV when the phone rang.

"Hello?"

"Ben? It's Becka."

"Hey, Becka. What's up so early in da mornin'? I just woke up."

"I couldn't wait for you to call about last night. So, what happened?"

Becka had orchestrated last night's pool hall meeting and Ben agreed because he saw no down side. He got to play pool, drink beer, see his friend, and find out information about Charlie for Becka. Also, if he could talk Charlie into a reconciliation of some sort, she would be in debt to him. Ben, being a debt collector, always liked to accumulate credit for some future perplexity that he could not see coming in the present. He liked to think of it as a rainy day savings account where credits were amassed for future withdrawals. He turned down the volume on the television with the remote providing uninterrupted attention to the call, but couldn't help having some fun at Becka's expense while he raided her funds.

"Well, we played pool. I won as usual. Had some beers, ya know . . ." Ben reported, being purposefully evasive.

"What did Charlie say, Ben?" There was some insistence to the pitch of her voice.

"About what?" Ben continued his evasive tact.

"You know, about me," Becka said, adding impatience to her rising intonation.

"Oh, yeah, about you, huh?" Ben said, laughing, unable to contain himself so early in the morning. "It's all about you. Isn't it Becka?" he asked, taking one final jab at her.

"Come on, Ben," she said, "stop fooling around."

"Okay. He said that you and him are history," Ben said bluntly, and then went on, "but get this, he said he talked to his mother over da phone. Can ya believe that?" Ben felt the skin on his forehead crease from raising his eyebrows.

"What? He's dropping me?"

"Yeah, he's droppin' you, but did ya hear what I said about his mother?" Ben thought this the more important item.

"Yes, I heard you. You're kidding, right?"

"No, honest to God," Ben promised, "and this is strictly confidential, Becka, if ya ever tell him I told you, I'll have to kill ya," he said, joking. "Either he's flipped or the stress is really gettin' to him or both. He said she told 'em that you weren't good for 'em and to break up with you. That you would, in some way, hinder his recovery. Talkin' da way he's been lately, I don't see a recovery. Do you?"

"I can't believe he said that, Ben. That's weird, really weird. And I can't believe he said, 'we're history' after all I did for him, that son of a . . . What about our wedding? What about all our plans? He's breaking up with me over a misplaced joke? I . . . I can't believe it. He can't mean what he said, Ben. He can't. I'll bet he needs more time or space. Maybe that's what he meant. You know how he has a hard time with emotional issues. But I'm worried about him if what you say is true. What should we do?"

"I don't know. What can we do? Give him more space and time to do what, recover? I think he's beyond the beyond, in the Twilight Zone or somethin'," Ben said. He sipped his coffee, then put his feet on the coffee table and shifted his bulk on the couch. The springs groaned under his weight.

"I don't know either. I'll have to think about it. What else did he say?"

"He said that you deserved to be dropped. You were makin' fun about his situation. 'Always jokin', he said, pissed him off, broke a coffee cup. That true?"

"Yes, he broke a coffee cup, tried to hit me with it. He came damn close, too. No, I wasn't making fun of him or his situation. I was trying to get him to smile, make him happy somehow. He's been so depressed lately. He seems so mad. I've never seen him so mad before."

"Yeah," Ben said, putting his cigarette in the ashtray on the table, "he can get real angry at times. He's got a bad temper, as you know, ever since high school. In fact, that's how I met him. Did I ever tell ya about how we met?"

"No."

Ben plunged into narration. "He was havin' an argument at school durin' lunch with some dick head Mexican who started in on Charlie. Ya know, sayin' Mexican shit, getting' into Charlie's face, antagonizin' him into a fight. Charlie was only too willin' to consent. Then, when Charlie stands up for himself, da rest of the Mexican gang joins in and they grab Charlie from behind. They held him while the one fucker started wailin' and beatin' the shit out of Charlie, four on one, typical Mexican odds. They'd never try anythin' alone unless they have a gun or somthin' to make da odds better. And Charlie was a loner, even back then. Didn't hang with anyone, so he was left to their mercy. Even so, he kicked and struggled and held his own for a while."

"So, what happened?"

"I saw what was goin' on, and me and another guy, Tony, you know Tony, we stepped in and broke it up. Saved Charlie from some stitches and a trip to da nurse's office or even da hospital. He's been sort of under my wing ever since. I've been friends with Charlie for, lets see . . . seven years now. During all those years, he's been angry most of da time, sort of buildin' this underlyin' infuriation, especially when it comes to Mexicans, and probably more so now, after a Mexican killed his parents.

"Ya should have heard him last night, Becka. Talk about angry, he went on a roll about how Mexicans are responsible for all kinds of problems da U.S. is havin', unemployment, healthcare, you name it, they're responsible. He thinks we should defend our border from da invasion by shootin' anyone caught crossin' illegally, even make it illegal to advertise or speak in Mexican. 'This is America and we speak English here,' he says. 'Deport all da bastards and put da military on guard.' I've got to say, he's got some points I have to agree with. But he ain't tolerant, not at all. And he's quite mad about a lot of things, especially da Mexicans."

"I knew about his Mexican prejudice, but he never said anything about the fight in high school," Becka said.

"Da maulin' is somethin' he's not proud about, but its one good reason why he's da way he is. It's probably one reason he exercises so much, like for protection. Ya never know when bein' in shape can save your life. Ya know?

"He's really a good guy when not stressed to da breakin' point though Becka, and loyal as they come. As long as you're not Mexican," Ben said laughing at his own joke. His large stomach heaved.

"I know Ben. We've gone on many romantic dates that I'll always cherish and he's got a sweet side to him when were alone. You know, holding doors for me and bringing flowers on special occasions. His thoughtfulness is one of the reasons why I love him so much. I just wish he could get past this joking thing. I still love him and won't give up on him. So, what do we do?"

"Ya mean, what do *you* do? He's not pissed at me. I'm still his friend. I'll help ya if I can, like I did last night. But I don't know what to tell ya to do," Ben said, thoughtfully.

"I'm sorry. I forgot Ben. Thank you, for your help last night. I was so upset hearing he doesn't want me anymore. I was hoping for a more positive answer from you though. Like, you convinced him of his error and that he said to call and we'd get back together. I leave messages for him all the time. I know he's getting them. I just wish he would respond, say something, anything. I can't stand the silent treatment. I need to talk to him.

"Oh, well, if he says anything in the future about me, you know, like he wonders what I'm doing or anything that you think is a step in my direction, let me know. Until then, I know he's avoiding me and I don't want to make him any more annoyed. Maybe I'll send him a card and explain what I feel since I can't tell him in person," Becka said.

"Hey, Hon. Who you talking to?" Tammy asked, entering the living room area from the bedroom. She scratched her disheveled hair into a more acceptable arrangement.

Ben covered the phone mouthpiece with his meaty hand and said, "It's Becka." He held up a finger to his mouth to shush her.

"That's a good idea Becka. I hope he reads what ya write. It can't hurt. Like ya said, 'It won't annoy him.' Who knows, he might read it and change his mind."

"I hope so," Becka agreed. "Well, I'll let you get going. I think I heard Tammy. Tell her I said hello. Thanks again for all your help. You, ah, wouldn't be opposed to throwing in a good word for me, would you Ben?" she asked.

"I already have Becka, I already have."

"Thanks Ben. Have a great weekend."

"You, too. Bye."

"Bye."

Ben hung up the phone.

"So, was that about Charlie?" Tammy asked, and took Ben's coffee cup. She sipped it slowly and then took a bigger gulp.

"Yup," Ben said, "and she's still in love with him. There's somethin' about that guy, she won't let go without a fight. Even though he's weird at times."

"Even if he wants *retaliation* against Mexicans? Would he still be your friend then?" Tammy asked, her face showing that she meant it sarcastically.

"Especially then," Ben said, laughing. Tammy giggled too.

While the phone was still in Ben's hand, he punched in Charlie's phone number.

"I think I'll call Charlie to see how he's doin'," he said to Tammy. "He wasn't feelin' quite himself last night. He was a little weird, weirder than usual."

He waited while the phone rang. On the fourth ring, the answering machine picked up the call.

"Hello. You have reached the McShane residence," Mrs. McShane's voice on the answering machine said, "We are not able to come to the phone right now but if you leave a message we shall return—"

Ben quickly hung up the phone. He said to Tammy, "Now that was weird."

"What?"

"I just heard Charlie's mom's voice on da answerin' machine. It freaked me out. I wonder why Charlie hasn't changed the greetin' yet?"

"He probably doesn't call himself so he doesn't even know it's there," Tammy said.

"Well, da next time I talk to 'em, I'll have to tell him about it. I don't like talkin' to answerin' machines as it is, and when ya hear a dead person's voice talkin' . . . well, he'll have to put his own greetin' on it," Ben said, putting the phone back in the charger.

"He's probably still sleepin'. I'll try him again later," Ben said, reaching for the remote. He turned up the volume on the television.

CHAPTER 7

THE NIGHTMARE

Charlie woke with the sound of the ringing phone. It was on the kitchen floor three feet from his head. The battery cover was missing from the handset as a result of being dropped last night. It was near the refrigerator tucked under the cantilever edge of the kitchen cabinet. The out of place batteries were still attached to the phone by two thin umbilical cord wires. The keypad and caller ID panel were illuminated due to the incoming call.

He heard the phone before he could see it. Three rings sounded before he considered answering. He opened his eyes, turned his head, and focused on the object causing the alarm. He maneuvered his right arm and slid it across the floor on the fourth ring, and his index finger touched the battery end of the phone. It spun on the floor slightly further from his grasp, as if miles away instead of at arm's length. The phone stopped after the fourth ring. The answering machine clicked on and beeped.

He remembered last night's call, his father's angry voice, and the pain, especially the pain. His body felt stiff. Residual soreness and a murky consciousness were the day-after result of his father's lesson in *retaliation*. He retracted his right hand from the now silent phone to rub his bleary orbs. Another day in paradise, he sarcastically judged, then imagined lying on a golden sand beach in some exotic island location. In spite of wishful thinking, the hard unyielding surface of the floor forced him to direct efforts toward his immediate removal.

He concentrated his faculties on reorienting his sore, achy body to the comforts of his bed. The next five minutes witnessed a crawling maneuver out of the kitchen, which graduated to a hands-and-knees shuffle down the hallway toward the master bedroom, and ended in a climbing action that eventually landed him in bed. He rolled over on his side and saw that the alarm clock on the nightstand read 8:58. Light emanating from the window indicated morning. With the satisfaction of successfully reaching his immediate goal, he closed his eyes, drifted into sleep, and dreamed.

Charlie found himself lying in bed in a plain windowless room. The walls of the room were bare institutional-green and a small florescent light illuminated a steel door partially open to a hallway. He was coerced to sit up and take notice by sounds of shuffling feet and murmuring voices outside. He left the bed, made his way across the small room, and peered out of the cleaved opening. Men and women paraded up and down the corridor dressed in robes, plain white pajamas, and slippers. Their eyes and faces were expressionless. He eased the door open further to gain an unobstructed view and asked, to anyone in earshot, where he was. They remained unaware and ignored him. He reached out to grab one of the paraders by the arm and, as he did, the forearm changed into the outside door handle of a vehicle. As Charlie's hand held the grip, he bent down to look through the passenger window observing the driver.

The engine rumbled in the corridor and fumed, but nobody noticed or cared. The man behind the wheel beckoned Charlie to get in. He did. He saw the driver plainly once inside the vehicle. Bewildered, Charlie gazed upon himself, except the guy had a beard and longer hair and dressed in street clothes. Charlie noticed the man's eyes were solid black, as if his pupils devoured the iris and white of his eyeballs.

The driver had one hand on the steering wheel. The other turned on the radio and flipped the station dial to create a blur of sounds until he found Blue Oyster Cult playing *(Don't Fear) The Reaper.* He winked at Charlie with his right black eye and with both hands on the wheel nailed the accelerator.

Charlie heard rubber skid marks being burned on the slick tile floor in the hallway. Tire smoke seeped into the vehicle as they sped down the expanding passage narrowly missing the parading multitude that neither flinched nor moved aside. Charlie's attention refocused from scanning the near-misses outside to concentration on the mad man behind the wheel. He considered buckling his seat belt, but his hands were frozen in fear. He clutched the seat, feet pressed hard against the floorboard. He no longer cared for anyone's safety but his own.

He watched as the driver's face and head developed into a grotesque deformity barely resembling the human head it had once been. Large mounds of flesh blossomed on his face and folds of skin grew here and there; bony protuberances destroyed smooth surfaces, as if craters formed by meteorites on the moon's Sea of Tranquility. The driver produced a guttural, hideous, and jeering laugh as the corridor evolved into a dark wet street. Prisms of beaded water on the vehicle's windows retreated in the battle against the wind.

"Baby I'm your man . . ." the song played on the radio.

Facing Charlie again, the deformity's eyes changed and now glowed a vibrant blood red. They protruded and bulged from its disfigured face, as if squeezed like a stress doll by some unseen hand. A putrid, rotten stench emanated from the absurd laughing jaws and made Charlie nauseous. In response, he wrenched his left hand from the seat to cover his nose and mouth.

A creeping chill ascended the steps of Charlie's spine as the second chorus of the song played on the radio.

Suddenly, the deformed face of skin and flesh melted off its bony foundation to reveal a bloodstained skull. The dripping ooze covered the driver's shirt and created puddles in his lap and on the seat. The deformity continued to stare at Charlie with its blood red eyes, ignoring the road and swerving the car. The hideous laugh bellowed in a fever pitch. Charlie cringed and leaned against the door in an effort to get as far away as possible. Jumping had crossed his mind, but he seemed glued to the seat, frozen, forced to continue the ride of an unwilling roller coaster passenger.

The song lyrically told Charlie not to be afraid.

The skull's bony jaw drew up the flat teeth into pointed fangs that dripped saliva mixed with blood. The mouth opened wider and wider until the jaw seemed to separate from the skull like the disjointed cartoon mandible of Stanley Ipkiss in *The Mask*.

The song became louder.

The mouth of the demon, full of sharp fangs, was now wide enough to consume Charlie's head. It lunged at Charlie engulfing him in total darkness.

Blue Oyster Cult sang the chorus.

Charlie screamed inside the thing's mouth. Fangs punctured his neck.

"Don't fear the reaper . . ."

Charlie rattled in the pitch black with an abrupt jolt and sound of a crash. The vehicle must have finally drifted off the highway and ran head-on into something.

"Reaper . . ."

Charlie felt himself being thrust forward.

He awoke in his familiar bed at home sitting up in a cold sweat, eyes wide open. And he heard the sound of metal crashing against a hard surface. The sound reverberated in his head.

It repeated.

Charlie perceived the haunting nightmare in particularly vivid and glowing color. It lingered at the edge of his consciousness. It seemed so real, but it was rapidly fading, taunting his memory with fewer and fewer scraps of images. Without effort he remembered the skull, the crazy ride, and the song but details were evaporating.

He looked around the room. The clock read 4:07. He slept nearly all day. He was parched.

He got out of bed, went to the bathroom, and turned on the light. He filled the glass on the sink with water and drank it completely. Then splashed water on his face and dried with a towel.

Charlie's wrinkled, unwashed clothes smelled of dirt and body odor reminding him of the smell of old age and the homeless he had harassed in solitary trips to downtown Phoenix in the recent past. He went on days when feeling particularly frustrated with life while living alone, days when Becka had been called away from his company.

It was fun kicking the transients as they slept on the pavement, pouring soda on their heads, telling them to get jobs and take baths. He anticipated and welcomed confrontations that never arose. Charlie felt power from the incidents flourish like weeds. It helped him to cope. A new sense of strength seemed to sprout from underneath rocks of arrogance. The invigorating excursions were never discussed with anyone.

He looked in the mirror and saw tired puffy eyes, sunken and shadowed, his face white, as if painted by a practicing Geisha stricken with terror. He smelled himself standing before the sink and decided he needed a shower. He didn't need anyone to kick him and tell him that.

He watched his bloodshot eyes squint in the mirror as the metallic sound repeated outside the house somewhere.

The words of the song remained in his head and he said, "The reaper." He couldn't remember the name of the group, but he pondered that question as he stood in the bathroom.

The phone rang interrupting his thoughts. He noticed the sound seemed louder than usual which indicated his senses were still working at a higher proficiency. He remembered the way his senses reacted to the lights on his drive to the pool hall the night before on the way to answer the phone. He walked to the nightstand by the bed where the phone charger was located. He reached down to pick up the handset when he noticed the caller identification read "RESTRICTED." He stopped and pulled his hand away as if sparks threatened electrocution.

If the call's from my parents, then I don't want to talk, not now, maybe not ever.

It was the first time he felt this way about his parents. Anger and resentment welled up inside. He wondered why their lesson had to be so painful. Even death might have been more merciful. He decided not answer this call. He waited for the rings to stop, then for a message to be recorded. No message was left.

The metallic sound repeated outside the house again.

He stripped off his shirt throwing it in the corner near the closet where the laundry basket overflowed. He kicked off his Vans.

The phone rang again.

He stopped briefly to speculate who the caller might be then checked the phone display. It revealed: "MARSHALL, BEN" and the number. Charlie answered the call.

"Hello?" he said, standing with the phone cradled in his ear, trying to unbuckle his belt at the same time.

"Charlie? What are ya doin'?" Asked Ben.

"I was going to take a shower. Why? What's up?"

"Da playoffs man. Ya comin' over?"

"Naw. I just woke up, Ben. I can't."

"Just woke up! We weren't out that late last night. What happened?"

"I don't want to get into it, Ben," Charlie said, as he reviewed what happened in his mind. He didn't want any more punishment. He lied, "I couldn't sleep."

"Ya know, Tammy talked to Becka this mornin'," Ben said. "She invited her over to watch da game with us. She wants to get back together with ya. Maybe ya can come over, talk to her, ya know, maybe patch things up."

"Ben . . . no Ben. I'm taking a shower. Since I slept so late, I still need to do some things today . . . and I don't want to see Becka, not today."

"Okay, Charlie. If ya change your mind, we'll be here. Ya know you're always welcome."

"Thanks Ben. I'll call you sometime during the week."

"See ya later, Buddy."

"Bye, Ben," Charlie said, and disconnected the call. He placed the phone back on the charger.

The metallic sound repeated outside.

It annoyed and disturbed Charlie to the point of investigation. He had to find out exactly what was making the pain-in-the-ass repeating sound. It was more important than the shower.

He went to the living room window, raised a few slats of the blinds, and squinted as he looked through to see outside. There, at the house diagonally across the street, children were playing baseball in their driveway using an aluminum bat. Each time they dropped the bat on the pavement, it made the metallic clanging sound that echoed throughout the neighborhood.

Charlie's eyes fixed upon the kids with loathing. They were Mexicans.

"What the fuck! Why can't they go to the park to do that? It's not even baseball season . . . dumb fucks," he said into the dusty white plastic slats.

He watched for a while longer, when the front door of the Mexican's house opened to exhibit a squatty, overweight, brown-skinned woman that wore a brightly colored sundress in bare feet. She shouted something to the three boys and motioned with her stubby hand that made the back of her arm skin flap. She held the door open as she yelled. Suddenly, their dog dashed out between the doorjamb and the woman. Charlie thought it was an act of magic since the woman's bulk covered the space in the doorway like a goalie covered the net in a hockey game. Somehow the dog puck got through and scored a freedom goal.

The dog appeared to be a mutt to Charlie, a white mutt with brown ears and one other large brown spot that covered its hindquarters except where a white tail protruded. Obviously a mulatto, even the dog is Mexican!

The animal ran around frantically thrilled in its newfound freedom. It leapt like its tail was on fire and its ass was catching as it circled and jumped on the kids. The boys appeared to think this was the most fun they had all day. Laughter and excitement prevailed, but the Mexican woman was now out of the house, directing anyone who would listen to round up the dog and bring it back inside the house. The spectacle across the street went on longer than Charlie wanted to watch. His back began to ache from bending over and he stood to rub it. A cigarette break was in order.

His search of the house for a cigarette started calmly but became frantic until he remembered he left his cigarettes in his truck last night. By the time he returned to the window to view the progress in the dog diversion, it was over. The kids and the dog were nowhere to be seen and the bat finally stopped clanging. Peace and quiet reigned.

PART 2

THE SKIRMISH

The misery which they suffer is communicated to a large circle of friends and the whole neighborhood is indirectly disturbed by the malady of one.

Samuel B. Woodward, 1821

CHAPTER 8

CHAQUITO

Charlie showered in the afternoon that he first had his nightmare, as he told Ben he would. He shopped for cigarettes and beer later that afternoon, nearly filling an entire shopping basket with only these two items. Angry with himself for forgetting where he left his cigarettes during his nicotine fit, he decided to purchase an unusually large amount of cigarettes, cartons of them. He reasoned that he could afford to buy in quantity now that a bank account, with a substantial balance, remained at his disposal, thanks to the lawyer who recognized some need in his financial affairs. He also wanted to avoid the near panic that resulted from not having a smoke when needed and daily trips to the store would be eliminated.

After shopping, he distributed cigarette packs throughout the house and in his truck. Prior to today, he only bought a pack at a time. The cigarette insurance Charlie purchased made him feel protected, like his father undoubtedly felt when he purchased life insurance for family security.

Charlie never understood the concept of insurance before. Why would any sane person pay hard earned money for something they would never get to spend? As a result of the recent cash influx into Charlie's account, he had a different opinion now, not only of insurance but also of his father's foresight and concern. The security came in handy and Charlie began to realize the benefits extra cash on hand offered.

He didn't know why, but recently he felt more secure with a cigarette in his hand, sort of like when he was a baby and sucked on the corner of a small blanket. His mother called it "the blankie" and there were pictures of him in albums packed away somewhere holding and sucking on the blanket. To wean Charlie off the blanket, it was cut into increasingly smaller pieces until finally gone. His mother told him the story many times. She thought it was cute. He thought if he ever would consider giving up cigarettes that this would be the way to stop, a little at a time. But cigarettes were very important to Charlie, essential in fact, and now was not the time to consider breaking the habit.

In the days that followed, he received many more restricted calls. It seemed his parents were very persistent. They didn't leave messages and he didn't answer. He knew, by virtue of the restricted caller ID, not to pick up the phone.

In response to this onslaught, his angry imagination gave birth to banshees of wind, shrieking tornados sent down from heaven to whisk away his parents and their pesky judgment. This treatment was uncalled for, beyond the nature of his infraction. Peace and quiet: That's what he wanted. No more threats of pain. No more sorrow. *Wouldn't it be great to have that power?*

Trailing in the anger-storm aftermath came disappointment. First anger then depression. Laboring with feelings such as these, not answering the phone seemed a less dramatic and easier way to handle the situation.

His parents had failed him. He had such vaunted expectations for the next call, too. It proved the exact opposite of what he wanted, needed. They seemed to prefer thwarting his progress, his recovery. They couldn't see that he was in pain, pain caused by their actions. He wanted to close the door on them, shut them out, and make them feel sorry for what they did to him.

Thoughts of the World Trade Center disaster surfaced again, but this time he focused on what President Bush did, or didn't do, in the aftermath. Charlie, like Bush, was shocked at first. It was to be expected. When he received news of the death of his parents, he collapsed to the floor in Becka's arms. He remembered sitting in silence considerably longer than Bush did in the Florida elementary school, while the world raced along waiting for action. That's right, everyone was waiting for action. The only action Bush took was to retreat to Air Force One and isolated security as Vice President Cheney took control of critical events. Charlie retreated to the isolated security of his mind as Ben Marshall took control of events helping him to cope. The patterns coincided remarkably well.

Charlie spent a great deal of time considering what the President did in the months that followed. The leader of the free world, being a worthy role model and sitting at the helm of the most powerful country on the planet, would be able to advise by deed alone. Charlie needed that elder guidance in his life now that his parents were gone.

He developed an interest in recent history and took notice of the actions taken by George Bush during a time of trouble, when those responsible for evil died in the atrocities they committed. Here truth, pure and piercing, presented itself to Charlie with advice he could glean from no other source. All Charlie had to do was imitate and follow. Excited by this new awareness and guidance in his life, he dwelt on the actions of the president.

Bush, along with trusted advisers, made bold aggressive moves in the world. He attacked groups thought to be responsible, pushed through tough but necessary legislation at home granting unprecedented, uncontested power, forged war against an elusive phantom enemy, and conducted numerous acts of brutality in foreign lands, all the while ignoring world opinion. He adhered to a well thought out plan bringing justice to evildoers. Bringing justice to evil, that was the key.

Charlie must take control, become powerful, right the wrong, make his parents proud, and, into his cloudy dismal circumstances, bring justice from the darkest depths into the glorious light of day.

The real light of day became too bright for Charlie's eyes now, so he wore sunglasses all the time, even at night. Dark lenses reduced the remarkably florescent colors and their mesmerizing effects that were always visible. He always wondered why some people, like movie and rock stars, wore sunglasses at night. He found out first-hand and it made sense. He understood. It had something to do with power, the power to transform the future, to mold a new reality.

Charlie sat in his chair by the window and sipped his hot coffee as he pondered the future.

He drank cups of coffee during the day and bottles of beer at night. His nightmare became a regular event now recalled in its entirety. He felt it was the cause of his insomnia, or maybe the pressure of molding a new reality. The beer seemed to relax him, and helped him get to sleep; to stay asleep was a different matter. He found the nightmare would wake him at all hours of the night and afterward there was difficulty getting back to sleep. In spite of the alcohol, he stayed up later and later each night. He began to fear sleep due to the dreams. His mind, an active whorl of thoughts and sensations, became difficult, if not impossible to control. The result, of course, was that he needed larger doses of coffee during the day to wake up and stay awake, and greater quantities of beer to sleep. He was concerned about this new pattern in his life, but then there were so many concerns lately. What was one more problem, give or take?

Eating habits also suffered: Junk food, or anything he could make fast and easy, became his staple. Most times, he ate at fast food restaurants or brought the food home; boxes, bags, and wrappers littered the house. Garbage collected steadily and the house became cluttered, defiled. Good nutrition was impossible. He now longed for his mother's home-cooked meals and would even welcome the microwave version of leftover food, which he grudgingly ate many times in the past.

Most weekend days and late afternoons found Charlie in his comfortable easy chair in the living room facing the window with the shades pulled up. He smoked, drank, gazed out the window, and wore his trusty sunglasses. His attention was directed toward the neighborhood in general, but specifically focused, often fixed, on the Mexicans across the street. A house of hatred was being constructed in him by virtue of his inconsiderate Mexican neighbors. Nails were hammered each time their aluminum bat clanged, a ball landed in his yard, and when he saw that pain in the ass dog running around his yard.

"How could they hurt me?" He repeated over and over when thinking of his parents.

"What a nuisance they've become," he said whenever the phone rang with the restricted number. "Why won't they leave me alone?" he yelled, as he held his head between trembling hands. "Can't they understand I'm making them sorry for what they did?"

And he thought about the recurring nightmare. He rarely had nightmares before and now this. "Things are getting very odd around here," he said to himself more than a dozen times since the nightmares began.

Last week alone posed a series of challenges: Mornings were difficult to negotiate for work, and driving the delivery van became harder, too. Directions, paperwork, everything turned into draining challenges. Charlie was late for work one day last week, and he accomplished less while at work. Concentration had become nearly impossible; even conversations were hard to follow. Asking people to repeat themselves was a common occurrence.

He didn't like what was happening to him but was powerless to stop it. Frustration ruled the day, and nights for that matter. Steering wheels took a few blows as the baffling behavior continued while driving. He held his hands in a fist when failing to follow conversations at work. The bull stare came back with a vengeance.

Video games and television, former amusements, became chores, hard work, hypnotizing. Game scores were negligible and quickly lost. Television forced him to stare in unrewarding, useless concentration. Programs seemed to change without notice and ran into each other so that he remembered relatively nothing about what he watched for hours. He came to view both amusements as wasted time.

To simply sit and watch the world outside was easier. He listened to music trying to relax and sooth his nerves. It seemed simple. All he had to do was listen. So the radio stations played quietly on the home stereo, his truck, and in the van at work. Ultimately, he spent time in search of stimulus reduction.

On Monday, January 29th, Charlie called in sick to work. He stayed home planning to get needed rest. At seven in the morning, he sat in his chair by the window and turned on the stereo tuned to 98 KUPD, one of his favorite stations that played rock music on the morning show. He sat with his coffee, smoked, and tried to relax. He was dressed only in shorts ready to accomplish absolutely nothing.

"Charles," a voice called to Charlie over the sound of the softly playing stereo.

Charlie turned around, so quickly, he spilled coffee on his thigh. He didn't notice the hot liquid. The voice seemed to come from behind him. He expected to see someone in the living room, but nobody was there. He paused with his head turned around toward the room and inspected the space. His wary eyes darted from the couch, to the television, to the hallway in an uneasy search. He listened intently and hoped to hear something; anything to verify what he had heard and what fully occupied his attention. He reached for the remote to the stereo and turned the volume off. He listened.

"Charles," said the voice again.

Charlie spun his head forward to look about with the same result.

"Charles. It is a smart thing you have done not to answer our phone calls," the voice said.

Charlie's eyes widened. He felt his brows rise further up his forehead. He stared while his cigarette burned quietly between brown-stained fingers, the smoke rising straight up in the air. He listened hard.

"Yes, Charles, it is your mother speaking. You have forced me to communicate with you in this manner. I approve. It is much safer. No one can overhear our conversations this way."

Charlie closed his eyes and sighed.

"Your father and I are very sorry that you were harshly corrected. However, we stand behind what we did . . . what had to be done. I know you are angry and have been avoiding us, but as I have told you before, we have a plan for you that cannot be avoided. Your training, your work will begin today."

"Hello, Mom," Charlie said, with some relief. "You're right. I have been avoiding you . . . your calls. I didn't want to talk. Dad hurt me."

"We know son, but it was for your own benefit. If we could have avoided hurting you we would have. But I think you are well aware of the seriousness of the situation now and future lapses will be eliminated . . . for good. I am sure you would not wish to repeat that lesson again."

"No. I guess I'd avoid it at all costs now," Charlie said, and put out his cigarette in the nearby ashtray. She didn't like his smoking habit. He braced for the complaint about smoking in their house as he put down the remote and picked up his coffee cup sipping it slowly.

"Good, Charles. Now, remember I told you that we have a plan. The plan is quite simple really: You will begin by trimming unwanted elements from your neighborhood. By removing the already dead and wasteful members, you will help the parts that remain to grow stronger. You will perform your work and become the gardener of society. Humanity will benefit, be grateful. Even the President will approve Charles.

"The plan has two stages, two sections we must address: The first section will test your resolve. You must develop courage and devotion; demonstrate strength of purpose in small matters first. Then you will be able to transfer your attention to more weighty matters in the second part of the plan, where the real benefit to society will be realized. First, you will work locally, in the neighborhood, and then you will deal with Arizona at large.

"As I said, your work will begin today, section one. Your operative word, the word you will recognize to spur you to action will be 'reaper,' for you will reap the dead-wood, stray animals from the neighborhood. You will remove the dog and cat strays from your neighborhood because they sap the strength and vitality from the community and must be eliminated. This is your initial work. You will start immediately. Events are coming together as we speak.

"Time is short. Remember, Charles, 'reaper.' When you hear this word you will know what to do. I have to go now. Your work begins."

"Bye, Mom," Charlie said calmly looking to the ceiling.

He no longer felt bewildered. A sense of purpose pulsed through him again like the blood in his veins. He was glad his mother had apologized. The silent treatment seemed to work. He considered the word "reaper." His thoughts were interrupted by the sound of the aluminum bat hitting the concrete driveway across the street.

"The fucking little Mexican brats are at it again . . . and on a school day no less," Charlie said, as he directed his vision across the street.

They *were* at it again, and they instantly pissed him off. He stood up from his chair in anger and clenched his teeth. Every nerve tingled in his body from the sound of that metal bat. He couldn't believe they were doing this at seven thirty in the morning.

He watched their mother open the front door to bellow instructions to the kids. She pointed toward the garage door and as she did it opened. The father got into the car. Before the woman could close the front door, the dog bolted through a crack and ran into the street. It looked as though the dog ran with a purpose, to chase a cat perhaps, and ran down the street until out of sight.

Apparently, the Mexican family cared little for the welfare of the dog as they refused to chase him. Charlie guessed that they were headed to school or work and didn't want to be late—priorities. They had no time now to chase the dog. It had vacated the area anyway and was long gone. The family piled into the car and backed out the driveway. The garage door closed and they disappeared down the street out of sight.

Charlie sat back in his chair and drank his coffee, relishing the solitude of the moment. He turned up the stereo volume again and lit another cigarette.

On the way to the main thoroughfare, most of the neighbors on the street drove past Charlie's house to their destinations and by nine thirty the neighborhood became quiet.

At this time, the dog returned. It meandered and sniffed in a random pattern, but always closer toward Charlie's house. It sniffed a tree on the lawn of Charlie's next-door neighbor and deposited a urine sample. Wandering, the dog eventually sniffed a spot in the grass of Charlie's lawn; it squatted down to relieve itself of last night's dinner near the corner where the driveway and sidewalk joined. He watched with detest as the dog bent its torso in a sitting stance. The feces began to drop to his property one by one. Before the last fell, the song in his nightmare, *Don't Fear (The Reaper)*, played on the radio.

The dog finished its business and headed up the driveway to the left side of Charlie's house.

Familiar words poured out of the stereo speakers.

Charlie jumped up from his chair in the living room and ran to his old childhood bedroom behind the garage to follow the dog from inside the house.

"Seasons don't fear the reaper . . ."

Charlie heard the action word from the stereo in the other room as he opened the shade perpetually closed in his old bedroom. He watched as the dog pawed at the gate, open a crack, but not latched. It pushed the gate open far enough to sidle through, and the spring tensioned gate closed behind. This time the latch clicked shut.

"Now I've got you . . . you little Mexican bastard. It's time for a nice little Mexican payback," Charlie said, as he left the window on his way to the kitchen door leading to the back yard.

As soon as Charlie opened the kitchen door, the dog tramped from the block wall that surrounded his property straight to the patio door where Charlie stood. The dog was playful. Its white tail wagged back and forth slapping Charlie's legs and everything else nearby. The dog's mouth was open, panting, and the tongue hung over its teeth. It seemed happy to see Charlie.

He held the door open and the dog went eagerly through, no coaxing at all.

"This was easier than I thought it would be," Charlie said closing the door behind him.

"It's like you're willing to pay the price to keep the reaper satisfied," he said to the dog as it sniffed the area near the garbage can and closely inspected old fast food wrappers on the floor. The tail still wagged excessively hitting the wall and garbage can as he wandered about; its dangling brown ears swayed with every shake of its head.

Charlie went to the knife rack and grabbed the largest, sharpest Farberware knife available. It had a nine-inch, honed blade and a black, plastic handle. Charlie thought it seemed up to the task. He then went to the refrigerator and fished out a slice of Kraft American cheese from the package on the door. He peeled off the wrapper and held the orange slice of cheese in the air above the dog as bait. He headed to the bathroom off the hallway and the dog followed; neither broke step. Charlie figured it a more controlled space, easier to clean. When they were both inside, he closed the door.

The dog looked up at him with begging eyes as it sat patiently on the floor near the bathtub anticipating the cheese snack. Charlie noticed the dog had a collar. He placed the cheese and the knife on the sink beside him and bent over the dog. He read the information on the dog tag: "*Chaquito*, if found return to Manual Garcia . . . hum . . ." There was also a phone number that he didn't bother to read. "You won't be needing this anymore, *Chaquito*." He removed the collar.

Chaquito seemed pleased to be rid of the collar as he scratched his unencumbered neck with his right back foot and then sat patiently still.

Charlie reached back to the sink, put the collar in the basin, and collected the knife and cheese. He then pushed open the bathtub curtain completely to one side out of the tub.

"Let's see if you're as stupid as you look," he said to the dog and threw the cheese slice into the bathtub. *Chaquito*, without hesitation, jumped in. He licked the slice of cheese that landed flat on the bottom surface of the tub. When that didn't work for ingestion, he attempted to bite the cheese with his front teeth. On the third attempt, he successfully began chewing the tasty orange square.

With the mutt's attention diverted, Charlie slipped the keen blade under its neck. With one forceful motion, he slid and pulled upward on the knife slicing the front and left side of *Chaquito*'s neck wide open. The knife cut clean to the spine, slicing through skin, muscle, and tendons. Blood immediately squirted out of the gaping wound. After a brief time delay, *Chaquito* choked and gasped in a yowl mixed with gurgle sounds as he scampered around in the slippery enclosure. He lunged into the white walls that surrounded the tub, his head lolling off to the right side. The wound exposed red muscle fibers and white tendons. Blood splashed in a random pattern.

Charlie backed away from the dog toward the door to watch the spectacle unfold from a safer, cleaner position.

Charlie felt no sign of horror or joy; the work was performed unemotionally, mechanically. He held the blood-smeared knife in a defensive position in case the dog somehow made it out. It did not.

In less than thirty seconds, *Chaquito* stopped moving. His short white hair matted in a pool of sticky blood, blood that conveniently dripped down the walls, across the floor of the tub, and into the drain. His head twisted backward beneath his body.

Charlie watched the mutt's diminished effort to breathe. The air no longer filtered through the head but came directly from the exposed, bloody neck. When *Chaquito* exhaled for the last time, red bubbles burst from the blood-filled windpipe and a sliver of orange cheese, surrounded by red blood, protruded from the dead dog's throat.

CHAPTER 9

DISPOSAL

During the clean up operation, Charlie, in an all-businesslike manner, focused on the messy chore. So quick, careful, and diligent, he could have been mistaken for the owner of a restoration company specializing in crime scene clean up.

The animal weighed approximately thirty pounds and one bag, Charlie estimated, would not be sturdy enough. He didn't want tares or leaks to warrant additional cleaning, especially if blood dripped on the carpet or in the truck pickup bed, where the bag would eventually be placed for further transport and disposal. *Chaquito's* limp body unwillingly slipped into a doubled-up, thirty-gallon trash bag.

Most of the blood, confined to the tub, washed down the drain easily as planned. Splatters on the floor, walls, and toilet bowl were wiped down with a sponge. There were no carpets or throw rugs to clean or rinse. The shower curtain came clean with the showerhead spray. Every inch of the bathroom, even the ceiling, inspected and made spotless. The tiles gleamed. Except for the smell of bleach, no casual observer would have ever guessed that a bloodletting took place in this setting after Charlie finished cleaning.

"The room needed a good cleaning anyway," Charlie said to the dog inside the garbage bag. The bathroom emerged the only spotless place in the house.

"You know *Chaquito*," Charlie considered out loud nearing the end of his mundane task, "maybe I should have given you more time to eat the cheese, a sort of reward for making your elimination so easy for me. Ah, but what does it matter?" he reconsidered. "You're only a dog. You can't understand the concept of mercy or reward. Can you? You're just a dumb animal like your owners."

Charlie kicked the bag for a response.

"What difference does it really make in the big picture?" he said staring at the black bag. "Beside, you're dead now. Aren't you?"

Charlie removed and saved the dog tag and placed *Chaquito*'s collar in the trash bag along with the mutt. He didn't want the ID found by some remote chance. He planned to bury it somewhere in the back yard at a later date. The evidence temporarily went into the silverware drawer in the kitchen, the rinsed knife into the dishwasher.

Charlie felt no sentiment about what he had done. The job accomplished and completed in a suitable manner. He followed his mother's earlier instructions to the letter, and performed his duty without witnesses. Some credit he gave to *Chaquito* for the success because the mutt was a willing sacrifice. Admittedly, things could have been harder.

Elimination of strays to make the community better had begun. The dog would appear to have vanished from the neighborhood, a runaway. He completed the first step on the road to bigger tasks, his resolve proven.

At eleven o'clock, under cover of dark on this Monday night, the time seemed right to take care of the final detail, disposal of the evidence. The simple plan provided for finding an appropriate, unsupervised dumpster and making an imperceptible deposit, like night deposits made at banks. He'd drive to the stores down on Eighty-third Avenue, have a look around, make his drop, and do some shopping, thereby serving two necessities at once.

Charlie checked the neighborhood from the front window. Everything appeared desolate. In his truck, he adjusted his sunglasses while looking in the rear view mirror and backed the truck out of the garage. Houses in the neighborhood were dark, as expected, with the exception of outside lights. Most houses in the area, including his, displayed illuminated porch lights to discourage crime. Charlie's parents had done this for years. Who was he to break a successful habit? As he passed the Mexican's house on his way to the store, Charlie wondered what conversations they had during the day about their precious dog.

"Think anyone was blamed for your loss?" Charlie said looking into the rear view mirror toward the truck bed. "You know, *Chaquito*, they did attempt a feeble search for you during the day when they returned from work and school. I saw them from my chair by the window." The back of the truck remained silent.

"They didn't knock on anyone's door though, merely walked around calling for you and then went to other areas out of sight. I think your owners got what they deserved," he said as he passed the Mexican's house, "and if they don't like it, they can just move back to Mexico. Right?"

Charlie turned south on Eighty-third Avenue.

"It's not your fault, anyway. Your dumb owners are the ones to blame. Next time, maybe they'll think twice about letting their animals out, defiling the neighborhood."

During the uneventful ride down Eighty-third Avenue, Charlie only passed one slow car that traveled in his direction and only one vehicle, a motorcycle, passed by going north. The extremely bright light of the motorcycle vibrated in passing over the uneven pavement. Charlie shielded his vision with his hand. One house displayed mesmerizing Christmas lights. He wondered why the people still displayed them so long after the holidays. Traffic lights, also vibrant to him, were green all the way on his three-mile trip. He didn't stop once. "This should be the way the lights run all the time," he said to himself.

The supermarket and concentration of stores were located on the corner of a major intersection. The first business he came to was a bar located in a strip mall with other stores, including a gas station. He drove slowly around the back of the building and there, ahead on the right, stood a dumpster.

This was perfect. Charlie eased the pickup even with the dumpster. Just then he saw a crew of pavement sweepers in three trucks cleaning the parking lot on the far side of the building. Lights were flashing making the activity level too high. His search continued.

On the other side of the intersection stood a drug store, an auto parts store, and another strip mall with mostly fast-food restaurants, in each case, the dumpsters well lit. One overflowed with trash, another locked. Charlie couldn't believe the difficulty involved in finding a place to get rid of the evidence.

The supermarket across the street was open, and the various other stores were either closed or had lights on but no customers inside. Very few cars occupied the parking lot, a good sign. He had been to all these stores many times before, but never in search of dumpsters behind buildings. Around the back of the supermarket, he passed by derelict baskets stacked like cars in a junk yard, shelving that would never see the inside of another store, and trailers backed up to loading docks like soldiers standing at attention waiting for a drill inspection.

Near the back corner of the building, an alleyway appeared flanked on either side by two large and open metal doors. He drove by the well lit outside area and tried to see down the alley, but darkness obscured the view. That was good. He removed his sunglasses and, with the help of brake lights, found the illusive dumpster all the way against the back wall of the alley.

Charlie inspected the walls all around for cameras or windows; there were neither. He turned off the truck's lights and left the pickup running as he got out to inspect the dumpster on foot.

To the left, against the building, generators and air conditioners hummed behind a chain link fence. On the right, against the opposite wall, weeds grew, some a foot tall, in a narrow dirt strip interspersed with rogue trash that escaped garbage truck collection. Pebbles and loose debris cracked under foot on the pavement as he headed back to the dumpster that smelled of rotting food.

The eight-inch opening of the compacted dumpster forced Charlie to stop and calculate whether the bulk of the dog would fit through the opening. Suddenly, he heard loud clicking sounds behind him off to his left. Alarmed, he turned around expecting to see employees, but viewed nothing but the humming machines against the building. His heart pounded against his sternum as he listened, eyes frantically searching the alley. The air conditioner compressor clicked on again while he watched making the same sound as before. A false alarm produced the noise, but his heart continued to race. In spite of his growing concern about the possibility of being caught, he decided to take a chance that the dog would fit.

He jumped in his pickup and backed down the dark alley that afforded better cover for the truck and convenience regarding dog transportation. He moved quickly to the camper shell door at the rear of his truck, and felt pressure, a need to rush, as though he had been there too long already. He opened the camper door, grabbed the trash bag, turned around, and threw the bag into the opening. It didn't fit.

Charlie swore under his breath and felt beads of sweat form on his brow. Frantically, he arranged the dog's parts inside the bag so that the head went into the opening first. It slipped in easily, but the dog became stuck at the shoulder. Urgency mounted as Charlie looked around while he first shoved then began pounding harder on the animal's remains. The beating maneuvered the dog's soft tissue and hard bone into the slot, one leg at a time, and he exerted considerable pressure to crush the chest through. Jumping to gain more leverage and his heaving breath produced considerable noise that he hoped would not be heard. Finally, the mutt slipped completely through.

He mopped his wet face with his shirt as he ran to the driver side door and got behind the wheel. Thoroughly stressed, he put back on his sunglasses, drove out of the alley, and turned on the lights, glad to be done with the job.

He parked the pickup in the front parking lot of the supermarket and turned off the lights and motor. He took out his pack of cigarettes, and with trembling hands, lit one. He sat in the truck a while to calm and gather himself. The disposal process raised his blood pressure and he felt a need to prepare to shop. When ready, he got out of the vehicle and headed around the front of the truck toward the store.

Looking toward the store entrance, Charlie noticed a man exiting the store. The guy watched him as he passed the front of his truck and seemed to be walking straight toward Charlie, looking directly at him. He briefly broke eye contact with the man and detoured a few steps, but the man made necessary adjustments in his gait to continue toward Charlie.

Extremely nervous, Charlie considered running in another direction, going back to the truck and leaving. He knew that this was not a mere customer, but the store manager who saw everything at the dumpster via a hidden video camera. He surprised himself how quickly he envisioned an arrest and being detained in an office while the police were called to the scene. An investigation would be made. Mexicans and animal rights activists would descend upon him. Charlie's mind raced.

He stopped walking. He took one last drag off his cigarette and tossed the butt on the ground waiting for the man to pass. The man did not pass, but walked right up to Charlie and grabbed his arm. *I should have run while I still had the chance. My life is over.*

Charlie experienced a sinking feeling in his loins, as if all blood in that area of his body drained to his feet. His legs begin to quiver and his head became faint.

"You left your camper shell door open, son," the man said, as he held Charlie's arm and pointed with his other hand toward the pickup. "If you got anything of value in there, I wouldn't leave it open this time of night."

Charlie turned on the spot. He saw that he indeed forgot to close the door after visiting the dumpster. He gave a nervous laugh, said nothing in response, and walked back to lock the door. On his way, Charlie felt some relief, but the guy got a good look at him and could be a witness at a missing dog trial. The observant man would never forget Charlie's worried face. It would be the clinching testimony the all-Mexican jury would need to convict him.

His concern did not diminish on his way back into the store and he wished he were invisible. He watched everyone and even considered shopping at another store to avoid a possible confrontation.

He accomplished his shopping task without incident glad to be standing at the checkout counter. He paid the bill in cash dropping some loose change on the floor that he didn't stop to pick up, but made a hasty retreat back to the truck.

In his grocery bag, nestled among other necessities, were cans of dog and cat food.

CHAPTER 10

DISMISSAL

Although portions of *(Don't Fear) The Reaper* stubbornly repeated in Charlie's memory, he forgot large portions of the song. For complete future inspiration and ease, he bought the CD permitting discretionary listening enjoyment as needed for the important job of eliminating neighborhood strays. Charlie frequently played the song on the house stereo while he went about the stray elimination business for nearly two months.

During this time, Charlie developed a twitch, in which his head turned jerking slightly to his left while neck muscles pulled downward on the left lip and his left eye closed slightly. It occasionally occurred in one quick and involuntary motion. Whenever it happened, communication sessions with his parents ensued giving Charlie encouragement, instruction, and focus.

During one of these messages, Charlie's instruction involved shopping for plywood and other construction materials to erect a paltry shed in the backyard against the house, near the covered patio. Fabrication forced him to use earplugs to muffle the sounds of saw and hammer, which were too loud for his extremely sensitive hearing. He didn't need goggles though since the ever-present sunglasses protected his eyes from sawdust and the Arizona sun.

The ground around the shed remained littered with hundreds of cigarette butts and numerous discarded empty coffee cups until final cleanup. Some of the cups claimed cigarette filter trophies firmly stuck inside the cup by evaporated brown goo. The project kept him busy during time away from his courier job until early February, when completion of the shed allowed reaping work to begin in earnest. Charlie's time and effort now focused upon stray elimination, the important work, and left the courier position neglected to a continually increasing extent.

Many affairs and circumstances went heedless the whole month of February and nearly all of March, including Ben's petitioning for attendance at the yearly Super Bowl party and the annual St. Patrick's Day bash held mostly in Charlie's honor, being of Irish decent. Charlie answered Ben's calls, but attended to little else, to Ben's dismay.

With a lapse of attention to the caller ID on one occasion, Charlie answered the phone when Becka had called. She sounded so happy when he answered the phone that he didn't have the heart to hang up on her. He missed her but found his schedule too demanding now to see her even though sometimes he desired her company. She was concerned about him so he eased her mind saying that he was very busy at work. She also wondered about the wedding plans and their future together to which Charlie, against his mother's wishes, indicated that things were still okay in that regard, but would be necessarily delayed due to the demands of his work.

Because of Charlie's increasing attendance problems and other factors, an inevitable encounter with management at the courier company transpired on March twenty-third, an otherwise unassuming Friday afternoon.

*   *   *

The manner in which Art Feldman dressed corresponded in similarity, not surprisingly, to his desk and office. His stained beige shirt, not completely tucked in his pants, revealed the naked milk-white skin of his copious flanks. Overtaxed suspenders strained to hold up abbreviated pants held taut at the waist by excessive stomach flesh, thus paying the debt of length owing to the effort. Curly black hair grew down the back of his wide neck, which he mostly gave up trying to keep shaved and groomed until it was haircut time. There was a demarcation line bordering a clean-shaven face and chest hair. He felt a need to shave at least; a beard for a businessman was out of the question.

His forehead was rather high due to a receding hairline and tiny little indentations on either side of the bridge of his nose proclaimed the use of reading glasses to all who saw him. They were located somewhere under the mass of papers strewn about his workspace. Dark brown eyes focused wantonly on a half-eaten, open bag of chocolate-chip cookies on the desk, systematically devoured while talking on the phone. As crumbs dropped to the desk surface, a fleshy hairy hand swept them from papers in a spurious endeavor to inflict order amid turmoil.

His office boasted inexpensive prints in respectable frames and dated award plaques hung randomly about the walls, an effort in decoration. Unadorned windows framed a view of the dry Salt River bed in the airport industrial community of downtown Phoenix, with silhouettes of bold high-rise buildings and mountains in the distance and delicate palm trees in the foreground. Randomly placed buildings lined the imaginary bank of the desert riverbed casting long shadows in the late afternoon sun.

Mr. Feldman spoke loudly in a valiant struggle to overcome his tendency to mumble even while on the phone to his private secretary in the adjacent, outer office.

"Is that problem employee, ah . . . what's his name . . . McShane, back from the field yet?"

"Yes, Mr. Feldman," the secretary cooed into the phone. "Should I send him in now?"

"Well, what the hell do you think?" the hard-driven owner of Maricopa Couriers asked, then stuffed another cookie into his mouth. He felt his jowl shake as he chewed thinking that someday a diet would be in order.

He dropped the receiver back into the phone cradle and reached for the diet soda on the desk to wash down the dry mouthful.

With the knock on the door, he wiped his moist lips with the back of his hand, and tossed the empty soda can in the wastebasket under the desk.

"Come in," the three hundred pound man over-filling the executive leather chair bellowed.

Charlie McShane entered the office. He closed the door and advanced within feet of the owner's desk. He stood between two matched and worn leather chairs.

"Mr. Feldman?" McShane asked.

"Yes, McShane. Sit down," he ordered, then motioned with his thick hand to one of the black chairs that faced across from the enormous mahogany desk.

McShane did as ordered. He sat quiet and attentive, hands folded in his lap, with both feet firm on the fraying carpeted floor.

"McShane," Feldman began. He always called employees by their surname if he knew and could pronounce it. If not, a formal address would be avoided in favor of a simple pronoun.

"McShane," he repeated, "I've been receiving reports, disturbing reports from your dispatcher, that you've been arriving for work consistently late. H.R. tells me you've used all the sick days allotted to you and still you continue to take days off, without pay I might add. Your work performance and productivity has suffered considerably in the time you decide to actually show up for work, especially in the last month. Your work performance is unacceptable. I've also received complaints from H.R. that fellow employees say you've been acting strange, saying things that don't make sense; seems they think you're creepy lately. Two of my customers have complained to me about you specifically, for the same reasons. It seems they would rather do business with another firm than have you delivering their packages."

He paused for a moment trying to size up his wayward employee. The effort was quickly suspended.

"I sure as hell can't afford to lose customers and I won't have a disruptive employee causing trouble in my operation. Now, I know about your parents, the tragedy you suffered over the holidays, but it's now near the end of March. I've given you plenty of time to get yourself together, but frankly, I just can't afford to give you any more time."

Feldman waited for a reaction. None was forthcoming.

"Therefore, effective immediately, I will no longer be requiring your services," he said in a businesslike, cut and dry, loud manner.

Feldman gave himself to speculation and puzzled over McShane's non-commenting manner during the last few minutes. McShane had said nothing during the entire speech, nothing in defense, no interruptions, no questions; he had no reaction physically and his face remained placid. Feldman considered this firing to be the most unusual in all his twenty-three-years experience. And now, after all the accusations and being fired, he still displayed no agitation.

Feldman looked into McShane's eyes. They showed visible signs of stress. They shifted endlessly, seeming to betray a multitude of thoughts that, for some strange reason, remained unexpressed. Concern grew as he watched McShane at length sitting in silence. He wondered if the employee had heard anything he said.

"McShane, do you understand what I just explained to you?"
"Yes."
"Do you have anything to say?"
McShane asked, in a laborious manner, with obvious pressure beneath the calm exterior, "Would it make a difference . . . if I said . . . something . . . anything?"

Mr. Feldman peered in uncharacteristic silence over his paper-strewn desk at McShane and felt a strange mounting tension. At first he considered the kid's point. There would be nothing he could say to make a difference in this meeting's outcome.

Then he focused on how McShane seemed to choose his words with extreme care, with too much deliberation, as though each syllable needed to be considered individually. The guy was in slow motion mentally, or at least appeared to be, and his ability to speak and work hindered greatly . . . by what? Was the kid sick? Feldman didn't know the answer, but he now knew at least, why McShane's productivity plummeted, only able to complete a quarter of the work previously accomplished. In addition, this, no doubt, caused the employee reaction, why they found him to be strange and weird.

Feldman watched McShane's eyes focus about the room like a spastic ping-pong ball. The kid hardly ever looked directly at him. A sudden trepidation drenched Feldman completely from head to toe; a sense of urgency mounted, gripped him, and it now became priority number one to end the meeting as quick as possible, to vacate this McShane time-bomb from his presence before something bad could happen. Feldman sensed something evil and wanted no part.

"No. No it wouldn't," Mr. Feldman agreed, "but it's what I expected, that's all. What most people have done do in your situation."

McShane's raised eyebrows became the only response Mr. Feldman could view and then he lifted his hands from his lap, palms up, in a "what now" gesture; his eyes glanced out the window then back toward Mr. Feldman briefly.

"Well, you can leave now. My secretary will give you final instructions and a box in case there's anything you want to take of a personal nature."

Feldman originally decided not to give Charlie any more money than earned. But he said, to appease what he felt was like a volcano ready to erupt, "I feel, in spite of the circumstances, you should receive a severance check. And I wish you luck. You were, at one time, a valued employee here. Close the door on your way out."

Mr. Feldman watched as the odd, young man rose from the chair and left. On his way out, McShane did not close the door. Feldman felt lucky that this small act of defiance became all the kid could muster.

CHAPTER 11

SNARE

After being fired and during the drive home, satisfaction and relief circulated in Charlie's mind like ice cream and milk in a blender. What a fortuitous development. The courier job was tedious, dull, unworthy. He shivered at the thought of driving all day, making deliveries, and the meaninglessness of a life thus spent. Although he worked at the job for nearly two years, making deliveries was not his first choice for employment. The position opened and he needed money. He took the work out of desperation.

Courier driving made him feel as though he were a lab rat tortured for months running randomly through the Phoenix metropolitan maze. Feldman, the mad scientist, took notes concerning the efficiency and adaptability of the hapless specimen. With successful scampering, no electrical shocks were administered, but woe to the misguided, tired, and harried.

Charlie never desired to be a courier. He held contempt for his fellow employees that complained about all aspects of the jobs they did, but remained in the rut. He remembered hearing about the labor of love and how people are most happy when they're devoted. Charlie, fond of helping society and making his parents proud, looked forward to loving a full time position in the elimination business.

The extra time afforded as a result of being fired would provide an opportunity for real progress to be achieved—a pleasurable occupation that meant something in the big picture of life on this planet. Slaving for that fat pig of a boss illustrated a most revolting waste of time. Feldman didn't deserve Charlie's time. No more moonlighting as a delivery driver. It was time to move on.

And what did his fellow employees know, anyway? They had nerve to complain about him: Him a problem? Pah. Being Mexican, now that would be a suitable definition of a problem. Strange? They didn't know what the word entailed. They're the odd ones, always talking about him behind his back: Wagging tongues, whispering, pointing when they thought he wasn't aware. Charlie saw them write on their pads about him whenever he entered the office. They scribbled memos, prepared accusations, spied on him. They're the troublemakers. Better to leave them to their mundane lives. Let them find somebody else to prattle about.

"Yes, I'm glad that dumb fuck fired me," Charlie said, as he smoked a cigarette watching the glowing vibrating red traffic light through his windshield. "Saved me the effort of giving him my resignation. Why should I allow myself to be watched over like a caged rat? Or be persecuted one minute longer. And for what? Pennies? Chump change? I don't need them. Not any more."

When the light changed green, Charlie accelerated and adjusted his sunglasses. He couldn't wait to get home. Important pleasurable work waited.

*   *   *

Whenever Charlie returned home, checking the snare in the shed he built in the backyard became his first and most important task. The process reminded him of fishing, checking the line with a yank to find out if anything got hooked. For this purpose, a peephole allowed a view of the inner space of the shed without opening the door around back unnecessarily.

The hastily built shed consisted of flimsy plywood walls that blocked the view of the curious. Polyethylene foam backing the entire structure muffled noises from inside. Canned cat food, tuna, and peanut butter seemed to work best at luring small dogs and cats that could fit through the swinging trap door at the bottom of the shed. The snare, triggered by a strong spring, set the noose located at the far end from the entrance.

Most animals caught by the neck died of strangulation. The more they struggled, the tighter the noose became. When this occurred, Charlie would only be responsible for disposal of the evidence. In other cases, a front leg would sometimes be snared. This necessitated a bloody visit to the bathroom. The trap worked remarkably well for such a primitive device. Charlie and his parents were satisfied by the results.

The snare constantly occupied him in his pursuit of perfection: The establishment of the perfect, stray-less community. He thought of the auto commercial on television that used those words to advertise their diligent work to make the perfect car while he slid aside the peephole cover.

Charlie held the cover with his hand, looked through the eyehole, and viewed another cat caught in the snare by a right front paw. In the thrill of the moment, he decided not to play the song about the reaper, as he had always done in the past. Instead, he reached for a pair of leather gloves located on an exterior shelf. He flapped the gloves out to remove potential insects of the biting, stinging variety and worked them onto his hands.

Entering the shed, he saw a pure-white, longhaired adult cat crouched in the corner of the trap. The snare's wire stretched to full length. The cat's hair puffed out in anger made it look much bigger. The distracted animal gnawed the wire seemingly unconcerned about Charlie's presence. He closed the door and reached down to hold the cat in place while attempting to remove the wire noose, a procedure accomplished safely a number of times in the past two months.

The passive cat suddenly rolled over on its back and burst into a frenzy of sharp claws and teeth. The spontaneous action took Charlie by surprise. In desperation, the cat bit into one gloved finger and held tight while kicking its back legs, claws flashing. It scratched long bloody grooves into Charlie's arm without glove protection. He let go of the animal screaming in pain. The violent whirl of sharp edges and teeth retreated back to the corner. It's angry, green-yellow eyes stared up into Charlie's startled face. It hissed, spit, and growled with ears folded back.

Charlie held his injured arm to his body. Inspecting the wound, he saw no veins were opened. Just numerous long but shallow flesh wounds burned a deep red. Anger built as he glared at his white assailant. This represented the first time any animal put up such a fight.

Injured, Charlie shrieked, "Fuck you!" He kicked with ferocity at the cat. "You little, fucking son-of-a-bitch," he yelled. Spit emitted from his mouth and fell upon the wailing creature. He steadied himself with his hands holding the walls while he kicked with his right foot. The assault required numerous blows to subdue the feline. When finished, the cat lay motionless. The once white fur turned red and brown from a mixture of blood and dirt.

His uncontrollable rage was not over. A knife from the kitchen would finish the job. Back in the trap, he stabbed the animal in a wild assault that ended with decapitation. Unceremoniously, he held the head and body beneath his feet accompanied by slight crunching sounds. He hacked with the knife until the ragged bloody neck released the head from the body.

Later, in a calmer atmosphere, Charlie regretted the loss of control. The bloodbath, now in the trap instead of the bathroom tub, presented problems. A major cleanup became necessary in order to insure other animals would not smell the scent and become wary. The job would necessitate meticulous cleanliness because of the strong sense of smell animals possessed. Even a spotless cleanup may not produce the desired result.

Charlie eventually got around to reading the cat's collar tag. Its name was Charlie—an omen he thought—a bad omen. A cat bearing his name would somehow be trouble.

*   *   *

At nine o'clock that evening, Charlie sat in the kitchen and drank dinner (his last beer in the refrigerator). He filled the trash bag that contained the cat's remains with the overflow of garbage on the kitchen floor. Still not satisfied with the bulk, he removed the old garbage bag out of the can and put that in also. He needed to take the trash out anyway. Today's work alone in the bag was too obviously a dead animal. The added weight and bulk concealed the evidence.

Charlie was fastidious about capture and disposal when he began his work. He did as his parents instructed with strong resolve and a steady purpose. It felt good to follow orders, have objectives. Although he was now experienced, a thoughtful, logical workman able to avoid pitfalls, today was not a good day. He didn't act logically. He made some changes in his routine and, as a result, that fucking white pain-in-the-ass screwed things up.

The problem might have resulted from being fired or that he didn't play the reaper song. But whatever the cause, he resolved to improve his effort. He would become more resourceful and control his temper. He couldn't imagine what caused him to lose his cool. He didn't like being upset. After all, he loved his work.

Charlie wanted to prove his value and graduate to the next step in his parents' plan. The sensation of a job well done no longer gratified. He desired to move forward, take the next step, make his parents proud. He stood ready for advancement in spite of what happened today.

His mother always told him that if you had a good reason to do something and did it well, then there could never be any wrong in it. His parents rewarded him by communicating from beyond the grave. How many people could say that? He didn't know how they did it, but the fact that they did made them sort of demigods. He worshipped them and remained duty bound attending their demands, which became his goals. He felt honored to comply. After all, they said that he would reap all the glory.

Charlie finished his beer in one long draft then fit the can into the trash bag through a hole furnished by the loosely tied yellow straps at the top. It was night now. Darkness provided cool temperatures, cover, and security. It seemed to be a time when he performed his best work.

With keys in hand, Charlie carried the trash bag to his pickup parked in the garage. Charlie began sweating as he tossed the bag in the truck bed. The temperature at this time of year was still warm long into the night with the garage door closed. He snapped the door to life with the remote and it grinded and strained along the guide rails. He lit a cigarette and watched the rear-view mirror a while to insure secrecy. He backed out and closed the garage door when everything seemed clear. He drove to the supermarket, his destination as so many times before.

The supermarket parking lot in front was busy and full of activity, but around back quiet prevailed, where the trash bin lodged. Careful inspection months ago verified there were no video cameras spying near the bin. A survey of the area showed no potential problems or witnesses. He backed the truck to the wide-open compactor bin, turned off the truck lights, and finished his cigarette. He waited, watching. In less than a minute, satisfied the time was right, he opened the camper shell door and made the transfer. Tossing in the bag, the smell of rotting vegetables wafted up from the near-full bin like a sour puff of wind blown into his face by the mythological god of landfills, protesting yet another undesirable deposit.

In his mind, Charlie saw the white cat crouched in the corner of the trap, hissing and spitting and he thought of his forearm scratches. In memory of the animal, he spit into the bin.

*   *   *

The bad omen the white cat represented to Charlie proved well founded in truth. In spite of his efforts to produce a sterile, non-revealing environment, no more animals entered the trap. It seemed as if Charlie had posted a sign in universal animal language "Beware—No Trespassing Under Penalty Of Death." The event of butchering the cat named Charlie in the shed signaled the end of an era.

Charlie gave chase to the last animal to even enter his backyard, a black cat. It ultimately escaped disappearing over the block wall surrounding his property. Only a six-inch, black-tail remnant remained clenched in his fist as witness of the pursuit, and then, nothing. Like the deserted, calm sea became windless and desolate in Captain Ahab's search for Moby Dick, Charlie's backyard became a forsaken wasteland.

CHAPTER 12

CHARLIE

The Gardner family lived in a house similar to Charlie's. They were neighbors in the same development, one street west and six lots north. Their house hugged the front end of a large triangular-shaped, cul-de-sac property. A gentle breeze blew from the southwest like nature's fingers playing a symphony on wind chimes hung from the backyard covered patio eave. Planters filled with marigolds and petunias splashed red, purple, and gold around the house. They brightened the landscape, but were destined to become dried brown cascades of death within two months. The Arizona sun can be brutal.

The weather was already warm but pleasant this early April morning. Mrs. Gardner opened the sliding glass door allowing fresh air mixed with the sweet fragrance of petunias to waft into the kitchen through the screen. Carried along with them came the soft and dreamy and restful sounds of the chimes.

Mrs. Gardner, influenced by magazines and advertising, considered a shopping spree to buy new wardrobes for her family. Easter, both the religious holiday and season, signaled spring fashion shopping to the masses. The season arrived early this April. She anticipated crowded stores. The day promised to be pleasurable, at least for her and Callie, her daughter. Her son, Jacob, might complain, but a bribe related to skateboards would silence the whining.

Today, a teacher's workday, meant more time off from school for the children. Mrs. Gardner transported her thoughts back to her own school days while pouring another cup of coffee. She couldn't remember getting so many breaks. Schoolteachers today had weeks of special disruptions allotted to various reasons and causes. She briefly wondered how children actually received an education at all, very undisciplined and wanting. The result frustrated her, caused additional expense burdens, and decreased her productivity at work.

Mrs. Gardner forgot about the day off until Jacob reminded her earlier this morning when she woke him. By then, it became too late to cover her responsibility by making arrangements with her retired mother, who lived quite a distance away in Sun City West. She did the only thing a creative mother could do in this situation. She called in sick.

The family participated in the morning breakfast ritual amid the background noise of meteorologist, Brad Perry, reporting pleasant weather details on the plasma TV in the empty living room. Mr. Gardner, dressed for work in snappy-casual business attire, ignored most of what happened at the table while reading the morning paper. His children verbally fenced between mouthfuls of cereal. Mrs. Gardner monitored their verbal thrusts and parries while dispensing the morning meal and otherwise catering to everyone.

Today's arguments, and for the past few days, concerned Charlie, the family's pure-white longhaired cat. Mrs. Gardner realized the need for discussion about such an emotional matter, but the parley became abusive.

"It's all your fault," Jacob said, and pointed a finger at his younger, blond-haired, blue-eyed sister dressed in yellow pajamas.

"Is not," Callie replied, and slapped Jacob's wagging finger away from her face.

"Is too. You're the last one to let Charlie out," he said, with a frown. "She's gone now for good because you're stupid."

"No, I'm not."

"Yes, you are. Stupid Callie, stupid Callie!"

Before Mrs. Gardner could perform her official family referee duties, Callie screamed, "I hate you!" She stormed out of the kitchen stamping her feet and wept all the way to her room. The sound of her upstairs bedroom door slamming shut signaled her arrival and the desire for privacy.

"Why'd you say that to your sister?" Mrs. Gardner asked, Jacob. "You know she's not stupid. Charlie's been out hundreds of times before. She always came back. You've let her out yourself. We all have."

"I know," Jacob said, "but I'm mad, and sad, all at the same time." The eleven-year old's sullen face quickly turned downcast, his tearful eyes betraying his current emotion.

When seven, Charlie, became Jacob's first pet, at the same age as his sister was now. Jacob's responsibilities to clean, feed, and care for Charlie proved the animal really his. He gave the cat a male name not knowing the animal to be female. Friends and family thought the error endearing. Jacob did a wonderful job over the years to love and care for Charlie. He became extremely attached to the animal he considered a sister, one that didn't argue and annoy him, as he informed his mother on numerous occasions.

Jacob loved Charlie dearly. The entire family did. Charlie became a Gardner family member. When she could not be found, feelings of anger, loss, and grief filled their aching, empty hearts. Jacob cried at night in his bed over the loss. This Mrs. Gardner heard, but she would never admit it to Jacob.

Jacob put down his spoon and pushed his cereal bowl away. He was almost finished anyway. "I don't feel like eating anymore," Jacob said. "Are we going to go to the pet place again today? Maybe someone found her. We haven't gone since yesterday. Can we, Mom, huh?"

"We'll go to the animal shelter later. But first, we've got to do some shopping for other things. We'll leave as soon as your father goes to work and we're all finished eating breakfast and getting dressed . . . in about an hour. Okay?"

Mrs. Gardner said to her husband, as she pushed her chair back and stood up from the table, "I'm going upstairs to make sure Callie's okay. Don't leave until I come back."

"Okay." Mr. Gardner said from behind the paper and turned another page.

"I'll make sure he doesn't, Mom," Jacob offered.

"Thanks. I'll be back soon."

Mrs. Gardner ascended the stairs to Callie's room and slowly opened the door. She witnessed Callie crying into her pillow in the fetal position on her bed facing away from the door. In silence, Mrs. Gardner sat on the edge of the girl's bed and laid her tender hand on the child's trembling shoulder. A calm soothing squeeze with just enough pressure told the girl, "Roll over and hug me." Callie did as encouraged. They held each other in silence for sometime until the sobs subsided. Mrs. Gardner wiped Callie's wet flushed cheeks with her thumb and kissed her hot forehead.

"Your brother can be hurtful at times, Callie," Mrs. Gardner said breaking the lull, "but you know what, he's hurting just as much as you are, maybe more. It's just his way of dealing with the situation. You cry and he gets ugly, and he . . . he wants to blame someone for Charlie's disappearance. But it's not your fault."

"Do you think Charlie will come back, Mom?" Callie managed to ask between sniffles, her red, swollen eyes focused on her twisting fingers.

"You and your brother make Charlie a happy kitty. Just like you both make Daddy and me happy. We all love her, very much. She loves us, too, even your father," she said, with a perfunctory smile. "She has a good home here. I'm sure she'll be back soon. We have to be patient and pray God will care for her until she comes back. You know she has a collar. And when somebody finds her, they'll call us. Then we'll go pick her up."

"But, why is it taking so long?"

"Well, maybe Charlie runs and hides when strangers come near her. Or she can't find her own way back by herself. We just need to be patient. You know what patient means?"

Callie shrugged her shoulders.

"It means we can't hurry what God has planned for Charlie."

"But, I love Charlie. I want her back now. I miss her. I miss petting her and playing with her. I want her in my arms so I can kiss her, right now."

Mrs. Gardner hugged her daughter again, more for her own good this time than for Callie's benefit.

"We all miss her, sweetie. She's part of our family. She's our kitty angel. Isn't she?" Callie shook her head in agreement as Mrs. Gardner wiped away her own silent tears as discretely as possible behind Callie's back.

She wanted to be strong for Callie, but she thought that after two weeks away from home, the odds of a safe return were not in Charlie's favor. The odds got longer each day. Yet she wanted to give hope to her daughter. But positive vibes were a very difficult expectation under the circumstances.

Mrs. Gardner recalled the last two weeks events in silence: The hours spent in search of Charlie, mourning her loss, distraught emotions, discussions with neighbors, posting signs on poles and mailboxes around the neighborhood, and fruitless trips to the Arizona Humane Society. Everything performed with a heavy heart, all ending in frustration.

Not knowing what happened to their beloved Charlie became the hardest part. There's no closure. Bad feelings continue indefinitely, hope shattered. The animal seemed to have vanished like a patented Arizona mirage. Mrs. Gardner couldn't help but feel that seeing Charlie again would be tantamount to a miracle. But she could never let Jacob or Callie know her true opinion about Charlie's return.

Mrs. Gardner feared the worst as she viewed pictures of Charlie she helped Callie make on the computer. They were taped to the wall of Callie's bedroom. Cherished memories of happier days with Charlie passed through her mind as the air conditioner snapped to life and vibrated the roof above their heads.

She wondered if closure would ever be realized. The hollow feelings, sadness, and suffering would probably last a lifetime.

CHAPTER 13

SHADOW

The Be Cool Air Conditioning service truck crept at a leisurely pace along the surface street in a residential section of Peoria mildly drifting left and right, as if the driver had one beer too many for lunch. But lunchtime wouldn't be for another two hours. The man behind the wheel turned the vehicle aside to the right curb abruptly and paused. Red brake lights glowed in the brilliant sunny day as the driver, Bob Spiker, turned down the truck's radio to concentrate on a cell phone call.

"Okay, that's better Hon," the owner of Be Cool said into the cell phone. "Now what about the insurance?"

"I *said*," his wife Penny began to repeat, "I found a company that will insure us both for three hundred dollars less than what we're paying right now."

Bob heard excitement in her voice and thought it absurd, like she had won the lottery. He wished that winning the lottery was the real reason for the call.

"That's great Babe. I'm glad you called to tell me, 'cause I was about to aim the truck straight at a light pole and step on the gas," Bob said jokingly, with a smile on his face. "Maybe an accident would put me out of my misery. But saving that much money sounds like a better choice."

Bob knew Penny had begun a diligent search to obtain competitive rates because of a recent troubling increase. Apparently, one agent gave preliminary figures to Penny that sounded too good to be true. She was reacting to the good news. Bob was more realistic.

"But don't get your hopes up too high," Bob continued. "Remember we're dealing with insurance companies here, the pariah of society. Actually, it's a dead heat between them and the medical community. You know why doctor's call their business a practice, don't you?"

"Yes, Lovie, I know. Because they really don't know what they're doing and they have to *practice* on you."

"That's right," Bob said, thinking he taught her well.

"But if we can really save three hundred dollars a month?"

"Remember, Hon, they're cherry pickers," he said laying down the brutal facts of reality. "You have asthma. Good deals and asthma don't go together. I turned fifty-five. You know the day you turn fifty-five, somehow it makes a big difference. According to them, you immediately have heart attacks and any other ailment that's expensive. What do you always say about your ass?"

"The crack in your ass is pre-existing," Penny said.

They both laughed at their private joke.

"Well the guy needs to see us in person, so I made an appointment for next week, Wednesday at 6:30. I don't expect you to write it down right now so I'll remind you later when you get home. Okay?"

"That'll be fine, Honey. Anything else?"

"That's it Lovie. Have a good day. Be careful. Love you."

"Love you, too. Bye." Bob flipped the cell phone closed.

While parked, Bob consulted the map again refreshing his mind about the location of his customer. Finishing, he tossed it on the passenger seat and checked for traffic in his mirror. The phone rang again.

He answered. "Be Cool Air–"

"Bob, come home right now," Penny interrupted. Her tone of voice sounded distressed, borderline hysterical.

"You just called, Hon. What is it?" Bob asked, concerned. Her urgency reached through the airwaves, seized Bob's ear, and wouldn't let go.

"It's Shadow. His tail is . . . he's bleeding . . . half his tail is . . . is gone."

"What? Okay, okay, I'm on my way."

Bob hung up and called his appointment. In the midst of a U-turn the customer answered.

"Hello?"

"Mrs. Benson?" Bob asked, as he stepped on the gas.

"Yes."

"This is Bob Spiker from Be Cool. I'm sorry, Mrs. Benson, I have to cancel our appointment today. An emergency has come up at home. I'll reschedule your appointment later," Bob said and hung up, hoping he didn't end the call too abruptly.

Bob drove like a madman on the edge of his seat for the next ten minutes.

*   *   *

Bob found Penny at home talking on the phone while consoling Shadow, their black longhaired cat, keeping her hand away from the maimed tail. Three quarters of it lacked fur and skin only bloody flesh remained, raw meat exposed to the air. The injury looked as if someone wanted to skin the animal alive starting with the tail. Bob remembered how much pain he felt when a simple raspberry-type scrape from a sports injury burned as if on fire. The thought made him compassionate as the cat whimpered in a low constant groan.

His eyes focused from Shadow to Penny. She seemed to have it together now discussing the situation with the animal hospital personnel. Her calmer demeanor forced him to pull himself under control. He withdrew in search of the pet-carrier and a blanket for the trip to the vet.

*   *   *

Bob and Penny waited impatiently in the animal hospital waiting room while the doctor treated Shadow as an emergency case. Other pet owners in attendance informed about the cause for emergency were aghast. Conversations between the Spikers and others in the small room ensued covering the subject. Guesses were made about what would cause such an injury.

Grief seemed to wash over the Spikers like a torrent; their usual tranquil demeanors were ripped apart. While waiting for the vet's report, Bob thought how Shadow became Penny's empty nest baby.

"You remember when Shadow was a feral kitten?" Bob said to Penny. "How he smelled so bad and was so scrawny and underfed when the girl next door brought him home from the vacant lot next to the bowling alley?"

"How could I ever forget?" Penny said. "But we always endured his odor well."

"*You* always endured his odor. I remember thinking something was wrong with him. But you, you always loved him, right from the start. In spite of his filthy, matted fur, incredibly huge ears, and tail longer than his body. It was way out of proportion. He looked like a wingless bat with a tail," Bob said smiling.

"Yeah, but I love bats with tails. Shadow was the ugly duckling only I could love. I washed him, cleaned and brushed him, held my breath and hugged him even closer when he gassed. You think our son's girlfriend would have done that?"

"No. That's why she brought him over, so you would take care of him."

"That was her mistake, her loss. I knew as soon as I met him, he was my animal soul mate. He's a 'fur person,' you know, *my* fur person."

"Yes, and I think your relationship, at times, encroaches on my feelings of jealousy. Seriously, I'm in constant amazement how the two of you act together. How he snuggles up under your chin at night and only rubs your face with his, like your kissing or something. You don't love, Kittyboy, like Shadow," Bob said accusingly.

"You're right. Kittyboy's just a cat. I'll always regard Shadow as my lucky acquisition, our son's girlfriend's greatest contribution to my eternal happiness. He's a beautiful animal. Everybody loves him."

"He grew into his ears and tail well proportioned over the years."

"His tail! Bob, I'm so upset," Penny said starting to cry again.

"Don't worry, Hon. He's in the care of the vet now," Bob said reassuringly. "Shadow's earned a place in my heart, too, you know. I don't like what's happened any less than you do. Many times I remember working at my desk in need of a break. And at just the right time, he jumps up and plops down right on my papers purring. It's his way of giving me his special love."

Penny said through her tissue, "But who would do such—"

"Mrs. Spiker?" the doctor broke into her question. He stood in the doorway to the office. The Spikers rose to meet him.

"Shadow will be fine," the vet informed them. "He suffered no other injuries and he's resting now under sedation. I'm sorry to say that his tail had to be amputated up to where there was skin left."

Penny pulled Bob's shoulder to her face and cried turning away from the doctor. Bob remained silent.

"It appears that Shadow got his tail caught in something. It wasn't a dog though. There aren't any bite marks. Anyway, Shadow will remain here overnight for observation. Please call tomorrow for a follow up report on his condition. If everything goes well, you can bring him home tomorrow. I'm very sorry."

"Thank you, doctor," Bob managed as the vet returned to his office.

*   *   *

Back home sitting in the living room, the Spikers couldn't understand how Shadow's injury happened because everyone in the neighborhood loved him. Visitors would inquire about him when he was out of the room. They would comment on his kind manners and soft fur and held him on their laps until their legs got numb.

"Who would do such a thing?" Penny asked yet again, still flushed with a tissue in her hand.

"I don't know," Bob said, "but the doctor said that it looked like Shadow got his tail caught in something. It wasn't a dog, no bite marks."

"It wasn't caught *in* something, Bob. It was pulled *by* someone. Someone tried to grab Shadow and all they got was his beautiful tail. Shadow got away, but I'll bet it was a life or death struggle. Poor thing."

"I know." Bob said. He reached across the leather couch for his wife in a silent embrace.

When they parted, she unfolded her tissue and blew her runny nose.

"You know," Bob said, thoughtfully, "I just remembered seeing some lost-and-found signs posted on the mail boxes getting the mail yesterday. They've been there for days. I didn't think to read them before, but now . . . I think I'll take a walk, see what they say. Each one was about a lost pet. I think there were three of them the last time I looked."

"Sounds like an epidemic," Penny said.

"Yeah, it does," Bob agreed, and wrinkled his nose at the thought.

Bob always envisioned himself as a can-do sort of guy. According to Bob, there were two basic types of people in the world: Those that got things done and those that made excuses, and excuses were like assholes, everybody has one. Bob made sure he always took control all his life; he had a purpose, even the way he moved exuded confidence. The situation demanded Bob's attention.

"Think I'll go and check it out. You okay for a few minutes?" he asked, fetching his keys off the kitchen counter.

"Yeah, I'm fine," Penny replied while picking up the phone. "Find out what's going on."

"I'll get to the bottom of things," he said confidently, as he walked out the front door. "Starting now."

Bob returned with the "lost" announcements. Penny had called a girl friend to discuss the day's events in the bedroom. He knew she would be busy for quite some time.

On his business phone line, Bob called the pet owners who had posted the announcements commiserating with each. Three of the notices involved cats and one concerned a dog. None had been found yet. And one offered a reward.

He began collecting information and started a file. He called nearby friends. Inquiries were made of the police and he summoned a city council member in his district.

Bob ultimately formed a project to assemble the community together in a town meeting and worked this angle with the cooperation of government officials. A meeting was scheduled at 7:00 on Thursday night, the nineteenth of April, in the local elementary school auditorium. It would bring about twenty-five concerned families together. Joining them would be a council member and a police officer from the Glendale Community Action Team. Everyone expressed concern about the outbreak of missing pets. The meeting would address these disturbing issues.

CHAPTER 14

UPRISING

The small auditorium doubled as a cafeteria for the elementary school serving Charlie and Bob Spiker's neighborhood. Cafeteria tables were stored and metal-folding chairs occupied the floor space arranged in orderly rows of two distinct sections. An aisle down the middle provided walk space between the two sections that furnished seating for sixty. A large white screen hung from a ceiling boom over backstage and an overhead projector stood at the ready located on a portable stand near center stage casting a red-letter message of welcome on the screen. The auditorium and stage were well lit and six folding chairs were lined in a row on the stage off to the right of the projector. A dark wooden podium was stationed stage right near access stairs to floor level. Two men occupied the chairs on stage, one dressed in a police uniform, the other in a bargain basement suit and a loosened tie with the top shirt button open.

A diverse, ethnic throng of interested and involved neighborhood residents gathered during the last half hour. Some assembled standing and talking around the chairs in small cliques. Others had already found their seats and sat waiting for the meeting to begin. Children played games in the corners and far reaches of the floor space excited to be in school without teacher supervision and away from their parents for the moment.

A few minutes after 7:00, three thump sounds emanated from the public address system; an obvious test the cordless microphone had passed. A rumble sound followed as the microphone was lifted from the podium stand and held by the hand of a slender, six-foot tall gentleman dressed in dark slacks, polished wing-tip shoes, and a light-blue, Hilfiger shirt.

Bob Spiker was not a professional public speaker, but had past connections with men's clubs and excelled in a college speech class. This equipped him with provisional serenity standing before an audience. He held the microphone to his mouth and took a deep breath.

"Can we all find our seats now? We'd like to get started so we can all get back home soon," he said standing behind the podium.

Bob waited about fifteen seconds until everyone found their seats before continuing. He focused on Penny sitting in the front row. Her smiling face and eye contact gave him confidence.

"Most of you know me, but for those of you who don't, I'm Bob Spiker. I'm your neighbor here and I own an air conditioning business called Be Cool Air Conditioning. Sorry, I had to get in a shameless plug," his animated smirk lent further description to the spoken words enunciated in clear diction. "But I'm not here to talk about air conditioning tonight. I'm here because I'm a concerned fellow citizen like you," he said with a gratifying voice, waving his open hand palm up toward the assembly.

"I organized this meeting because of my concern and I want to start by thanking you all for coming here tonight, taking time out of your busy evening to attend this meeting."

All eyes of the audience were now looking right to the podium. The previous murmur among the crowd had stopped.

"I've talked to most of you, either by phone or in person, concerning a problem we're having in our neighborhood:

Our pets are disappearing," he said rocking to the balls of
his feet. A habit Spiker developed over the years to help
emphasize spoken words. The motion also involved pushing
his hips forward and bending at the knees making him easily
understood, credible, and persuasive. "I've come to find out
that it's a bigger problem than most realize. It's certainly
bigger than I thought initially."

He walked from the podium toward center stage. The
audience followed him with turning heads. Someone in the
third row sneezed.

"It seems there's been a rash of vanishing pets taking
place. During my recent investigation, I've documented
twenty-one pets, that I personally know of from talking to my
immediate neighbors," Bob announced rocking on his feet on
the word twenty-one and waving toward the audience with
an outstretched hand.

A murmur in the crowd started and heads began to wag
left and right as the assembly confirmed what they heard
with their seated friends. Spiker gave them the opportunity
to react and paused for calculated dramatic effect.

"That's right," he said shaking his head in the affirmative,
"twenty-one of our pet friends, our loved family members,
that I know of."

Bob raised his hands to quell the crowd that reacted
increasingly concerned as questions began begging interruption,
"Please, reserve your questions until after our officials have
spoken. Thank you.

"Now, the purpose of this meeting, the reason why you
took time from your valued evenings, is to inform you about
what's happening in our neighborhood. What's being done
about it and to form a neighborhood watch in the future.

"We've all seen the *lost animal* fliers taped to the
mailboxes I'm sure. But truthfully, not all of us had posted
announcements when pets disappeared. We all went about
our busy days thinking the problem affected only a few, not
worth being concerned about. But there is good cause for

concern. Some may have a missing dog or cat that we don't know about. We want your information, your input. So please, get with one of us here on stage after the meeting to help give us a full picture of what's happening."

Bob turned to give a thumb up sign and a nod to the men seated behind him.

"Okay, now, we have tonight, as our guest speakers, two people who are concerned and committed to helping us with our problem," Bob said smiling holding his hand out in a reference gesture. "First, on the left, is our district city councilman, Tony Zimmermann." Tony raised his hand in acknowledgement. "And to the right, police officer Jack Dunn, who heads up the community action team in our district.

"We'll start with officer Dunn. Officer?" Bob said. The policeman stood, walked to Spiker, and took the microphone. Bob sat down in one of the chairs on stage.

"Good evening ladies and gentleman," Officer Dunn said walking to the projector. "As Mr. Spiker said, I'm in charge of our community action team. Your police department knows about the situation. We have received many calls in this district since I first spoke to Mr. Spiker about two weeks ago."

He removed the "welcome" page on the projector and inserted a map of the area in question. He turned to face the map. "This map shows the boundaries of this district. The area I'm in charge of. The area most of you live in. The red dots represent households of those who have reported a missing animal. There are more missing pets than dots because some families have lost more than one dog or cat. Our hearts go out to those of you who have lost a pet." He turned again to face the audience.

"Now, the question I've been asked repeatedly is: What are the police doing about it? Well, it's a loaded question. First of all, your police department is doing all that it can in regard to this problem. But we face a difficult situation because there are no reports of related suspicious activity, such as animal cruelty, or reported evidence that have been called in by the community. We were not aware of any unusual activity going on until Mr. Spiker here called. Since then we have had a barrage of calls. We've responded by creating a presence in the community, sending more squad cars more frequently. But frankly folks, without evidence or eyewitness accounts, we don't have anything to work on. We need you to be our eyes and ears. Keep your heads on a swivel, have eyes in the back of your heads as the saying goes."

Officer Dunn pulled a red-laser pointer from his front shirt pocket and turned. "Getting back to the map, as you can see, the dots are concentrated in this area." He highlighted the dots on the map with a glowing red circle. "I don't want to alarm anyone here tonight, but it's most likely someone responsible that lives in this area here, possibly a neighbor. Everyone needs to be watching closely what happens in this section of town. Which brings us to the neighborhood watch.

"Everyone needs to become involved. Like I said before, *'we need your help.'* Your police force can't concentrate exclusively on this situation. We have to protect a much larger geographical area from more serious types of crime. However, that being said, we are here to help. But you need to first help yourselves and obtain physical evidence, and report visual sightings of animal abuse or suspicious late night activity.

The problem could be caused by any number of reasons: Coyote attacks, hit and run car accidents, and runaways. But we think, because of the sheer numbers involved, that trappings and kidnappings are the most likely reason for the outbreak."

"You mean to say someone is killing our pets?" some guy to the right shouted out.

"Maybe," officer Dunn answered looking in the man's direction, "or kidnapping them. Which is why we must set up the neighborhood watch."

Bob thought the accusation over the top for a moment, that it might incite a riot, until the audience seemed to take the comment in stride. He gave a knowing look to Penny. The police opinion supported her view.

"There are some things that can be done in the way of prevention," the officer continued, "other than the watch group, that we all can do in an effort to work on this problem."

He went on to list suggestions involving leashes, keeping animals indoors, rice-sized microchip implantations, and tags.

Officer Dunn removed the map from the projector and inserted another page of information.

"These are addresses and phone numbers you need to know. There is no need to write them down. We have copies for you to pick up after the meeting." He outlined the list and left the numbers on the screen. He moved away from the projector putting his laser pointer back in his pocket.

"I will be happy to take questions now," he announced.

"I have a question," someone in the back row said.

All heads in the audience turned toward the thirty-something black man that stood with his hand partially in the air like a schoolboy awaiting permission from the teacher to run to the bathroom.

"Go ahead," Officer Dunn said acknowledging the man.

"When did all dis first start? I mean, we lost our cat, Stimpy, 'bout two months ago and gave up runnin' to da shelters lookin'. I hate ta say it, man, but I think he's gone fo good."

"The question was: 'When did all the disappearances first start?'" the officer repeated for the benefit of those in the audience that could not hear the question. "The answer is," he continued, "about, as best we can estimate, the beginning of February. Around the time your cat vanished sir, thank you. That point needed to be addressed. Any other questions?"

The man in uniform waited a moment and then continued, "Okay. I'd like to give the microphone to Mr. Zimmermann who has some things to say. Mr. Zimmermann?"

Councilman Tony Zimmermann made a statement of support and told the assembly that the Mayor was made aware of the situation and that he, the Mayor, regretted that he could not be at the meeting due to prior commitments. He indicated that the city was committed to doing all that could be done, and that the meeting was a first step forward sponsored by the city. He outlined the neighborhood watch as officials envisioned and requested volunteers to sign up for the program. The projector was offered to anyone who wanted to show pictures of their pets to the audience. A number of families prepared for this aspect of the meeting took the stage; among them were the Gardners and the Garcias. Spiker showed pictures of Shadow, before and after, recounting the story of the cat's signature black tail—now a stub.

The meeting adjourned shortly after. Many stayed after the formal portion of the meeting to volunteer and to commiserate with others about their pet disappearances. Bob was pleased with the response the neighborhood showed displaying a controlled uprising, not like the violent torch-carrying mob after the Frankenstein monster, but a civilized people with the same intent.

Meeting results were reported in a nearly full-page article in the free local newspaper delivered to all residents in town. The headline read: "Glendale Community Mystified By Missing Pets." The article addressed the missing pet issue and reported an updated figure on the total of vanishing pets after the meeting's tabulation which shockingly stood at twenty-five. Pictures taken at the meeting by reporters were included with a map. Testimonials from distressed former pet owners were quoted.

When Bob read the piece afterward, he beamed with pride at the credit given to him for organizing the meeting and noticed the correspondent didn't fail to mention the names of the council member and the police officer also in attendance.

Safety tips were listed. The numbers and addresses to the various helpful agencies were outlined including a hotline phone number for reporting suspicious activity, the Arizona Humane Society Clinics for installing microchips, and a Compassion Connection for help dealing with loss. An appeal was made to keep watch over pets and keeping them indoors if possible.

The article was a stirring, heart-wrenching account of a horrible trend in society that did not fail to concern the community.

CHAPTER 15

ARTICLE

Charlie sat in his chair set up near the living room window smoking a cigarette regarding the world outside his house. The wearisome view generated contemplation of another day's useless energy spent, alone, waiting for over due contact and direction from forgetful parents. As he reached for the ashtray, the shimmering glare of a cylindrical object located on the front lawn pierced through his sunglasses and arrested his keen peripheral vision. Upon closer examination, he observed it to be the twice-weekly free newspaper that became his only means to obtain local information, since he could no longer stand to watch TV and radio stations offered so little in terms of news.

Striving to be inconspicuous, Charlie claimed the rolled up publication from the brown, mostly-dead-grass lawn and headed directly back inside out of the heat of the day.

He removed the rubber band and unwrapped the paper revealing a front-page story concerning missing pets. Knowing the news to be locally generated, his curiosity peaked. "This ought to be good reading," he said as he sat down to see what the newspaper had to say about his work.

Charlie's eyes were drawn, at first, to a photo of a man the caption listed as Bob Spiker. The picture appeared distorted to Charlie, like viewing the man's face through a convex lens, and it jumped out at him causing him to jerk the paper away, startled.

Suddenly, Charlie's mind transported himself ten days in the past. He no longer saw the picture in the paper, but was peering through the peephole of his front door. His heart rate climbed with fear and terror while he stood watching the man reach for the doorbell again. Bing-bong—the sound reverberated in Charlie's head announcing an attempt by some investigator, some enemy trying to pry into his privacy.

"Do not answer the door, Charles," his mother's voice said as his twitch returned. "This man cannot be trusted. Mark my words. He will only bring trouble. Avoid him, Charles. Avoid him."

The word "him" echoed in Charlie's memory as he found himself still holding the newsprint in trembling hands staring at Bob Spiker's image. He smiled as he recalled the wise decision not to answer the bell while facing fear through the viewfinder of a peephole. The grin quickly withered, as he scanned the remaining pictures of cats he freely and intimately recognized and a map he knew to be of his Glendale neighborhood. Charlie started reading.

"Almost every day," the article began, "Mrs. Gardner and her two children, Callie and Jacob, visit the Arizona Humane Society . . ."

However, for the first time in his life, written words in the article became a stiff challenge to read. Charlie perceived the words differently now. He held the newspaper with hands that seemed distant, almost disconnected from his arms. When he brought the page closer, the letters looked funny, too big. As he moved the page back and forth in an attempt to focus properly, the words appeared psychedelic: First too big then too small. It was disconcerting, like being on acid he imagined.

He rubbed his eyes in an effort to improve vision. Next the print looked excessively black and much too bold. Charlie's concentration was impaired to a great degree by the simple appearance of the letters that made reading the article difficult. He dwelt on unreliable visual data flooding his mind and fear gripped him with the sensation of hundreds of spiders scurrying along his spine. With an unnerving sense of awareness, he tried to read the article no longer grounded in reality. The lightening bolt of torment that the simple act of reading had become struck overwhelming confusion into Charlie, who was without the aid of a diverting rod. He felt like retreating into an emotional roly-poly bug to keep at bay the negative sensations the act of reading presented.

The vexatious power of fear pressed him ever tighter into a solid metamorphic stone from which he would never emerge he feared, forever lost, vanishing into the strange characters and figures on the page he held shaking.

"Shit." He tossed the newsprint aside in frustration first clutching his head and then closing his eyes with the fingers of his right hand.

The phone rang bringing Charlie out of his distress with a jolt. He ran to the phone in the kitchen only to see on caller ID that it was Ben. He waited for the answering machine to take a message. Ben hung up.

"What is it this time Ben?" Charlie asked looking at the phone on the kitchen counter. "What are you doing Charlie? Want to come over Charlie? Get a job yet Charlie? Becka still loves you Charlie. When are you ever going to give me a break, Ben, and stop the interrogation? Huh?"

He grabbed a beer from the fridge and returned to the living room where he sat thinking how nice it was to be able to sleep through the night again. He felt refreshed now. The recurring nightmare had faded from his mind, like a silver full moon skating across a progressively overcast sky. The clouds obscuring phantoms in a blanket of omission allowing sleep without the torment of the creature or the crazy ride.

Dreamlessness gave way to relative but boring peace for the last few weeks. A conservation of energy and recharging the batteries ever since the stray elimination stopped.

After corralling his fear for a long while, Charlie picked up the paper again. He saw words that looked perfectly familiar; like old friends from high school whose faces he remembered well, but whose names he could not recall. The lightening bolt of confusion that struck his mind seemed to be influencing memory. He labored through one paragraph ten times before finally remembering the words of the message, piecing the puzzle together. The entire article became an extreme exertion in patience. Multiple breaks were utilized to reduce the building stress. His afternoon thus spent endeavoring to read. It was the last time Charlie would ever attempt reading for a long time.

Once the panic attack released Charlie from captivity, he realized why the animals ceased to enter his yard. At first, he figured, it was due to the bad omen, of killing the cat with the name Charlie, his name. But now another unexpected reason became clear. The fact that the neighbors no longer let their pets out induced Charlie to declare final victory over the stray population problem, a job well done. The community responded confirming and assisting him with his work and, in a strange way, helped to eliminate the problem of the strays. Their deeds spoke louder than words. Because of their help, they approved his efforts.

But the author of the article seemed to disapprove at the same time and an underlying hate, spawned by the police, welled in the neighborhood. Charlie imagined neighbors rising up in revolt against him for some reason he could not understand. Fear of persecution engulfed his thoughts. He needed protection.

He vowed to stop looking out his front window and began to consider how future attacks could be handled. He got up to close the blinds on every window in the house.

"Hostile neighbors are plotting against me. A defense is necessary," he said to himself as he lowered the front window blinds, twisting them shut. "I've got to install an alarm system right now in case I'm attacked. I'm responsible for my own safety, nobody else. Certainly not the police."

He wound up in the kitchen closing the last of the shades where his search for an alarm system started. The barriers conceived against potential enemies came at a time when he felt himself sinking for lack of meaningful work. He was glad about the new direction. He remembered the words of his mother warning him of this very thing. Enemies *were* all around him. Why couldn't he see this before? She was right.

The article proved one fact that Charlie had known for some time: The first phase of the work was over, and the next phase, the more important phase according to his parents, was about to begin.

VISITATION

The month of June in Arizona is hot, very hot. The sun, reigning monarch of fire, seemed to have relocated 50 million miles closer to earth. The blazing furnace clocked overtime and the temperature soared to over 115 on sunny days, which happened to be every day for the past two weeks. Eighteen-wheelers and tanker trucks squeezed the softened asphalt into ruts resembling those made of mud after a heavy rain, especially at stoplights. Moisture wrenched out of all things alive or dead. Waterless plants and animals mummified within hours in the piping-hot temperatures and over time became bleached skeletons in the desert collected by treasure hunters and sold as southwest décor. The brown, desolate landscape of the ever-expanding desert confirmed the sun's tight, global-warming stranglehold as Arizona drains the mighty Colorado River of water to survive the onslaught.

Phoenix is the only major U.S. city to preserve hideous weather records; monuments erected by the baking sun, dedicated to the heat god and those who worship the increasing number of days in a row the temperature century mark is eclipsed. The records are like trophies awarded to the broiled residents for enduring triple-digit temperatures for triple-digit days.

Yet, in what almost seems like collective spite, over two million humans are willing to live in the torrid, sultry heat, a number that increases year by year along with the desert and heat records in this precarious man made, some would say, paradise.

The news program, *Good Morning Arizona* used the heat as the lead story. Heat makes the lead story daily unless a major disaster occurs and especially in the midst of a record-breaking heat wave in which the Valley was currently involved. June typically ushers in the record-breaking dry heat and July follows with more of the same combined with humidity, called the Monsoons, a lethal combination.

Charlie McShane was having a nightmare while sleeping on the grimy couch in his living room. Sweating and cold at once, his hands wildly grasped the air in torment. His right dangling leg flailed kicking the nearby coffee table, which knocked over multiple empty beer cans. One half-full beer spilled making a warm puddle that meandered to the edge and dripped in a steady stream to the carpet.

The sounds of bouncing empty beer cans and the struck table woke Charlie from his nightmare. He sat up and squinted at the surroundings. At first bed came to his mind, but then realized he was on the living room couch. He sat up and rubbed his face with both hands. He concentrated on his eyes trying to rub clear sight back into his tired orbs. Breathing deeply, he recalled his sleeping torment.

The dream was back again, nearly the same vision with which he became well acquainted prior to the first phase of his work with the stray animals. The nightmare that recently stopped recurring after he ended that first stage of his work.

In this new version of the nightmare, Charlie switched places in the vehicle. He stopped the vehicle in front of a door located in a long corridor, picked up a person who bent down to look through the window at him, and sped down the corridor narrowly missing parading pedestrians.

Charlie was the one that winked at his passenger and flipped the dial of the radio creating a blur of sounds until a new song played, *Mr. Crowley* by Ozzy Osbourne, during which the passenger evolved into the grotesque deformity while Charlie drove.

The song played on the radio while Charlie laughed wildly and observed the passenger's transformation. He was the one in control. He was the driver and the morphing creature with sharp teeth his passenger.

"Oh, Mr. Crowley, did you talk to the dead?" Ozzy forcefully sang louder.

Suddenly paranoia gripped Charlie in the oppressive heat as he drove recklessly, avoiding a mounting evil. Sweat ran down his face as he swerved and took turns way too fast, his head on a swivel searching for enemies and pending confrontation.

All the while, the song continued to play louder.

In darkness rain developed making the heat humid and driving conditions nearly impossible, yet Charlie drove faster. The bloody skull of the passenger next to him, the dripping fangs, and the ever-widening mouth forced him to scream as he floored the accelerator in a feeble attempt to flee.

The song played at a deafening pitch.

As in the first nightmare, the vehicle veered in the end with an abrupt crash and jolt. Charlie thrust forward.

"Mr. Crowley . . ."

Charlie sat on his living room couch clasping his head in an attempt to suppress waves of fear and confusion. He shuddered pondering the nightmare. Thoughts of the dream brought back memories of other horrors. A wave of revulsion crashed over him as he watched the videos replay the World Trade Center disaster, the explosions, the carnage, and the terrorists committing evil and unpunished transgressions.

This in turn brought back memories of his parents dying at the hands of the unpunished Mexican terrorist, that drunken illegal bastard. He recalled how George Bush took care of the terrorist problem and Charlie pledged to follow the example. Revulsion gave way to hate which rose up from the depths of his mind like Jaws breaching for chum at the stern of the *Orca.*

"I need a bigger boat," Charlie said reaching to the coffee table for the comfort of a pack of cigarettes and the lighter. They both occupied a dry spot on the table. He rummaged through the pack, found a cigarette, and lit it. He tossed them both back to the table, but they went sliding across and fell off the far edge joining the puddle remnants of beer on the carpeted floor.

Items on Charlie's floor were not unusual. There were plenty of things on his floors most people kept on tables and shelves: Magazines, coins, spent matches, food packaging, CD's, cigarettes, lighters. All were just as accessible there as anywhere else. He tried to relax by smoking and watched the beer drip as uneasiness from the nightmare lingered.

Like laser beams, the noon sun stabbed through cracks and holes in the living room blinds clothed in a sweater of dust. Charlie shivered in the air-conditioned house as the sweat from the nightmare evaporated from his skin. The thermostat, set to seventy degrees no matter how hot it was outside, was never attained and the air-conditioner ran constantly. It was Charlie's way to say, "Fuck you!" to the *sun*-of-a-bitch, especially on days like this when the noon temperature was already 109 degrees. Huge electric bills were heedlessly paid now that money was of little concern.

The house was gloomy inside. Blinds never opened anymore. There were two advantages: Keep the heat from filtering through the windows, and keep curious eyes from peering inside.

In the dim light, Charlie reached over to the bent shade lamp and twisted the light switch to look for the ashtray. It was on the floor near the couch perfectly upside down with all the other table-less items. Once found, he rubbed out the first of many cigarettes of the day. He left the ashtray on the couch while he made a feeble attempt with his foot to spread the ashes and butts left on the carpet in a sloppy, circular mess.

Once the nightmare and resulting emotional attack ebbed like a murky mist in a slight breeze, Charlie wanted to get up from the couch, but his body hurt. So he just sat staring across the living room. He thought he could use a beer, but he was only thinking right now, not doing.

Depressed that he had not worked for weeks at any job, time moved slowly and his mind's condition was tremulous at best. And now the bad dreams had begun again.

Charlie thought: What the hell does the returning nightmare mean? "Do I need to occupy my time constructively, get back to work?" The gravity of the situation gnawed at him. He needed a plan of action. His cheek began twitching for the first time in weeks. Then came an interruption.

There were many things Charlie hated in his world, in varying degrees, but few objects of hatred ranked with the sound of phones and doorbells. His face winced at the sound of the front door bell that rang right after the twitch. With the sound, he realized that a bruising headache had taken hold. He sat motionless hoping the caller would go away, but the doorbell repeated.

"Incessant mother fucker. I'm going to kick the shit out of you," he said, feeling the headache more acutely.

With the prospect of violence looming, Charlie stood from the couch and staggered to the front door. With one eye closed and the other squinted, he looked through the peephole into the glare of the noonday sunlight. On the other side of the door stood his friend, Ben, who reached out to push the doorbell again.

"What, Ben?" Charlie yelled through the door, wishing to stop the bombardment of sound.

The ploy didn't work. The bell rang one more time. The door handle commenced jiggling. He put both hands and forehead against the warm door as Jack Torrance did while locked in the storeroom talking to Wendy in *The Shining*. While looking down he shouted, "Ben . . . leave me alone!" The extra effort made his head pound harder.

Ben shouted back through the door, "I'm not goin' to stop ringin' da bell 'till ya open da door, Charlie." He rang the bell again.

"Ben. Ben, please. I . . . I don't . . . feel well."

"Open da door, Charlie." Knocking and pounding joined the assorted cacophony of head splitting sounds.

"Okay . . . okay," Charlie said, in a lower tone of voice as he clicked open the top lock and stepped away from the door. "Just stop the noise."

The noise stopped.

Charlie thought that perhaps Ben reconsidered and left now that quiet prevailed. He hesitated opening the bottom lock with this hopeful thought. After a short lull, the doorknob began to jiggle and the pounding resumed. Charlie gave up hope and opened the bottom lock avoiding round two of the noise Olympics. He turned away from the door and headed back to the comfort of the grimy couch.

The door swung open, with a blast of heat and blinding light, as if a bomb exploded knocking over numerous pots and pans stacked like a rampart against the front door. The sound was ear shattering to Charlie, but confirmed the effectiveness of his recently constructed alarm system. Ben quickly closed the door and observed the assorted metal scattered at his feet within a three-foot radius of the door. Then he looked at Charlie who just dropped down on the couch.

"Ya better get away from me, ya bastard," Ben said. Profuse sweat ran down his face as he lumbered toward the couch. "What da hell ya doin' leavin' me out in da heat so long for? I could have melted on your door step."

"Well . . . that was . . . the idea," Charlie remarked, choosing his words carefully. "What ever happened to . . . common courtesy? You know . . . someone calls . . . before barging in . . . or makes an appointment . . . or—"

"Why should I call? You never invite me over anymore," Ben interrupted in anger. "I don't even know why I'm concerned about ya anyway. Ya don't care about anybody but yourself. Ya don't know what's meaningful and what isn't anymore. Ya don't understand what people are tryin' to ..." Ben stopped, performing a double-take, looking at more pots and pans stacked on the window sills in the living room. "What's with all da pots and shit stacked in front of da windows and doors, Charlie?"

"Grab my smokes and lighter . . . will you?" Charlie said, ignoring the question. "Over there," he indicated with his eyes.

"What? Ya haven't heard a word I've said. Have ya?"

"Yeah, yeah . . . cigarettes, Ben." Charlie continued to stare at the cigarettes on the floor.

Ben left his stand by the couch to follow the request, bent down on the other side of the coffee table, and picked up the cigarettes and lighter. He lit two cigarettes and handed one to Charlie, then placed the pack and lighter on a dry spot on the table. He paused, to brush away some old torn wrappers and stale crumbs before he sat in the chair on the opposite side of the table.

Charlie stared at Ben from the couch and blinked to focus because Ben vibrated and glowed. Ben also wore long jeans. He watched a glowing drop of sweat form on Ben's chin and became fixated on the occurrence. It was obviously too hot out for long jeans. What was Ben thinking?

Ben took off his hat, drew his hand across his wet forehead, and wiped the bead of sweat on his chin with the back of his hand. He put his hat on the arm of the overstuffed chair.

Charlie cleared his throat, "So, ah . . . what are you . . . doing here?" he asked in a raspy voice.

"Come to see you, fool."

"Why?"

"I'm checkin' ya out. Haven't heard from ya since ya got fired last month. I was wonderin' if ya were all right. I see ya look like shit."

"Yeah, I'm okay."

"Find another job yet?"

"No." Charlie said, thinking that he finished the first step of the plan and was between the first and second part of his work.

"Ya lookin'?"

"Yeah." Charlie was hoping that the twitching he experienced just before Ben's interruption would be the long anticipated communication from his parents. He couldn't wait until Ben left and wondered how long it would take. He considered what to do to speed the decision along.

"Bullshit. You're lyin'. Look at yourself. Ya got a three-week-old beard. Ya smell like ya haven't showered in days and your hair . . . I don't even want to go there. And you're tryin' to tell me you're lookin' for a job . . . like that?"

"So . . . come over to . . . bust my balls?"

"Somebody's got to do it and I guess I'm elected. You won't talk to Becka or anyone else. Who else cares?"

Charlie shrugged his shoulders.

"Look at this place. It's a pigsty. I can't believe how bad ya managed to fuck this house up since your parents died. Everything's dead outside, even da weeds. Quite an accomplishment, Charlie. And what's up with da pots?"

Charlie took a puff of his cigarette, and blew the smoke upward. Feeling harassed, impatient, and disturbed, he ground out the butt in the ashtray with exacting resolve, determined to crush the life out of every last ember in frustration. As he mashed the cigarette, Charlie's began to wonder what he could do to get Ben the hell out of his house. His cheek and face began twitching.

"And what da hell is that?"

"What . . . is what?"

"Ya got a twitch now?" Ben asked, as he reached for the ashtray and dropped in his butt.

"Got a what?" Charlie knew to what Ben referred, but he thought only he was aware of it and was surprised Ben could see. The twitch was supposed to be the *secret* way he communicated with his parents, ever since the phone calls stopped. He was angry that Ben saw his twitch and felt his privacy violated. He seethed at the thought and then panic began to take hold, not a good response.

"Not now, Mom . . . I'm busy," he mumbled, in a low tone of voice. His eyes darted back and forth as he tried to subdue the twitch. He feared the pain of correction if Ben knew what was going on with him and his parents. He twitched a second time and his hand went to cover his cheek.

"There, ya just did it again. And who do ya think your talkin' to? Your mother? Still?" Ben asked in a mocking manner. His face showed disbelief.

"Fuck you, Ben! You've been . . . on my case . . . pots are . . . protecting . . . ever since you . . . least I . . . you're one . . . to talk . . . hair . . ."

Charlie's mind started to misfire and he struggled to maintain some sense of what he was trying to say. His mind formed the words haphazardly and they came out of his mouth the same way. He paused and went on, "Who the hell you think . . . about my mother . . . I've got hair . . . you . . . you . . ."

Charlie stood up shaking vigorously. He stopped himself from speaking further. He knew there was little sense to what he was saying, but was at a loss to correct it. His face tensed as he stood clenching his fists at his side. He twitched and shook and didn't know what to do. He watched Ben's eyes stare in horror at the spectacle.

Ben reacted by jumping out of his chair. He moved out of the living room away from his friend's startling behavior.

When at a safe distance, Ben said, "I don't know what you're talkin' about, Charlie, but you're scarin' da piss out of me, literally. I've got to use da bathroom."

Ben maneuvered his large body quickly and easily down the hall toward the hallway bathroom.

Charlie snapped, "Don't . . . not that one . . . Ben . . . my bedroom." He moved around the coffee table and pointed down the hall. Just as Ben arrived at the bathroom door, Charlie shouted, "No!" He pointed toward his bedroom with vehemence this time, so Ben would, without doubt, follow his instruction.

"Okay, okay" Ben said, looking up at Charlie with a furrowed brow for barely a second, and then turning continued to follow Charlie's demands.

Charlie couldn't remember if evidence of his work butchering animals in the bathroom was properly cleaned and he didn't want Ben in there.

Once Charlie saw the detour executed properly, he went into the kitchen to get a beer from the refrigerator. He resented having to exert himself this way. He opened the door and stared into a blank abyss, the light occupying his mind and overwhelming his senses as he drifted in thought.

When he finally came back to reality, he saw that Ben had returned to the living room where he paced the floor rubbing his baldhead while waiting for Charlie. Ben's face appeared absorbed in thought. He picked up a lavender, multi-colored rhinestone animal collar on the floor in the corner of the room and examined it. Ben brought the collar into the kitchen.

Charlie stood, still at the refrigerator, watching Ben with the door open.

"What's this, Charlie?" Ben asked, holding the collar up as if it were a confiscated bag of narcotics. "Charlie?" Ben said shoving Charlie at the shoulder.

"Can't do it, Mom. Not now," Charlie murmured.

"What?" Ben asked.

"Ah . . . nothing," Charlie said, as he came back to reality. He looked at the collar Ben held up in front of his face. "Just a collar I found . . . some time ago." He finally reached into the refrigerator for a beer, popped open the can, and began drinking it.

"I'll have a beer," Ben announced smiling with apparent anticipation.

Charlie closed the refrigerator door hoping Ben would get the message.

Ben looked at Charlie with disbelief, anger, and contempt written in bold letters on his face. Then Ben noticed nasty scratch scars on Charlie's forearm.

"What happened to your arm, Charlie?" He asked pointing at the scratch marks with the hand holding the collar.

"Scratched . . . on bushes . . . outside. Yard clean up . . . yard." Charlie paused, to consider the speech problem that would not stop. "Writing a book?"

Ben seemed to ignore Charlie's comment reading the collar.

"So, have ya tried callin' da owners of . . . Charlie?"

"No. Told you . . . just found. Nothing important. Saving . . . it has my name."

"Okay, but why do ya have all these pots and pans stacked up by every door and window in da house? At least answer that," Ben said, as he jerked his head toward the windows of the kitchen.

Charlie's twitch came back again. In a cover-up effort, he slammed his beer on the kitchen counter splashing liquid from the can.

"Look, forget it!" Charlie demanded, and snatched the collar out of Ben's hand. He threw it across the kitchen near the overflowing trashcan.

"You're freakin' me out, man," Ben said, backing away from Charlie. "What are ya doin' pilin' up all those pots and pans? You're . . . you've become a nutcase, Charlie. What da fuck's wrong with you? I'm getting da hell out of here. You're crazy."

Ben backed out of the kitchen. Charlie followed him step for step, twitching as he walked.

"Not now!" Charlie shouted, looking up. Then, "Get out!" he roared, at Ben. "Get out . . . don't come back!"

Ben headed for the front door. He opened it and let in the blast furnace heat. He turned kicking a pot and said sharply, "Ya need help, Charlie. I'm tellin' the truth. For God's sake, go see a doctor, before it's too late. You're really fucked up."

Charlie shoved Ben out the door, slammed it shut, and secured both locks. He turned toward the furniture and noticed Ben's hat on the chair. He collected it and threw it outside in the heat. Then he rearranged the pots and pans in a meticulously stacked pile against the door, his warning system against enemies reset.

"Good, I'm glad I'm rid of him," Charlie said to himself, once again in control of his speech. "Don't need him. Don't need anybody. I can take care of things myself."

Charlie sat at the kitchen table and drank the rest of his beer. His twitch returned.

"Mom," Charlie said, expectantly, "sorry I couldn't talk while Ben was here. We want our conversations to be secret, right?"

"That is correct, Charles, secrecy above all else. It is time to embark on the second phase of your work, section two. You did a commendable job on the first phase and your father and I are very proud of your accomplishments."

"Thanks, Mom. I worked hard. I want to begin the next phase."

"You proved your metal. You are courageous, devoted, steadfast, strong-willed. We are certain you will do just as well in the real work ahead, the important work you have been preparing for all this time."

"You know I'll do my best."

"Indeed you will, Charles, indeed you will."

Charlie tossed his empty beer can at the trash heap. It landed next to the lavender collar.

"The new key words will be *Mister Crowley*. When you hear these words, you will begin work on the new objective that of eliminating the infectious virus which has invaded the body of our state, our country. You will rid Arizona of the foreign invaders that have besieged our borders and have made our homeland sick. Like the strays you were so successful in eliminating from the neighborhood, the results of your new job will start a chain reaction that will spread across the nation like wildfire. You must succeed, Charles. Do you understand?"

"Yes, Mom."

"Good. Remember, we will be watching you, Charles, so do what you are told, what you know to be right. Follow the worthy example set by President Bush when he set in motion the wheels of war against the World Trade Center terrorists. Your boot camp training has ended. It is time to forge war against the illegal disease invading our land. Repayment for atrocities committed against us and other Americans. The evildoers must be made to pay for their crimes. Remember the example set by George Bush. Continue to make us proud. We love you and desire your success above all else. Fulfill your destiny."

"I will, Mom."

The twitching stopped.

CHAPTER 17

APOLOGY

"I'll do it if you think it's a good idea, Dad," Charlie said to his father. "When should I make the call?"

"Now. It's Sunday, in the morning, and Ben will probably be home after a night of playing pool and hard drinking. He'll most likely not be glad to hear from you after the way you threw him out yesterday, but he'll come around after he listens to your apology."

"I had to throw him out Dad," Charlie said with his cheek twitching and his left shoulder rising slightly toward his face. "Mom wanted to talk. I couldn't hold a conversation with her while Ben was here. He'd overhear us talking and then you'd be mad. I didn't want to go through another *correction* session like the last time I talked to Ben about you guys. I had to get rid of him."

"You did the right thing, Charles, but now we have to smooth matters over a bit, otherwise it might lead to trouble. You know how Ben likes to talk. We need to ease his mind, give him confidence that you're in control. Make him understand that you need more time to do your work and get yourself orderly. Then, when the time is right, you can get together with him, like before your work started. After all, you did warn him through the door that you weren't feeling well. He came in anyway. Didn't he?"

"That's right. I did say that. Didn't I?" Charlie agreed, remembering what he said to Ben yesterday. "I pleaded with him to go away and he forced his way in. So, it's practically his fault for not listening to me. I'll make sure to remind him about that."

Charlie made his way to the master bedroom where he picked up the phone and punched in Ben's number while he laid down on the bed. He waited for the call to be answered.

"Hello," a female voice came over the line.

"Tammy? It's me . . . Charlie. Is ah . . . Ben there?"

"Charlie? Yeah, he's here. I'll see if he wants to talk to you. He was pretty pissed off with you when he got home yesterday."

"Well . . . that's what I ah . . . want to talk about. Can you get him?"

"Hold on." A brief pause followed.

"What do ya want, Charlie?" Ben's asked.

"Ben, I . . . I called to apologize . . . about yesterday. I told you . . . I wasn't feeling well . . . but . . . but you came in . . . anyway. The door bell . . . I . . . I hate it . . . hurts my ears." This was as far as Charlie's thoughts on the matter took him. He tried to remember what else his father had told him to say. Ben broke his pause of silence.

"Apology accepted, Buddy. Look Charlie, it's just that I . . . we, we're all concerned about ya. Ya kind of vanished for da last few months. Ya won't answer our calls. We miss ya. Ya know?"

"Yeah, I know . . . been depressed," Charlie said reaching for his smokes on the nightstand.

"Ya ain't kiddin', man. We were discussin' ya most of da day yesterday. What to do about your situation and all. But we honestly don't know how to help ya. Ya have to work on this problem, Charlie. Ya have to go see a doctor. If ya want, I'll take some time off from work to be with ya when ya go.

But *you* got to make da appointment. *You* got to make da call. I can't do it for ya."

"I . . . I don't need . . . anyone . . . Ben," Charlie said not wanting to say the word doctor. It took him what seemed like an eternity to substitute the word 'anyone.' He took a long drag off the cigarette he lit while Ben was talking.

"Yeah, ya do, Charlie," Ben said. "It's just like alcoholism . . . ya have to see da need."

"Ben," Charlie said getting annoyed, "I'm okay. Really. I . . . I just need more time . . . to get over my . . . loss. I need you . . . to stop . . . worrying. Let me be . . . alone. Work things out . . . myself."

"Charlie, I'm tellin' ya—"

"Ben," Charlie interrupted, "I'm not calling . . . anyone. Just give me time . . . more time."

"Okay, Charlie," Ben said. "Ya take all da time ya need. But just remember, I'm here for ya. If ya need anything, call. Okay? Just tell me one thing."

"What?"

"What da fuck were ya doin' with da pots stacked up against the windows and doors, man?"

"They're . . ." Charlie caught himself. "I . . . I got to go, Ben. But . . . do me a favor."

"Name it."

"Tell everyone . . . I say, hi," Charlie said, trying to be thoughtful, showing Ben he cared and was in control. "Especially, Becka," he added for good measure knowing how much mileage he would attain from those two little words.

"Ya bet I will," Ben said emphatically. "Becka will be glad to hear that."

"Okay. Good. I got to go now . . . work to do."

"You got a job?" Ben asked.

Charlie hung up.

After the call, Charlie sat back in his chair where he used to watch the world unfold outside through the open blinds.

He now stared at the closed shades daydreaming about a time when all Mexicans in Arizona were eliminated—"pruned" to use a word from his mother—or got the message and went back to Mexico due to the result of his work. When politicians would commend his work and no longer be afraid to legislate laws to keep English the official language, to stop companies from advertising in Spanish and hiring illegals, to deport on a grand scale the illegal hordes that clog community services, schools, hospitals, health care, and pollute society. Having begun the important task of elimination, pruning, all America would catch on fire and become one great hive, working tirelessly in support of the vision his parents instilled into him. The plan, put into action following the examples of President Bush, would redefine what America is all about: A stronger nation, indivisible with liberty and justice for those who belong here, not those who sneak across the border, break laws, seek handouts and entitlements, and kill indiscriminately.

Charlie knew that he could not accomplish these lofty goals and reap the rewards his parents promised with Becka and Ben and his so called friends constantly nagging him to do mundane things like attending Super Bowl parties, playing pool, and watching DVD's on the couch hugging and kissing, making love. Sure these things were important to him way back when, at a time when he was not so occupied by the important work at hand. These things could and should wait. There will be time again for them later. He'll get married as he said he would, but not right now. His work demanded priorities.

He saw his life differently now. To his way of thinking, he had a purpose. Sure, things would be more easily accomplished if he had the power of President Bush, but he was willing to work in small ways at first, concentrating on bigger and better results with the help of others that see his parents' vision and eventually work toward the end result, like the way things happened with the animal strays. Instead of a gathering of community neighbors, he could rely on local political power, which always meant the involvement of the military or police to enforce the correct view. And the correct view was a state without illegal aliens and a country that would surely follow suit.

At least he was doing something about the problem, unlike all those internet e-mailers who can only bitch and complain and write scathing letters highlighting everything that's wrong, but do nothing to stop the invasion. They're wasting time and energy allowing the problem to fester and grow rancid by employing such passive methods of persuasion. Something had to be done, done right. His parents said that they got their information from the highest authority. God knows what's right. Most often people don't know why they think the way they do. They just do what the "bleeding heart liberals" (his father used to call them) tell them to do. The blind leading the blind, sheep led astray.

He had to maintain secrecy though, because God knows they wouldn't support his view, his vision. They don't realize the corruption, the drain on society these Mexicans represent. The pain and suffering they bring to all those with whom they come into contact. Misunderstanding will surely abound because they could not know the pain of losing parents to terrorist attacks from the Mexican invaders. They would cite human rights and God knows what else to prove their incorrect point of opposition. They would kill the vision at all costs and him along with it. Charlie was not about to let that happen. They were all plotting against him, his parents, even God. How daring. How reckless. How stupid.

As the afternoon waned, he became more excited about the work and accomplishing the second and more important phase of the task at hand. Confidence built within him and with the help of his parents he was ready to wage war, a secret war, a silent war for the betterment of society and for a more perfect union.

PART 3

UNDECLARED WAR

Lunacy, like the rain, falls upon the evil and the good,
. . . it must forever remain a fearful misfortune . . .

Inmate of the Glasgow Royal Asylum—1860

CHAPTER 18

THE INVASION

The meeting was held in a dilapidated one-bedroom one-bath hovel with a large closet and small kitchen. It occupied a tiny God-forsaken plot of ground in the kind of neighborhood where front lawns sprouted parking lots as well as weeds. The dwelling's exterior boasted peeling paint and rotting wood. Inside, the main attractions included frayed carpeting, curled linoleum tiles, and at the snap of a light switch, scurrying insects performing like fleas in a circus. The building, though marginally habitable by U. S. standards, provided a dry and covered place to live in a rough section of Phoenix for Lorenzo Perez and his two twenty-one year old borders, Armando Gonzales and Jorge Salazar. This residence represented luxury to Lorenzo compared to his house in Alvarado, Mexico, where he lived with his family before crossing the border without them.

For nearly eighteen months, Lorenzo worked his carefully laid plan of creating his fortune in Arizona. He was initially deposited, with forty other squatting undocumented entrants, in a sordid condition drop-house in a quiet subdivision of Phoenix, guarded by gang-bangers on the crime family payroll. From there, he established a local address as a border in a house with only ten illegal immigrants. The move represented progress.

Lorenzo worked his share of cash labor jobs, made valuable contacts, and eventually obtained false IDs, a necessary tool for further advancement. It was then, with the help of a friend named Efren, he landed a job in a local printing plant. The steady paycheck provided him preferential recognition and six months ago he became the proud renter of one of Efren's houses. Armando and Jorge met Lorenzo at church and arranged to move in almost immediately. Lorenzo brought payments to his landlord monthly, but since renting the house, Efren had not visited until today. The meeting was conducted in Spanish.

"Efren, this is Armando Gonzales," Lorenzo introduced the dark-haired young Mexican wearing an oversized plain white T-shirt and equally baggy jeans. "And this is Jorge Salazar," Lorenzo said, introducing the young man wearing an LA Dodger cap dressed in a Corona T-shirt and who could have passed for Armando's brother. The three shook hands and exchanged greetings.

"Please sit," Lorenzo said to Efren, with an outstretched hand indicating one of a set of four worn wooden chairs matched with a cleared oval table in the cramped kitchen. Soiled breakfast dishes awaited hand cleaning in the sink.

Efren sat and the others followed suit.

"So, my friend," Efren spoke first addressing Lorenzo, "I hear you finished paying off Don Pablo last week." The short man of forty-five, a living legend among the immigrant community in Phoenix and a friend to many emigrants, commanded respect from those who sat at the table.

"Yes," the twenty-nine year old Lorenzo replied, "finally after a year and a half of making payments to that stuffed pig." Lorenzo doffed his white cowboy hat and ran ink-stained fingers through his thick black hair. His Stetson and ostrich boots showed visible signs to others that Lorenzo was becoming a man of means.

"Stuffed pig?" Efren said. "Be careful how you talk about him. He's not only a hooker for the Huertas, he's also a blood relative. As you know, he makes deals to take people like you across the border and is a highly respected recruiter for them. If the wrong people heard you disrespecting him . . . they have people everywhere." Efren's brow furrowed as he shook his head. "It could make trouble for you. This is where the Huertas live, my friend."

"Jorge. Please, turn off the radio," Lorenzo directed. "I can hardly hear myself think." Jorge got up from his chair to follow Lorenzo's request. "That's better. I call him a pig for two reasons: Because he carries around that expensive gut, it makes him look like a pig. And because he had the nerve to threaten my wife when I missed a payment. Remember? Just after I got here."

"I remember," Efren said nodding his head in agreement. "You were very angry, my friend."

"I'll never forget that about him. Asshole. I'll never forgive him either. It took me time to find the print plant job. You know. But he didn't care. He just wanted his money, no matter what."

"Illegal crossings are a business, Lorenzo. To him, you're just another fish on a hook," Efren offered.

"I know," Lorenzo admitted. "But he didn't have to be an asshole about it. How the hell did he get the title of Don anyway? Isn't that title given to kings or something?"

"In his case, it's a word for respect. I know him well enough to have seen his house. When I finally got some respect from the Huertas finding people like you jobs," Efren passed his hand by the men at the table, "and making houses available, he invited me to visit him for a weekend. The guy's rich like a king. It's big business, Lorenzo. The Huertas got fixers like me working in Illinois, Florida, California, and Idaho, too. He's a partner in one of the most powerful crime families in Mexico."

"I guess most people see importance, a Father figure maybe," Lorenzo said.

"He deserves the title," Efren concluded.

"Maybe," Lorenzo added. "But he's still a pig."

"A pig who makes all the arrangements to help guys cross the border," Efren said. To Armando and Jorge he asked, "You guys crossed using Don Pablo, too, didn't you?" He alternated eye contact between them.

"We did," Armando spoke up, "but, man, the Coyote he hired to meet us in *Sonoyta* was an asshole. He was younger than us," he said indicating Jorge, "and full of shit, thinking he was better than us. Said he was proud to be offering a valuable service for Mother Mexico. Said he was helping to get back what was once our territory. You know, man, win the undeclared war and take back Gringo land one 'walker' at a time."

"That's right, man," Jorge, a welder by trade, agreed. "I heard him singing words to a rap song about the war. Something about taking back land at gun point."

"I don't know about any of that bullshit," Armando said. "Man, all I came here to do is work, make money, have an adventure, get some excitement. Any job is better than no job and the Gringos give us work. Maybe, if I'm lucky, find a rich girl. You know, get married, live a better life . . . like you Efren. What's wrong with that, man?"

"Who would marry you, you faggot?" Jorge teased.

"Shut up," Armando demanded, punching his friend in the arm.

"Okay, man, okay," Jorge said laughing and rubbing his shoulder.

"My guide was cruel," Lorenzo said changing the subject back to Coyotes. "He drove us hard. Gave us handfuls of Ephedra to speed up our walking."

"I know," Jorge chimed in. "Ours made us walk so fast that we left behind a family of four. Man, they just walked slower and slower until we couldn't see them any more. Armando brought it up to the asshole, but he just said, 'Fuck them if they can't keep up.' We don't know what happened to them. Never saw them again. They never made it to the pickup point."

"Wasn't the pickup crazy, Jorge?" Armando asked. "Man, it was so insane. You almost didn't make it in the van. The fucking driver started taking off and you had to jump in at the last second."

"Yes and I landed right on top of you, and thirteen other bodies."

Laughter filled the kitchen.

"You know what's amazing though," Armando said when the humor died down, "in spite of all the craziness on the border, you know, with the Border Patrol, the DEA, INS, cops, park rangers, angry Gringos in jeeps, it's surprising we were able to cross with out being seen."

They all laughed again.

"And isn't it funny, my friends," Efren said still snickering, "all that happens right near Kit Peak Observatory?"

From the looks on Armando and Jorge's faces, they were dumbfounded. Lorenzo, too, unable to follow what Efren had said, sat in an uneasy silence which ruled for the next few seconds.

Efren finally said, "I think it's funny anyway." He paused. "You know . . . Kit Peak is a place where the Gringos have telescopes so they can see things millions of miles in space." Still no reaction. "You dummies. If the telescopes were pointed at the ground instead of the sky, they would probably see the millions of us crossing the border coming to this land of opportunity."

Everyone burst out laughing again now that they all understood. The chuckling gave way to silence again, which Efren broke by asking, "So, are you happy you made the decision to come north?"

"Sure," Lorenzo was the first to reply. "Now that I got rid of Don Pablo, I can really start sending money back to my wife and family. I'm just one more worker in the great melting pot of America. It's nice to have health care and all the benefits we are entitled to as well."

"It's a matter of survival . . . no?" Efren asked.

"It was. I mean the uncertainty drove me crazy. I have a steady job now, get overtime and all, thanks to you," Lorenzo said to Efren. "What did I have back home? I worked as a part time soda bottler, when there was work. Did odd jobs around town. Grew my own corn, coffee, fruit . . . raised chickens and turkeys . . . but I never got ahead. The only vacation I got was when I got sick. Running water in my house was supplied by a pan . . . the running part was me, getting the water from the rain barrel under the gutter spout."

"Things are much better here, man," Armando piped up. "Back where me and Jorge are from, my family only had one radio and it was permanently tuned to the only station we could get. Here it's musical heaven, man, so many stations to listen to."

Efren asked, "What about you two? Have you gotten your false IDs yet?"

"No, man. No IDs yet," Jorge replied.

"My friends, you know I can't get you good jobs until you have IDs. It's almost impossible to find employers who don't ask for IDs."

"We can't afford them yet, man," Armando broke in. "Me and Jorge work for people that shop at the nearby Home Depot. Our English is not real good yet, but we manage and speak enough to work for small building contractors and homeowners. We like the work and are saving our money the best we can."

"It's hard to save when you keep drinking your money away," Jorge said looking at Armando.

"You're going to get a broken tooth, man, if you keep it up," Armando warned making a fist. "And then your English will really suck."

"What? Like yours?" Jorge countered.

"Better than yours, asshole."

"They were friends back in the Veracruz area," Lorenzo informed Efren while the two young men bantered back and forth, "but you would never know it. At times like this,

I wonder how they stay friends. They made the trip north together and they're good people. They pay their share of the rent on time, buy groceries, and do most of the women chores around here. So, if they say they're saving, I believe them. It's hard to save and party at the same time, though."

"Which brings me to the reason for my visit," Efren said. "I have another kid, another paying roommate to help you all save. He needs a place to stay for a while. Maybe you would consider him, as a favor to me. His name is Felipe Valverde."

"Yes?" Lorenzo, as head of the house asked, seeking for more information.

"He comes from a rancho called Cosamaloapan. It's a backcountry village located inland and south of Veracruz. It has thirty-nine people; all without electric . . . you can't even get there by car. Felipe told me you have to walk for two miles from the road. He's unskilled, speaks very little English, and is only sixteen."

"Sixteen?" Lorenzo asked. "He made the trip north at sixteen . . . alone?"

"He made the trip with his father," Efren continued, "but his father died on the way."

"Oh, too bad," Lorenzo said making the sign of the cross. Armando and Jorge wagged their heads.

"Felipe tells me he and his father, Carlos, entered Arizona in the Tucson sector, leaving Mexico a few weeks after Easter, in the beginning of May. His father may have been a little too old to make the trip, especially at that time of year. You know . . . too hot. He took too many breaks. They fell behind the group, like you said about that family, Jorge."

"It happens too often, I think," said Jorge.

"They were half way down a mountain ridge when they heard a plane. The main group, further down in the valley, rushed for cover."

"Don't tell me," Lorenzo suggested, "his father died in a fall."

"Well . . . when they saw the others running for cover, they did, too. Carlos jumped into an arroyo and found himself in a rattlesnake lair. Got bit before Felipe got to him. Felipe killed the snake with a stick, but Carlos was already dying."

Lorenzo thought back to a horrible scene he witnessed on his trip north in the desert, one he would never forget. It was the final resting place of a young mother and her two babies, who died along the way during their crossing. The setting had become the source of many sleepless nights and sorrowful memories for Lorenzo.

"Felipe said nobody in the group moved while in hiding, but as soon as the plane passed and it was clear, the Coyote continued on and everybody followed. Carlos and Felipe were left behind, alone."

"Wow, man, so the kid was left in a life and death situation?" Armando asked.

"Right. Felipe stayed long enough to watch his father die, but not long enough to bury him. That was the hard part. Felipe said Carlos told him to continue on to America, to work the plan they made to help their family financially. Carlos told Felipe he loved him, tried to make Felipe's decision easier, and said his good-byes. Felipe was angry that the Coyote would not rest so Felipe could bury his father. He told me that he thinks about it all the time. He's very depressed."

"Man, no kidding? Wouldn't you be?" asked Jorge.

"He feels guilty . . . letting Carlos bake in the sun, become food for scavengers, but what could he do?"

Nobody answered.

"So, he arrived here in Phoenix, hopeless. He's not sure what to do now, you know, stay or go back home. I was hoping he could stay with you, Lorenzo, until he figures it out."

"Poor kid. Sure he can stay here," Lorenzo said nodding his approval to Armando and Jorge. They gave their support nodding their heads as well. "Where is he now, Efren?"

"At my house. I told him I was going to search for a place for him to stay. I thought of you right away. It's settled then? He'll stay here?"

"Yes," the three men said together.

"What does he do for work?" Lorenzo asked Efren.

"He's fallen to panhandling, because he's unskilled. I made a sign for him that says, 'Will work for food.' He's been standing on street corners for two days now and people give him change. Sometimes he's given more. He hopes to actually get work this way one day. He doesn't complain and is quiet most of the time. He's trying to deal with his bad luck. He manages, but I think he could use a few more friends. Maybe he'll eventually go back home."

Efren got up from the table preparing to leave. "It was good to meet you," he said to Armando and Jorge and shook their hands.

They sauntered from the kitchen to the living room where all the windows were lined with old newspapers. Armando's sleeping comforts were met in the living room with plenty of well-used pillows, comforters, and blankets. Jorge called the large closet his bedroom and Lorenzo claimed the only real bedroom with a stained twin mattress and a plastic crucifix hung on the wall.

They stopped in front of the entrance near Armando's blanket. "You know," Efren said to Lorenzo as he opened the door, "an evil shadow has passed over Felipe. He's a stranger in a strange land, alone and lost . . . like an abandoned human stray. Take care of him, my friends."

CHAPTER 19

LOOKING FOR WORK

For Charlie and his father, weekends were never spent under the hood of a car or watching NASCAR races. They had no interest watching cars go round and round on a track. Both were not mechanically inclined and felt automobile breakdowns an inconvenience, never an opportunity to prove, improve, or brush up on mechanical skills. Horsepower never made an impression. Cars were merely a means to get from point A to point B and often a pain in the ass. Their interests didn't involve wrenches, air tools, grease, or oil. The only item any McShane knew how to fix on a vehicle was the fuel tank gas gauge—from E to F. No mechanical skills passed down, no joy of engine tinkering, no desire to teach or learn. When the time came to repair a vehicle, there was only one tool picked up by McShane men: The phone.

"Service. This is Woody. How can I help you?"

"Hi. M-my truck is . . . running kind of . . . funny," Charlie said unsure of his explanation. He began to think of a better description to use, but all that kept coming to him at the moment was "funny."

"Can you be a little more descriptive, sir?" A short pause developed into a long gap of silence. "Is your truck running rough? Are you having trouble starting it? Seem kind of sluggish?"

"Yes," Charlie finally agreed.

"Can you make it to the dealership?"

"Yes."

"Okay. What's your name and what's the year and make of your truck?"

Once Charlie began to answer questions the conversation went more smoothly. The service advisor told him he probably needed a tune-up, a new fuel filter, and an oil change to fix the problem, maybe more, but could not tell for sure without seeing the vehicle. The guy could have told him he needed a new engine and Charlie would have agreed for all he knew about mechanics. Charlie hated leaving the house, but a trip to the shop seemed to be forced upon him and an appointment was grudgingly made.

The unbearable heat of summer took its toll on vehicles as well as humans. Air conditioning, a most needed option in searing temperatures, always breaks down when needed most, and oil viscosity fails faster in excessive heat providing two valid reasons for increased service visits during summer. For these reasons and many others, the dealership, engaged in the business of vehicle sales and service, was extremely busy.

For Charlie, there were too many people. He was intimidated by all the hustle and bustle. He felt his eyes were big as saucers, which remained a constant facial fixture the entire time spent at the dealership. Speech was a challenge when he talked to the service advisor. He could only manage to say "Okay" and "Fine" between big chunks of the foreign language the advisor seemed to be speaking. Charlie couldn't grasp any of the technical information. At the end of their mostly one-way conversation, Charlie added, "and please hurry."

The service advisor directed Charlie to the waiting room down a long corridor to the left of the service desk. On his way, he passed numerous sales offices in the corridor that were empty and quite plain: A desk, a chair on one side and two on the other, a phone, a pad, and a calculator for each office. There were no advertisements or distractions of any kind to occupy a buyer's mind. It appeared to be a war room and, like the tables in Vegas, the odds were stacked in favor of the house.

Looking through the glass door of the waiting room, Charlie afforded a moment to observe the scene and saw four people scattered around in uncomfortable chairs. A girl of about ten temporarily watched a game show on the color TV located in the corner. She held the remote in the midst of an arduous process of mindless channel surfing through news programs and soaps on the limited selection of channels. She seemed to be in search of a non-existent cartoon station and frustration grew as stations repeated, but nobody in the room seemed to mind, except the girl.

Two men read periodicals, one a young thirty something the other way past his prime, well spaced apart in the seating arrangements. Each had a coffee cup in hand courtesy of the thoughtful dealership.

The last customer, a marginally attractive woman, talked on her cell phone with eyes fixed on the little girl with the remote.

The scene seemed innocuous to Charlie, at first. He decided to enter the room. Walking through the door, he noticed that none of the people looked up at him. This caused considerable concern and alarm for him. The beginning of another panic attack struck him in the same way his father used to slap him across the face when, as a young boy, he lied about trivial matters. The episodes sent him rushing to his mother, but he inevitably found little consolation there, as she never sided against his father in matters of discipline. The corrections never stopped Charlie from lying, but he eventually became a better liar. And in spite of his ability to tell better stories, he continued to seek his mother's sanctuary when hurt.

Stressed nerves sent alarms to Charlie's brain. It was obvious that the police instructed these people not to look at him and to be inconspicuous with his approach. His mind raced with an unnerving sense of impending doom. The little girl was a touch of genius by the police, so devious that it caused his heart to plummet like an express elevator and his bowels felt the sensation.

Charlie stood laboring at an impasse five feet into the room unable to take one step further. A silent invisible wall stood between him and his advance. While still undecided about his next move, he noticed one of the men sipping his coffee. The inaudible action was no less than a signal conferred to lurking hidden agents, a tip off to Charlie's presence, an announcement to converge. Immediately, he turned and fled the room, certain that uniformed policemen would soon prevail upon him. He noticed the waiting customers stir as he glanced back to make certain no one was poised to follow.

With the confines of the waiting room abandoned, Charlie was uncertain where to go. He looked for police around every corner as he moved down the hall. A nicotine fit forced a smoke break, so he found the nearest building exit that led outside and entered the 110-degree heat. There were "No Smoking" signs everywhere and Charlie didn't want to give the police any further reason to accost him. The time it took to smoke a single cigarette became dreadful, but he managed to recover from the storming fear in the relative solitude of the far reaches of the used car lot.

The waiting problem for Charlie became a three-hour endurance of alternating discomforts: Relatively secure five minute breaks outside in sauna-like heat exposure versus fearful, anxious, wandering in the air conditioned dealership where constant avoidance became his only goal. During a quiet interlude inside the men's room, he wondered if there were any companies that performed automotive house calls to avoid this stress and torture in the future. A mental note was made to follow up the idea in the future, but the thought passed to oblivion with the flush of the toilet.

Waiting for his truck to be fixed seemed an eternity of punishment and anguish. It all came to an end when the service advisor found Charlie outside smoking in the heat. He announced that the truck was fixed an hour ago, but nobody was able to find him. The man asked where he had been, but Charlie did not answer the question.

Charlie didn't examine the bill for accuracy or ask to learn what had been done mechanically. He was anxious to remove himself from the rack, the instrument of torture the dealership had become. He signed the credit card papers, almost forgot his receipts, and ran from the building to find his truck in the parking lot.

The pickup, easily roused to life, seemed to perform notably well; whatever the mechanics did worked. The cost was expensive, but the lawyer would approve money to pay the bill from the funds held until probate, contingencies being allowed. This had to qualify. He fired up another cigarette, observed that a mechanic turned off the air conditioner, and flipped the lever to high then pushed the button to turn on the air. He opened the closed, fully loaded ashtray he'd been meaning to empty for months and thought that they would have cleaned it as a courtesy, considering the cost involved. Courtesies didn't happen in Charlie's world.

Fearful of being tailed, he zoomed out of the parking lot, slowing down only for a strategically placed speed bump. Charlie tactically maneuvered through dilatory traffic and performed a planned, last-second U-turn to expose a possible threat of being followed. With that last assurance on his part, he slowed to an inconspicuous driving pattern and blended with the traffic flow. He turned on the radio as he approached a red light at the entrance to the I-10 freeway. The stereo was tuned to 98 KUPD and the disc jockey just finished saying something about Osbourn when gothic-influenced, organ-solo music flooded the truck cab and washed into Charlie's mind.

His attention simultaneously diverted to a young Mexican panhandler that stood on the median beside the left turn lane. The young boy held a homemade, cardboard sign as the truck rolled to a stop for the light. The driver's side window came even with the boy and allowed Charlie clear view of the advertisement hand written in black marker letters: "Will Work For Food." Charlie's sunglass-shaded eyes looked up from the sign to the boy's face. Their gaze met at the exact moment Ozzy Osbourn began singing the words to—*Mr. Crowley.*

Charlie heard the command words "Mr. Crowley" and, in an instant, observed the Mexican with precise study and workman-like evaluations. His eyes widened as fresh instructive knowledge and perspective rushed into his conscious thoughts, like a treasured computer download.

He rolled down the truck window to talk to the boy whose face was sunburned and streaked with sweat from the intense heat. The boy's crude-cut, mussed, black hair hung over his ears and stuck to his wet forehead. He wore an ill-fitting dirty T-shirt. Rumpled dark canvas pants covered spindly legs down to brown leather huarache sandals, almost indistinguishable from his deeply tanned feet.

The boy saw the window of the truck roll down and moved closer. He held one hand out to accept an offer of bestowed mercy. The sign, even though it read "Will Work . . ." seemed to Charlie more of a request for a loose change handout. The idea of real work ever being offered or accepted in this situation seemed a remote possibility.

"What went on in your head?" Ozzy sang as the song continued.

"You want a job?" Charlie asked, as the boy approached the truck.

The Mexican stopped and stood a few feet away with his hand still held out. To Charlie, he seemed somewhat mystified by the English language.

Ozzy continued singing on the radio.

"Do you . . . want . . . a job?" Charlie repeated, as if slower speech would somehow miraculously translate.

The words of the song about talking to the dead reverberated in Charlie's head.

"You know . . . job . . . work . . ." Charlie continued, pointing to the sign that had "Work" printed on it, still held by the boy with one hand. He reached over to reduce the volume on the stereo. It interfered with his ability to communicate.

The young Mexican bent his head down, looked at the sign, and, after some apparent thought, held the sign out to Charlie.

"No. I don't want your sign," Charlie said, with a frustrated frown and held his hand up in refusal. Under his breath he continued, "Dumb fucking Mexican."

Charlie thought communication would be enhanced by a visual aid so he reached in his pocket and pulled out what folded paper money he had. He held a dollar bill through the window as an enticement hoping the visual aid would disseminate seeds of understanding in the dim-witted Mexican's mind, currently a fallow field.

The boy smiled taking a step closer to the vehicle to accept the money.

Charlie pulled the money from the window back into the truck cab and, with his free hand, repeatedly curled his index finger in a come-and-get-it gesture, which ultimately led to a repeated directional point around the truck to the passenger door.

Charlie said, "Get in."

He racked his high school Spanish class memory for the right foreign words.

"*Esta aqui*," he finally said annoyed, pointing to the passenger seat. Charlie began looking around to see if anyone was witnessing the strange show unfolding at the red light. Nobody was around as far as he could see. That was not only good but also relieving. Another few seconds and Charlie was ready to leave with or without the boy.

Seeds of understanding grew just in time because the Mexican finally reached the passenger door and entered the truck when the light turned green. Charlie guided the truck through the green light arrow turning left onto the interstate entrance ramp.

Continuing with the press for Spanish communication, Charlie glanced at the boy and said, "Ah . . . *Tu trabajo?* You work? *Si*." He accelerated the truck to highway speed.

"*Si*," the young Mexican said, smiling with newfound understanding. A head bob displayed due reverence toward an employer, a superior.

"Good . . . *bien*," Charlie said, also accompanied by a smile, but one more sinister in nature.

They sat in silence for a while during which time Charlie searched for more Spanish words to ask how much money per hour the kid's labor would cost, providing payment would be made. Charlie wanted to encourage a secure feeling in the boy's mind about being driven to an unknown location, to give a false sense of security. Asking for the boy's name would accomplish this and he knew the Spanish equivalent for that. So he asked, while looking ahead driving, "*Como se llama*? What's your name?"

"Felipe," the young Mexican replied, then placed the sign he still held in his lap on the floor of the truck, near his sandaled feet. The air conditioned truck appeared to agree with Felipe as he put his hands in front of the air vent to cool off. Then he said something in Spanish.

Charlie heard the word '*donde*' and figured Felipe had asked where he was being taken. The word '*vamos*' was also familiar, but he couldn't quite remember what it expressed, maybe something about hurrying up?

"To *mi casa* . . . for *trebajo*," Charlie replied. "How much for your work? Ah, *Cuanto dinero* for *ahora* for *trabajo*? You know . . . money." He rubbed his thumb against his index finger to show a sign of money to Felipe.

"*Diez*."

"Ten! Per hour? No . . . no . . . no . . . too much. No *muy bien*. How about five . . . ah . . . *cinco*?" Charlie offered. He held up his right hand with all five fingers extended.

"*Cinco* . . . okay," Felipe agreed, still smiling accompanied by another head nod.

Charlie at first thought that Filipe was a greedy little bastard to ask for ten dollars an hour, but now that the boy took five dollars he revised his thoughts to what an easy mark. What impressive negotiation skills the young man displayed, he thought sarcastically. Maybe five dollars was too much to offer. No matter, now that the basic lure and snare were set.

Charlie no longer felt further communication necessary. To speak a foreign language here in the United States of America aggravated him. During the balance of the drive home, he allowed himself to drift into speculation about Mexicans and the similarities of catching stray animals to stray humans.

He wondered why Mexicans, who knew they were coming to an English speaking country, would never bother to learn the language. Unlike other foreigners that came to this country in times past, Mexicans never try to blend in, never acquired the identity of the country they entered, never lost their foreign ways of doing things. Either they were too stupid or too stubborn. Either way, the process of becoming part of America's melting pot is avoided. Their laziness caused difficulties for everyone.

In regard to catching strays, he thought: With animals, an appeal was necessarily directed toward their stomachs, the basic animal desire to eat and thereby produce comfort, satisfaction. With humans, the appeal was with money, but the root form of the appeal of money was still connected to the stomach; money is converted into food and is therefore the same appeal. The lure was ultimately food in either case. Strays were hungry animals whether they were dogs, cats, or Mexicans.

How perceptive and astute the education of the first phase of the plan was utilizing stray animals as the training foundation. It established a similar repeating pattern to be effectively employed in the real work with Mexicans. Charlie found a another reason to worship his parents.

How simple it all seemed looking back: The shed, his house, food in the snare, money for food, pure biological proclivity, fulfilling basic needs, comfort, avoiding hunger. All strays, animal or human, exerted simple patterns of unwanted stress on society, with the solution to this problem being, of course, removal. *That's where I fit in, my job defined.*

Charlie then considered hunger. He could not remember ever being really hungry his entire life. Sure, he realized, he became hungry when meals were missed, but true hunger, not knowing if or when another meal would be forthcoming or going days on end without food, that type of hunger was never experienced. He wondered if that kind of hunger would be scary. Would it make a person do stupid things? Would it make them break the law? The uncertainty was the real problem. Hunger, for money, for food, for a better life, would constantly preoccupy the Mexicans forcing certain actions without concern for society. The results satisfying only the basic need. Logic and concern for others is damned in the face of true hunger. It becomes more than stomach pain; it becomes a reckless driving force, a drain on everything around. Charlie became encouraged and steadfast about his role in the work at hand.

Before Charlie realized it, the garage door to his house opened as the truck idled in the driveway. He took a quick survey for witnesses, all clear. The truck advanced into the empty, two-car garage and he pushed the remote button to close the door and turned off the engine. Felipe made a motion to exit the truck but Charlie grabbed the boy by the arm to forestall a hasty exit until the door closed all the way. He didn't want to announce to the neighbors that he was about to have a visitor. Most people were still at work and otherwise unaware of what was happening at the McShane house today.

From the heat of the garage, Charlie and the boy embraced the cool air of the house upon entering through the door from the garage to the kitchen. Charlie led the way. He pulled out a chair from the kitchen table and directed Felipe to sit using hand gestures rather than verbal commands. The chair, he made sure, faced away from the kitchen door to the patio.

Felipe sat as directed, peered around the room, and seemed to pay particular attention to the pots and pans stacked by the window and door of the kitchen that lead outside to the backyard patio. He was about to speak, when Charlie shushed him to silence with an index finger raised to his mouth. He was now in control.

"You probably won't understand a word I'm saying," Charlie said, "but I want you to eat first, before you work." He pointed alternately from his mouth to his stomach remembering his thoughts on feeding the hunger. "Food . . . *primero.*"

Charlie found the cupboard empty of clean bowls so he cleaned and rinsed a dirty bowl and spoon from the sink with a soap filled sponge, both of which were, in due course, placed in front of Felipe sitting at the table. Cheerios were poured into the bowl, milk added, and a glass of orange juice completed brunch for one and a major distraction while Charlie made preparations.

"Eat, drink, be happy, for tomorrow, or maybe today . . ." Charlie said. "While you're eating, I'm going to the garage . . . for some tools you'll need to work with outside." He used hand signals in explanation and attempted to paint a translated picture for Felipe to view. "You just sit here and eat . . . *comprende?*"

"*Si, grasias.*"

Charlie knew that Felipe understood little of what he said, but as long as the boy continued to eat for the next few minutes, that was all the time he needed. He proceeded to the garage and collected some tools used to construct the shed months ago for the snare. He carried them in full view of the Mexican boy into the kitchen and kicked the pots and pans piled in front of the kitchen door to the patio out of the way making a racket. Felipe stood up from his chair in an effort to help Charlie at the door, but Charlie said, "No! Eat. Eat. You stay . . . eat. It's okay. I've got it." He directed the boy back to the chair.

Felipe sat and resumed eating.

Outside on the patio, Charlie dropped all the tools so that Felipe would hear, all save one. The hammer never made it to the patio floor. It remained in Charlie's sweaty hand as he stood looking into the kitchen, at the focus of his work. He paused and began to twitch.

"You can do this, Charles," his father encouraged. "You must. Now is not the time to consider your actions. Remember how your hero, President Bush, was always clear about his objective after 9/11, how he brought justice to evildoers and made our country safe? The stray won't be eating much longer. Do it. Do it now."

Lightening bolts of purpose surged up Charlie's legs as they propelled him through the door. His resolve being reassured by his father, Charlie carried the hammer back into the kitchen in his right hand behind his back. Felipe, still engaged at the table, with his back to the door, didn't turn to see Charlie step up behind him. Felipe's careless concern was his last.

In one swift motion, Charlie raised the hammer high above his head. With great force, he brought the tool of death downward planting it claw side down firmly in Felipe's skull. CRACK! A muffled noise, like a coconut splitting on a concrete floor sounded from the Mexican's head. It mixed with a guttural bellow of shock rushing out of Felipe's mouth, along with milk and chewed pieces of little round oats. The hammer penetrated through the long mussed black hair, skin, bone, and brain. Its descent stopped only by the blunt interference of the handle.

Felipe's head progressed downward preceding the hammer stroke. A knee-jerk muscle reaction in the neck and spine stopped the head shy of the cereal bowl on the table. His right hand clutched the spoon in the cereal, but jarred the bowl in a violent upheaval. Milk and Cheerios splashed upward into his face and to the right of the table. The splatter of white liquid, larger than the splatter of blood, eventually mixed to create a pink swirl on the tabletop. The glass of orange juice, half consumed, was miraculously unaffected.

Felipe's body quivered in the chair. His bent legs shot straight out with enough force to kick off one sandal. It flew upward to the bottom of the table and dropped to the floor.

Charlie controlled the trembling, fluttering body movements with the hammer handle still wedged in the skull. Shattered skull pieces on either side of the wound, in time, failed to support his control. The bony cradle disintegrated, owing to the jerky movements of the body. The falling tendency increased while Charlie held the listing torso by head alone.

Blood bubbled out of the jagged wound, poured down through black matted hair, and washed over the collar of Felipe's dirty-white T-shirt. Charlie attempted to remove the hammer, to allow the body freedom to fall to the right, but the claw stuck. Attempts to dislodge the hammer sloshed blood and bits of brain into projectiles and created a bigger mess. After holding the head and body motionless in a frozen fall with the head cocked touching the left shoulder, Charlie released the handle. The body collapsed to the kitchen floor. The chair jerked to the left upon impact.

Blood collected into a puddle on the tile floor and ran out along the straight lines where the tiles were joined, creating an ever-growing, geometric pattern of vulgar, bloody art. Charlie stood in silence as he watched the blood creep along the floor tiles for a minute, astonished to see how vibrant the red color was against the white tile floor. He removed his sunglasses for an unimpeded view.

After careful examination, he laid the kitchen dishtowel on the floor in front of the cabinets to stop the flow of blood from reaching baseboards, an area hard to clean. Then he sat at the table and put on his sunglasses. He surveyed the area to assess cleanup.

The mess seemed overwhelming from where he sat.

Suddenly, Felipe's bowels released their contents, fouling the air with a most putrid combination of body odor, rotting excrement, and urine. What a messy business, Charlie thought.

Cleanup started with the hammer. Charlie bent down to retrieve it and, with a twisting, pulling yank, the tool released. A slosh noise, like a foot removed from three inches of fresh mud sounded, as the lifeless head fell to the floor with a thud, oozing red and gray tissue. Felipe's lifeless eyes seemed to stare across the bloody mosaic, past the table legs, to the wall.

Charlie cleaned the hammer in the kitchen sink and dried it with a towel from the bathroom. He didn't want rust to ruin the valuable tool. He gathered the implements outside along with it and returned them to the garage. He collected the mop and pail, as he had done so many times before, and brought them to the kitchen. He restacked the pots and pans by the kitchen door and sat at the table to take a break. As he smoked, he pondered body removal.

Once again he digressed, and drew similarities between the animals and the dead boy, his first casualty of the undeclared war. *Chaquito* and Felipe died a similar death of ease. Even, Charlie, the hellish white cat, gave more of a fight than both of them put together. They both seemed willing sacrifices, too. Except this time, body disposal would be a bigger challenge.

Charlie dwelt on Felipe's removal for quite some time unable to decide where to start. The project now appeared too big, too sordid. The stench filling the kitchen was distracting and made him nauseous. Thoughts began to wander as he finished his cigarette.

His twitch reappeared and clear thoughts began forming about the cleanup, as if his mother directed his intelligence. She was not speaking, but he now knew what to do.

He decided to wrap the head in a plastic bag, tying the plastic drawstrings around Felipe's neck. That would stop the blood flow from making a further mess. Then he would clean the blood with the mop and paper towels, saving the body and the bloody paper towels to be rolled up in trash bags for last. Industrial tape in the garage would secure the slippery bags in place. Felipe could then be easily transported through the house to the truck. Lifting him into the pickup bed alone would be difficult, but not impossible. The pickup needed to be lined and protected against any leakage or bloodstains, but that would be easy. Then a drive to the desert, dig a shallow grave in a remote location and the job would be done.

He was ready to begin, but first, a beer. He lit another cigarette and grabbed a can from the refrigerator.

"The plan is good," he declared, as he drank. "The first Mexican stray, the first invader in the undeclared war, the first job in execution of the real work would soon be recorded in the unpublished book of heroics," he said. "The trimming and pruning of unwanted members of society has, successfully, begun."

He performed the work according to the flawless plan. In the late evening hours of Friday night, he arrived home exhausted but satisfied.

His parents would be proud.

He had been unemployed far too long.

It felt good to be back at work.

CHAPTER 20

UNANSWERED QUESTIONS

Lorenzo's kitchen—indeed the whole house, what little space it included—smelled more appetizing than a Macayo's Mexican Restaurant. Huge quantities of scrambled eggs, mixed with green and red peppers and spices, hissed and sputtered in one large pan that occupied the biggest electric burner on the small greasy stove. On a secondary burner, a pot of refried beans bubbled. Coffee finished percolating over an hour ago.

Lorenzo spent time earlier this morning setting the table with a bowl of hot tomato sauce prepared in a stone mortar and pestle. A small circle of white goat's cheese had been cut into bite-sized cubes and placed on a plate. It engaged the center spot on the table. The ever-present corn tortilla chips rolled into little scoops were served in a bowl. They filled a corner spot on the table. As there were few luxury item utensils available, the tortillas substituted for forks and spoons. Most meals were eaten using pieces of tortilla held by hand to scoop food. Lorenzo sipped coffee from a mug as he watched the feast cook.

Most weekdays, Armando, Jorge, and Felipe prepared the morning meal, but on weekends, Lorenzo cooked because he enjoyed making breakfast when time permitted;

it occupied him on days off from work. He also preferred his breakfast cooked a certain way and, on weekends, he set the alarm early.

When Lorenzo went to wake his roommates, he was surprised not to find Felipe in the house. He looked around, even outside. Although Felipe was rarely in the house during the day, he was always present in the morning. Lorenzo was puzzled as he reentered the kitchen.

The three men sat at the kitchen table and devoured the Saturday morning meal in between superfluous grunting, belching, and farting. The food was consumed within minutes. Afterward, they sat drinking coffee.

"So, ah, where's Felipe?" Lorenzo asked in Spanish, alternating his wide-eyed inspection from Armando to Jorge and back to Armando again.

Armando glanced at Jorge. "We don't know, man," Armando said, speaking for Jorge. "After dinner last night, we went to Ojeda's Bar. When we got back home, he wasn't here. We went to sleep thinking he would come back later."

"Yes," added Jorge, nodding his head in agreement.

"When was the last time you saw him?" Lorenzo asked Armando with a note of concern in his deep voice.

"Yesterday morning, man, before we left for work," Armando said. He seemed to look to Jorge to receive agreement or confirmation.

"Said he was going to panhandle when I talked to him," remarked Jorge.

"Man, maybe he got lucky with a girl last night," announced the young, testosterone-driven Armando, accompanied by a big grin and twirling a raised finger.

"No chance, Armando, and you know it," Lorenzo said, with a piercing stare. He continued, "Felipe could hardly talk to us. And he knows us. Your joking . . . it's not right. He could be in some sort of trouble. What if we were talking about you? I'm worried about him. Maybe the Border Patrol picked him up. That's what I think. I always told him panhandling was too out in the open . . . asking for trouble. It's stupid, standing on the street asking for money." Lorenzo wagged his head.

"So, what do we do about it, man?" Jorge asked thoughtfully then drained the last of his coffee.

"What can we do?" Armando asked in reply. He raised his thick eyebrows to occupy more space on his already short forehead and shook his head, "We can't just march into the police station and say, 'Where's my friend Felipe, who just happens to be a Mexican National here illegally. Can you do us a favor and look for him while not arresting me or deporting me in the process?'"

Armando was friendly with Felipe, as friendly as Felipe would allow anyone to get. He felt somehow responsible for Felipe's safety and was now in earnest about the disappearance. But his seriousness, as his roommates knew, was always tempered by a mischievous, sarcastic streak that ran as a predominant characteristic throughout his personality.

"What you say has some merit, Armando," Lorenzo admitted, "but I think we should question some people that might know what could have happened to him. Efren might know someone. He never stayed out overnight before. He's too young. I don't like it."

A note of solemn concern registered in Lorenzo's voice. He drew a deep breath through his nose and exhaled while thinking, then reached for his coffee mug. "You guys go up to Seventy-fifth Avenue and I-10 and check around. I think that's where he panhandled. See what you can find out. It's close to the store where you'll be." He burped. "I don't have a good feeling about this." The solemn concern in Lorenzo's voice had grown to distress. He sipped his coffee.

"Yes, sir, Captain Lorenzo," Armando snapped in ridicule, as he stood from the table. "Permission to leave the table and shit in the bathroom," he added laughing, then ran from the kitchen.

"That asshole needs a serious attitude adjustment," Lorenzo said frowning to Jorge who remained seated. Lorenzo did not enjoy his leadership role being ridiculed.

"Ah, that's just the way he is, man," Jorge said. "I've known him nearly all my life. He'll never change, man. He thinks everything's funny. He doesn't mean any disrespect. He talks without thinking," Jorge explained, with a quite, respectful voice. "And thank you for making breakfast. It was good."

"You're welcome, Jorge. I appreciate you saying so, unlike that ungrateful prick," Lorenzo said, wagging his thumb in the direction of the bathroom.

"Please make sure you ask about Felipe in your travels today. Like I said before, 'I've got a very bad feeling about this,'" Lorenzo said rubbing his forehead.

"So, what are you doing today?" Jorge asked, as he took the last cube of goat's cheese from the serving plate and popped it into his mouth.

"First, I'm leaving the dishes for you guys to clean. Then I'm going to shower and go down to Efren's. He has a friend who works at the Mexican Consulate. The guy may know whether or not Felipe was arrested or deported. If he's been deported, well, it may be an answer to his prayers. He wanted to go home . . . but maybe not that way."

"I think so, too."

"I've saved fifty dollars to buy a TV. So today, I think I'll go shopping for a used one . . . if it's within the budget."

"A TV? Good Lord!" Jorge said, enthusiastically. "Wait until I tell Armando. Man, he's going to shit . . . twice! Now I can't wait to get back from work. Maybe, nobody will hire us today and we'll get to come back early. What time do you think you'll be back with it?"

Lorenzo knew that Jorge watched TV only at bars and on special occasions. He had never owned one, nor lived with anyone who had. This was a big thrill for Jorge, for all of them. Being able to watch novellas, soccer, and game shows like most of his friends and to discuss and comment about them was an important social statement. Lorenzo had been quiet during those conversations because he had no idea what his friends reflected upon. He remained content only to listen and keep up on the current novellas that way. Now he'd know about everything and could contribute.

"Maybe by noon," Lorenzo estimated. "It depends on how long I stay at Efren's and if I can find something right away or have to search around. Figure by three o'clock to be sure. By then I'll be ready for dinner and I'll come back, with or without the TV."

"And I'll be ready to watch," Jorge said with a smile before running off toward the bathroom.

Lorenzo looked thoughtfully at the last of his coffee as he swirled the liquid around in his cup. His mind spun in a circle, like the coffee, in an attempt to answer his concerns when he heard Armando cry for joy from the bathroom. The good news officially delivered brought a brief smile to Lorenzo's otherwise troubled face as he finished his coffee.

*   *   *

The used, color television was pigeonholed on an unused section of kitchen countertop, the nineteen-inch size allowed it to sit under a cabinet and off to the side, away from the food preparation area. The fully extended rabbit-ear antenna sported aluminum foil crumpled near the ends to enhance reception. A copy of *TV y Mas* was on the kitchen table. The set was tuned to a Spanish station televising a soccer match. Lorenzo watched it drinking beer from a quart bottle.

Armando and Jorge arrived home past three o'clock carrying bags that contained their next meal and quarts of beer. Drinking provided an early start to the Saturday night festivities. When they opened the front door and heard the television playing, they rushed into the kitchen and left their bags on the kitchen counter. They pulled up chairs and watched the game in progress as they talked.

They informed Lorenzo that they worked for a homeowner building a wooden-deck on his house. They met the man in the usual manner, outside the building materials superstore where they spent two hours in wait on the outskirts of the store parking lot. The torrid, morning heat drained them as they waited for the opportunity to work. They were about to leave when the homeowner stopped to talk.

They preferred this type of work to what Lorenzo did because the temporary employers paid non-taxed cash, provided interesting places to work—usually outdoors—and were not time constrained; they managed their own time and worked the days and hours they wanted, usually mornings. They were also able to walk to work and avoid public transportation, an added expense.

"Ah, the TV is good, Lorenzo. Reception is pretty clear," Armando announced, shaking his head in awe and approval.

"Yes, but we can only get one Spanish station. No cable, so this game will have to do," Lorenzo explained.

"You kidding, man?" said Jorge. "This is great! It's better than radio all the time. Although, I like my *Cumbia* music just before we go out. We can move the radio to another room now that the TV is here in the kitchen. It's staying here isn't it?"

"Yes," replied Lorenzo, "but I'm already having second thoughts about getting it. It's going to take up too much of our time. Time we could be doing work or something else useful rather than sitting on our asses getting lazy."

"Ah, you worry too much, man," Armando said, as he waved his hand in a downward mocking motion. "It'll occupy time, yes, but we'll have entertainment in our own house. It's important to know what's going on, to laugh, to be . . . ah—"

"To enjoy ourselves," Jorge interrupted, finishing Armando's thought process.

"Just joking assholes," Lorenzo said laughing defensively. "I see your point. I agree. I've wanted a TV ever since I came here. And now, thank God, I have one." Lorenzo was a religious man, more so than most, and he credited God for blessings in his life.

"I don't want to abuse the privilege though or loose track of time," Lorenzo finished, trying to make a point.

"So, what happened at Efren's, Lorenzo? Did he know what happened to Felipe? Nobody we talked to today knew anything," Jorge explained.

"Well, Efren didn't hear of anything either. He said he would talk to his friend about it and let me know. I can't believe he hasn't come back. It's like he just vanished. I tell you guys, I don't like it," Lorenzo concluded. He felt like a father figure to the boy and had become frustrated with helplessness.

"All we can do is wait," Armando admitted, as he rose from his chair to get a beer from the bag on the counter. He placed the rest of the bottles in the refrigerator. He twisted off the cap, which made a hissing sound.

"Don't worry so much, Lorenzo. There's nothing we can do," Armando advised flashing a perfunctory smile. "So, are we going to sit here on our asses and get lazy watching TV or are we going to make dinner?"

Armando's insolent question raised a hearty laugh from everyone.

They watched the game and drank beer much longer than any of them intended.

*   *   *

Early the next morning, Lorenzo woke with a start. He had a bad dream, but couldn't remember it's content. The alarm clock was set to go off in another hour, so he turned over and tried to drift off. His mind, especially when he tried to sleep, wandered and reverted back to events during his trek through the desert, crossing the border to Arizona.

He was back in the desert. The day was hot and everyone that made the crossing viewed the same horrible scene. The bodies of a dead and mummified mother and her two babies burned black by the sun. The pregnant woman was totally naked. She had apparently torn off her clothes in the baking heat in a hysterical effort to find relief while her blood boiled within her veins. Bloated, stretched, and cracked lips, parted and peeled back, revealed white teeth framed by the black, oval-shaped border. The dead woman's dark hair, stiffened and brittle from old sweat, stood on edge from her scalp, like a punk rock hairstyle.

Her stiff body lay in an angular pose on the ground caught in a last-gasp, death-scream for help. The head was partially propped up against a small mound of desert sand near a palo verde tree. The woman's breasts, shrunken and withered in the sun, cracked open under the heat and had oozed red and brown fluid that dripped out, leaving a dried pool of confirmation in the sandy soil around and under her body.

The pregnant woman's bulging, cracked-open abdomen exhibited the bleached, white skull of an unborn baby that protruded through torn leather openings in her belly. Another dead, weathered child, about a year old, was still attached to its mother by mouth nursing one breast. It looked like a black-leather purse with four withered straps. The woman's shriveled arm held her purse-like child in a loose but loving grip.

Lorenzo averted his eyes from the woman's vaginal opening out of respect, but her eyes, he remembered in spite of every effort to forget, were burned an eerie, maroon color by the sun frozen in a ghoulish, blind stare. The hardened, leather spectacle looked like some roadside terror attraction. There was no odor, but the sight caused some spectators to loose valuable liquid in the desert heat, witnessed by patches of dried vomit nearby.

As Lorenzo viewed the woman in his mind, she began moving her jaw. A snapping, cracking sound accompanied by puffs of dust emanated from her crumbling, baked-adobe mouth, that caused Lorenzo to freeze in horror. He watched and listened as the dead woman groaned a disarming question, "Who is 'Mr. Crowley?'" as pieces of lip fell away to the ground.

Lorenzo woke to the sound of his alarm. He found himself clutching his worn and scratched, laminated picture of the

Virgin of Guadalupe, Mexico's patron saint. He had carried the picture in his wallet since he was old enough to have a wallet. "If you pray to her, she'll protect you," Lorenzo remembered his mother saying to him, when she gave him the picture as a young boy. He tried to remember how the picture ended up in his hand.

Lorenzo turned the alarm off. As he laid in bed, he blessed himself and began to pray to Saint San Martin for Felipe as he viewed the plastic crucifix on the wall above his bed. After finishing this pious duty, he considered "Mr. Crowley" and what the dream meant when, without warning, the crucifix fell from the wall and hit Lorenzo on his forehead.

CHAPTER 21

JULIO

"Charles, Honey, it is time to get up."

"Give me ten more minutes, Mom. Okay?" Charlie mumbled during a twitch, his face comfortably buried in the soft pillow, bed sheets pulled up to his neck. He rolled over to face away from the window shading his eyes intent on returning back to sleep.

Charlie earned this rest during the night after the dispatch and burial of Felipe. Slumber without dreams or interruptions due to fatigue that set in because of the physical labor of digging a hasty, shallow grave in the hardpan, desert soil, using a tool ill equipped for the task. The flat head shovel, his father hung from the garage wall between two nails years ago after spreading decorative rock, did not suit serious digging, but shoveling. He labored excessively while trying to chink the desert surface in a desolate area off Route 60 near Wittmann. He experimented with the flat-faced, square shovel by jabbing the corner into the ground, but the unbalanced attempts hurt his foot, ankle, and back. The arch of his foot ached from repeated kicks against the footrest of the shovel and he couldn't utilize his weight leverage to dig. Only small clots of soil removal became a reward for all his efforts. His hands blistered, his back ached. The heat, even in the dark of night, hovered around ninety-five degrees. The supply of bottled water was quickly drained.

The result was predictable: Instead of a shallow grave, the burial became a mound of scrapped soil heaped upon the young Mexican's body, hardly better than simply dumping the body in plain sight. The grave was noticeable, even to an untrained eye, easily identifiable, and not what Charlie intended nor desired. At least it was hidden behind scrub brush from the dirt road.

The entire affair drained him. The results were well below expectation, not a job well done. He had concerns about his parents opinion of the work performed and worried the entire trip back home. This was not a good start. He made concessions and excuses in case he needed to defend himself later.

"Charles. Wake up."

"Go away and let me sleep," Charlie blurted out.

"Do I have to call your father?"

"Okay, okay," Charlie shot back, not wanting to involve his father. Things could get ugly in a hurry and it was too early in the day.

Charlie woke at the crack of noon, with the shaded, filtered sunlight trickling into the bedroom and burning his oversensitive retinas. He lay in bed, body aching, as he listened to the mid-Sunday racket outside his house. A neighbor mowed a lawn somewhere; it sounded like the lawn being cut grew in his living room. The noisy chore forced him awake. He took a minute to adjust to the rush of data once again flooding his senses. Surrendering to the assault he closed his eyes. The darkness felt so good, so comforting, so—

"Charles!"

"All right, Mom. I'm up," Charlie said sitting up abruptly in bed. "See?" He slumped his head into blistered and sore hands. "Ouch," he said recoiling, looking at last night's damage.

"Charles, this is all your own fault, you know."

"Yes, Mom. I know," Charlie answered, "but all the sounds and colors, the lights . . . used to be thrilling, like I had super human ability . . . an X-Man or Super Hero or something. But now . . . it's draining." He thought back to when he first talked to his mother about the optical acuity and hearing capacity that fascinated him, the sudden and exciting perspective they revealed. "You were right, Mom," Charlie hated to admit, "I should've reserved my judgment and used caution dealing with these . . . these new abilities. It's getting harder for me to . . . process all the information . . . to sort things out."

Over the last few months, Charlie became increasingly unable to respond appropriately to the overwhelming stimuli. Coping changed his behavior, movements, and emotions. This altered state of consciousness was proving to be a curse, the bane of his alert, vigilant mind. Only in sleep did a respite occur. Pure joy became impossible while raging data flooded and tormented him.

"I am sorry, Charles. You know, if I were physically able to comfort you, I would."

The thought of resting his head in her lap while she tickled his back brought back fond memories. Loving memories lost forever because of that fucking Mexican terrorist.

"Any sound above a whisper rushes into my brain like a computer overload and excruciatingly loud sounds are all around, always," he said listening to the lawnmower. "It's like the flood victims I hear about in the news, Mom. The waters keep rising and, before they know it, the people are on their roofs, forced from their homes waiting to be rescued. I think the reporters call it 'the hundred-year flood.' I feel like I'm enduring the hundred-year data flood . . . my senses are forcing me out of my mind. And each day the problem gets worse."

"Oh, Charles, *you* are a drama queen. You are beginning to accomplish the most important work of your life guided by the actions of President Bush against evildoers, and now you are going to call in sick?" His mother knew him all too well. He knew what she was getting at.

"It's simple things, Mom, like the light coming in through the shade. It hurts my eyes," he said reaching for his wrap-around-style sunglasses on the end table. He put them on.

"It hurts my eyes," his mother said imitating his voice purposely lower by a full octave in ridicule. "So, are you going to quit the work, like you quit college? What would your father say if he knew?"

"Don't tell Dad we were talking about this. Please."

"Well then, return your mind to the work at hand. Forget about your problems and focus on solutions. You know that you did not prepare very well for Felipe. Look what the result is: Your back hurts, your hands are blistered, you are very tired, and your morale has been compromised. Plan, Son, plan. I have told you a thousand times before, 'plan your work and work your plan.'"

"I will, Mom."

"Your work is the only way to control and focus your mind amid the chaos."

The twitching stopped.

The first unobstructed thought that came to mind that didn't involve the surge of sensory data concerned last night's work. He felt his brow furrow as he forced himself to focus and now realized two areas that needed attention, improvement. The first of his concerns involved the purchase of a new shovel; a long-handled shovel intended to facilitate digging, something with a point; and maybe a pick.

The second concern required an implement appropriate for executions. The hammer, a suitable but extemporaneous, surprise-attack tool was adequate, but needed replacement; a machete would be more suitable to dispense swift, infallible, human butchery. He felt comfortable and experienced with knives from pervious work with the strays. A machete afforded tangible benefits and was available from any good tool store hassle-free.

Brief consideration for the service of a gun was made but thought beyond budget; it also made unwanted noise when used and posed purchase challenges. Fingerprinting and filling out forms would also make a record with the state and federal governments and give authorities something to check, a way to pry into his activities. The idea was quickly shelved.

Both areas of attention could be addressed and secured at the local Home Depot store. Another trip out of the house would be necessary. It would be a chore because of the pain he experienced, but that's why they call it work. If it was enjoyable all the time, it would be considered a hobby and, therefore, optional.

Additionally, he recognized a need to obtain a CD of the Ozzy Osbourne song *Mr. Crowley*, enabling timely performance of his work, not leaving anything to chance. The local electronics store where he obtained the previous CD of *(Don't Fear) The Reaper*, could be visited during the same trip for tools. Both sunlight exposure and driving would be reduced to a minimum.

The trip comprised his only plan for the day.

*   *   *

The CD was purchased at the electronics super-store and then Charlie drove further in the parking lot to the Home Depot store for the tools. On returning to his truck, he tossed the tools into the back of the pickup, inserted the unwrapped CD into the stereo, and began the drive home, a/c blasting.

He lit up a smoke and advanced the CD selection to the song he wanted to hear while he waited for traffic at the surface street. While he lingered, he noticed the approach of two Mexican men in their mid-twenties. They stopped at the driver's side window and gestured for him to roll it down. *Mr. Crowley* had begun to play softly on the stereo. He immediately knew his plans were in need of adjustment.

Charlie rolled down his window as requested to the excitement and joy of the two sweating Mexicans. One, a pudgy, assertive man with a thin moustache asked, "Need workers, *senior*?"

Charlie recognized the opportunity at hand and said, "Yes." He proceeded to back his unimpeded vehicle into the parking lot. The Mexicans followed on foot.

He stopped in the far corner of the parking lot near the exit and got out. The two Mexicans were already waiting for him near his door.

"You speak English?" asked Charlie, squinting in the sun even through sunglasses. He noticed the approach of three more Mexicans that came from a larger gathering near a bus stop about twenty-five yards away.

"*Si* . . . a little," said the pudgy Mexican, with a smile that revealed teeth with silver fillings. His dingy clothes sported perspiration spots.

"Okay . . . good," Charlie said, "So you need work, huh? You want to work?"

"*Si,*" the pudgy man said, still smiling.

"What do you do?" Charlie asked, holding one hand up to blot out the sun and took a drag off his cigarette with the other. The three approaching Mexicans were almost at the truck to join the conversation.

"Anything . . . what you need?"

"Me? Need? Oh yes." Charlie said, improvising and speaking at the same time. "I need . . . ah . . . landscaping work done. You do landscaping work?" He dried his sweating face with a raised arm, the heat nearly unbearable. He wanted to get this over as soon as possible and get back in the truck's cool air conditioning.

Including the three most recent arrivals, there were now five, sweating, soiled Mexicans that stood staring in a semi-circle around Charlie. They all smiled and rocked to and fro, some with hands in their pockets. The group intimidated Charlie measurably and he considered a change of plans, but then decided to see if he could reduce the gathering.

"*Si, si,* very good work," Pudgy said.

"Look . . . ah . . . I only need one guy. I don't have enough work for all you," he explained to Pudgy, with a sweeping hand motion. He hoped to eliminate the crowd that had gathered with one stroke.

"*Si. Uno . . .* one . . ." Pudgy said, to Charlie and then in Spanish addressed the others in the group and rattled off a few sentences in Spanish. Afterward, the three new arrivals turned and walked back to the bus stop.

"You need two?" Pudgy asked. "He is my partner," he said, pointing and wagging his thumb at his broad shouldered but quiet friend.

"No, no. I can only afford one guy. Can you work alone?" he asked Pudgy, trying to make his work for the day easier.

"*Si* . . . yes," said Pudgy, in reply. Pudgy's friend still did not leave.

"How much you charge . . . per hour?" asked Charlie.

"Ten dollars."

"Okay. What's your name?"

"Julio."

"Okay, Julio. The work is at my house. I'll drive you over and we can get started right away. Okay?"

"You sure . . . you need one, *senior*?" asked Julio. He looked at Charlie with puppy-dog eyes and threw a glance to his friend before he fixed his attention back on Charlie.

"Yes. I'm sure . . . only one. It amounts to only . . . about . . . ah . . . four hours work . . . total," Charlie said, making the figure up. He held up four fingers and hoped the offer enough to entice Julio. "I can probably have you back by . . . six o'clock or so," he added.

"Okay," Julio said, smiling and then turned to his friend and issued a few sentences in Spanish. The friend said a few words in reply, gathered himself, and shrugged his shoulders. The larger man waved good-bye to Julio then turned lumbering toward the bus stop crowd, head bent, hands in pockets, looking forlorn.

"It's okay, he's a friend. I said you want one worker. I said 'you don't get work today. I share what I make.' He's okay. He no speak English. He need me for job," Julio explained, once again smiling, silver glaring in Charlie's eyes.

"Alright. Get in. Let's go," ordered Charlie. He tossed his cigarette butt, turned, and reached for the door handle.

Julio and Charlie jumped into the truck. He drove the truck home, and along the way, the stereo played the rest of *Mr. Crowley*. The snare set yet again.

CHAPTER 22

TRUSTING IN RELIGION

Lorenzo popped up from his bed as if it were on fire. He found the crucifix while rubbing his forehead, kissed it, and hung it back on the wall, all the while saying the rosary without the wooden beads. He ran across the bedroom to the corner where he kept a small bottle of holy water and began blessing himself with it. He even sprinkled his bed while yelling for Armando and Jorge to come at once.

"What is it, Lorenzo?" Jorge asked arriving first.

"Demons, demons!" Lorenzo shouted. "Bless yourself with this," he directed, handing the holy water to Jorge.

"What the hell happened?" Jorge asked. "Calm down and tell me," he said following Lorenzo's orders. "In the name of the Father, Son, and Holy Ghost."

Armando stood in the doorway. "What's going on?" he asked. Creases formed on Armando's forehead watching Jorge bless himself. He looked surprised.

"Here." Jorge handed the bottle to Armando. "Lorenzo said we are being visited by demons."

"What?"

"It's true," Lorenzo finally said. He proceeded to inform his roommates about his dream, the laminated picture of the

Virgin of Guadalupe he still held in his hand, and the crucifix falling on his head. They inspected Lorenzo's hairline and found a small drop of blood emerging from the injury. They stood with open mouths and intense stares.

"Now, more than ever, I have a feeling danger is upon us," Lorenzo concluded, pacing the floor. "This Mr. Crowley . . . somehow we are cursed. And the situation with Felipe, something's weighing heavily on my soul. I fear for us all. I don't know how to explain it to you, but I need to buy Saint San Martin candles and place one in every room of the house. I'm definitely going to church today . . . to pray for protection. And if you have any sense, you will come with me."

* * *

Every Sunday, Lorenzo left his safe-haven rental house to attend church accompanied by Armando and Jorge, each dressed in their best clothes. Lorenzo did so out of respect for God and the priesthood. He thought that his younger roommates did so for a much different reason, one that involved women. Lorenzo, being a devout Catholic, listened with contemplation, made confession, brought his rosary beads, recited prayers, searched his heart, asked for forgiveness.

On the other hand, Lorenzo would watch, as Armando and Jorge snorted at the trite rituals and stock sermons. He saw them inspecting the congregation for agreeable women. For them, church was a single's meeting place. Finding women with whom they might share their lives became the primary reason for attendance.

They ranged far and wide, sometimes ten rows forward or backward, to 'share the peace of Christ' with an attractive prospect. They shook hands and cultivated friendships with the most alluring women found during the scanning process and invited them to church functions. They usually disappeared after mass escorting ladies to Church sponsored dances, leaving Lorenzo to walk home alone.

This Sunday, however, church attendance for Armando and Jorge seemed to reflect Lorenzo's religious posture. They all recited prayers with reverence and were much more introspective. Suddenly, church became a solemn occasion when the subject of prayer centered on a demon named Mr. Crowley.

CHAPTER 23

SHARPENING SKILLS

Charlie parked the truck in the garage of his home as he had done before with Felipe, unseen by anyone, like a quiet breeze blowing into the open garage.

Julio followed him into and through the house. The pile of pots and pans stacked by the kitchen door were moved aside to allow access to the backyard. Julio seemed perplexed about the pile of metal, but said nothing as he helped slide a stack aside with his foot.

They entered the back yard.

Julio trailed behind Charlie to the shed in the backyard where the animal snare used to be employed. In the oppressive heat of the day, Charlie explained what he wanted Julio to do. Both were drenched in no time at all.

Charlie ordered Julio to dismantle the poorly constructed building made of two-by-four studs and joists covered with one-quarter inch plywood. Anger and contempt resonated in his voice as he launched into a detailed explanation repeating many times for Julio's benefit where the wood should be stacked, how the nails were to be removed and thrown into the trash, and how care must be used not to mar the house during demolition.

Julio ran his hand through oily and wet, black hair as he inspected the job site. He asked no questions but seemed to be wondering what tools were at his disposal to accomplish the task.

Charlie took the opportunity to fetch the hammer from the garage. He returned twisting it in his hand and stood behind Julio as he watched the Mexican continue his inspection. Charlie gripped the handle tightly raising the tool from his side. For a moment, the idea of using it as before came to mind but was repressed. Taking care of business outside was too risky. He lowered the hammer and leaned it against the shed. The task would be accomplished later, away from prying enemy eyes, after the shed was dismantled. At least he should get some work out of Julio first. Instructions were repeated once more for good measure and then he left Julio to the task at hand.

Charlie breezed into the kitchen, spending five minutes enjoying the air conditioning while making a grilled-cheese sandwich that he ate with a beer. After, he had a smoke. Then he went back into the heat of the garage to inspect the machete taken from his truck.

The eighteen-inch, steel-blade knife wrapped in cardboard packaging advertised the knife to be a professional model, as opposed to the hobbyist or avid gardener versions. Charlie wondered if he would be considered a hobbyist or a professional. He knew he was not the avid gardener. The blade would be used in his work and therefore, professional would be the proper designation. He drifted into speculation: What of the lifetime warranty? Would it be in effect if he somehow snapped the blade hacking a body part? Would the manufacturer honor the warranty if the pieces of machete were covered in blood? Tree limb or arm . . . what difference would it make if the knife snapped in two? He would have laughed about the absurdity of the thought a year ago, but now it weighed heavily on his mind. He removed the machete and saved the packaging just in case.

Charlie eliminated a thin, black-plastic guard protecting the blade's edge and tested it with his thumb—sharp, but could and should be keener for the use envisioned. He found a sharpening-stone on a dusty shelf and began to hone the carbon-steel blade to a razor edge. Each stroke of the stone rang in his ears and head as he thought of the effect his work would eventually have on society.

Once the Mexican problem was eliminated either by execution, or deportation—ziiiing—or because they eventually got the message like the neighbors did with their animals—ziiiing—there would be no more Mexican murderers to kill parents on the road. Yes, this seems to be working well. Ziiiing—no more Mexican strays to clog the system. Man, this is really hurting my ears. Ziiiing—no need to print directions on packaging in both English and Spanish. Accommodating corporate advertising bastards—ziiiing—only English for an English speaking country and population from now on.

"English must be the law in the future, Charlie," his mother said while Charlie twitched.

"That's right, Mom. No more Spanish billboards or TV programs." Ziiiing.

I love my work. God bless America. Eh, President Bush? Ziiiing.

These ideas appealed to Charlie as he labored with increased vigor sharpening and honing the blade. Rivulets of sweat flowed from his pores and dripped from his nose and chin onto the hot steel as he toiled.

*   *   *

At the same time Charlie sharpened the machete, Julio wiped his hot, wet face in the backyard heat. He needed a water break for the first time since he began working thirty minutes ago. He dropped the hammer on the newly created pile of plywood across from the two-by-four wood skeleton that the shed had become and headed for the kitchen.

Inside, Julio heard a scraping sound emanating from the garage. When he closed the door, the sound stopped.

"*Senior?*" he called out.

His question was answered by another scraping sound, the sound of metal abraded by equally hard material. Julio took a few more tentative steps into the kitchen and asked in a louder tone of voice, "*Senior?* Are you there? Can I have water?"

This time his questions were answered by silence.

Julio didn't want to appear rude and simply help himself to a glass in the cabinet and water from the sink. He didn't want to be found rifling through the kitchen cabinets. It wouldn't look good. His upbringing required permission.

His cotton-like mouth formed white spittle at the corners of his dry lips. He wiped his mouth with the back of his sweaty, salty hand and edged nearer to the closed door leading to the garage. He paused to listen. Silence permeated the house.

He knocked on the barrier and twisted the knob. It was unlocked. He leaned back slightly to allow the door to open inward toward him. When fully open to allow entrance, he put his opposite hand on the jamb and leaned his head through the opening into relative darkness.

"*Senior?*" Julio asked again, with wide eyes trying to adjust to the dim environment.

Julio's improving vision focused at first upon Charlie's pickup truck still parked in the middle of the space. Out of the corner of his peripheral vision, he caught sight of Charlie, arms raised, elbows even with his head, hands together gripping something directly overhead. In an instant, the professional machete flashed in an overhead arc and whistled down through the air above Julio's head.

Julio tried to back away, but his reaction was far too slow, and instead of the blade hitting his neck dead center, the machete lopped off his head from the neck right at the base of the skull. It shaved a toupee-sized swatch of hair off the back of Julio's scalp in the process. The force of the blow cleanly removed the head in guillotine fashion. It caused a firework, aerial-bomb explosion in Julio's neck, that left a spinning, tumbling trail of pin-point, sparkling stars in his mind until his sweaty, thirsty head hit the concrete floor, sounding like a large cabbage. Julio's shocked and open eyes beheld nothing more.

Charlie watched as the stunned body staggered and trembled in the doorway, hands holding the jamb and the doorknob, knees locked in stiffened response to the jolt. Thick frothy red bubbles increased from the neck mixed with gruesome gurgles until Julio's hands failed to grip. The body, like a tree being felled, toppled forward and hit the concrete floor covering the severed head. A dark, wet stain developed in the crotch of Julio's tan cloth pants that, in time, grew larger along with the puddle of blood that formed on the floor issuing from his neck.

CHAPTER 24

THE CONSULATE

Lorenzo sat on the backyard stoop of his house on Forth of July morning drinking coffee and thinking about Felipe and Mr. Crowley. It was hot outside, hell it was hot inside, too, but he needed to be alone, to think. Armando and Jorge were inside and they were a distraction. They were too young to care about spiritual things and, since nothing happened to prove demons were at work, they began doubting the idea.

He was certain Felipe had met a tragic end. This accounted for his disappearance without a trace. He was equally certain that this Mr. Crowley was somehow responsible. Probably some person possessed by a demon. Proof to back these convictions was missing, but he felt them just the same. All he had was a dream, a nightmare, with little or no substance. No evidence. To an outside observer, the theory would be ridiculed. Disbelief had already begun, starting with his roommates. Who could listen with an open mind? He considered talking about this subject to Father Garcia the next time he attended church.

He lifted his gaze from the hardpan soil beyond the steps and looked into the barren region beyond the yard. He noticed the desert floor seemed to be spinning and squinted his eyes to see more clearly. Sand swirled into a frantic Sonoran kaleidoscope fueled by a strong, well-formed, and long-lived whirlwind. The resulting dust devil raised a vertical, upward, funnel-like chimney of loose debris as the super-heated summer air rose through a pocket of cooler air above. The self-sustaining vortex of surface friction grew before Lorenzo's eyes, like a looming tornado that intensified and traveled directly toward the small rental house.

As the precursor to the more violent Monsoon storms breached his yard, Lorenzo ducked inside the kitchen where Armando and Jorge sat at the table watching TV.

"A dust devil is coming," Lorenzo announced. Just as he closed the door, the house moaned under the force of spinning wind and a cloud of stinging sand.

Lorenzo joined his roommates at the table. "It's another sign," he said placing his coffee cup on the table and pulling up a chair. I watched the dust devil form out in the desert and it came straight for this house. Even the name of the wind shows that it's a sign about demons and we are in their path."

Armando and Jorge, engrossed in watching a news program, didn't seem notice Lorenzo or the passing sun devil. They were listening to a news program about the arrival of Monsoon season. Every year, the news media feel compelled to report about the storms with cautions and warnings to prepare viewers to deal with the violent weather during July and August; wind patterns that prove dangerous in many ways.

"Did you hear what I said?" Lorenzo went on, his face flushing as he spoke in frustration; his attention directed equally between the two men.

"I heard you," Armando replied, turning his gaze from the TV to look at Lorenzo, his face hardened in apparent disbelief. "I think you're full of shit about the demons and signs. For three weeks, we've been listening to you and nothing has happened to us. Felipe's disappearance has made you crazy." He turned back to the TV.

"You are wrong Armando," Lorenzo said with narrowing eyes. "Tell him, Jorge," he said pointing with his chin.

"Tell him what?" Jorge managed while still watching TV.

"Tell him about the demon . . . about Mr. Crowley."

Jorge turned to look at Lorenzo. "It's *your* vision, Lorenzo. I see nothing demonic about the cross falling off a loose nail or dust storms. I agree with him," he wagged a thumb toward Armando. "You're letting this make you crazy. Leave it alone. Felipe went back home."

"You are both mistaken," Lorenzo said smugly. "You'll see . . . nothing good will come of Felipe's disappearance." He got up from the table and tramped back outside to sit on the porch.

When the news program finally went off the air, Lorenzo headed back to the kitchen and asked, "So, what are your plans for today?"

"Today is a holiday," blurted Armando. "We're going to find work."

"What's the holiday called again?" Lorenzo asked.

"Independence Day," Jorge answered.

"Oh, yes," Lorenzo said. "I remember now. So you're going to try to find work on a holiday when everybody is having cookouts and watching fireworks?" He still felt annoyed with them for not believing his view about demons.

"Yes," Armando said. "Cooking is done by women and the fireworks are at night. What else do men have to do, but work around the house on their day off?"

"It's a perfect day to try to get some things done when you don't have to go to work," Jorge explained. "It's like a weekend day to gringos with projects planned. The day should be very profitable."

"I see," Lorenzo said feeling a bit jealous of their plans. "So, where do you—" A knock on the front door interrupted him.

Silence immediately permeated the discussion, and, before long, the television fell silent as well, contributing to the hush; a typical response for illegal Mexican emigrants to surprise visitors. Unexpected visitors don't like unexpected visitors and unanticipated visits coerced them into a knee-jerk reaction to conceal their existence. Like frightened rabbits prepared to bolt, they sat nearly motionless at the kitchen table and glanced from one to another with alert eyes, even though this was not the first time a surprise jolted them. Concern grabbed hold.

Lorenzo whispered, "Either of you expecting anyone?"

Both men shook their heads.

"Get in the backyard," Lorenzo instructed, "and listen to what happens. I'll check the front door. If it's *la Migra*, I'll join you and we'll sneak out the back. If it's anyone else, I'll see who they are and what they want. If it's trouble, leave. Okay?"

Armando and Jorge bobbed their heads in affirmation. Without a sound, they slipped to the back door as directed and eased outside, leaving the door open. Lorenzo crept to the front window of the house covered in newspaper. Additional harder raps caused him to jump while there. He peeled away an intentionally loose flap of newspaper that covered the window, revealing a makeshift peephole. Through the opening, he saw his friend Efren standing on the front step. Lorenzo sighed in relief and let go of the flap. He opened the front door and invited his friend into the house.

With the excitement of the surprise visit now over, the four men gathered at the kitchen table, occupying all four wooden chairs.

After preliminary formalities, Lorenzo asked mildly, "So, why have you come to visit, Efren?"

They looked on with interest as all eyes focused on Efren, who sported a three day old beard connected to a permanent moustache.

"I'm here," the well-dressed man began looking at Lorenzo, "because about three weeks ago, you came to me asking me to contact my friend at the consulate about Felipe, to see if he was deported."

"Yes," Lorenzo confirmed, jerking his head.

"Well, as you already know, he has not been deported. That hasn't changed. The consulate has not heard anything more about Felipe, except that you reported him missing. If Felipe was deported or arrested, they would know," explained Efren in a clear, steady voice that sounded dry but sympathetic.

Efren earned respect from these men because he had enjoyed ten successful years of living in the land of opportunity. He commanded regard as well with piercing, dark-brown eyes along with a peerless-age-status; at forty-five he was old enough to be their father and no fool.

"However," Efren continued, "they suddenly have a great deal of concern for learning more about Felipe."

"What do you mean, suddenly?" asked Lorenzo. He raised his eyebrows and cocked his head slightly to the side.

"Well, it's been three weeks since I talked to my friend. And now, suddenly, I get a call asking me to arrange a meeting with you. He would not go any further into detail, just that he needs to see you personally."

"What? Why?"

"I guess now they want more information from you, about Felipe. So, I have to ask you, Lorenzo, can you go down to the consulate and speak to José? José Fuentes is his name."

"I suppose so. When?"

"As soon as you can, tomorrow. He seemed very anxious. They're closed today because of the holiday, but they're normally open Monday through Friday from eight o'clock to twelve thirty. I wrote the address and José's name on this piece of paper for you," Efren said, as he took the slip of paper from his front shirt pocket and handed it to Lorenzo.

"Okay, then. Just go and ask for José when you get there," Efren said with encouragement and a contagious smile.

"Would you like some coffee or a glass of water, Efren?" suggested Armando.

"No, thank you. I've got to go," Efren announced leaning forward to push his chair back with his arms. He stood from the table.

Lorenzo sat on the brown cloth couch located directly across from two matching armchairs. A wooden coffee table, with Latino magazines scattered about, divided the seating arrangements. José and Jane occupied the chairs. "So, we have a mutual friend Mr. Perez . . . Efren. He told me about your roommate Felipe and his disappearance some time ago. All I could tell him at the time was that Felipe . . . ah . . ." Mr. Fuentes consulted a document handed to him by Ms. McDonald, "Valverde was not deported. Unfortunately, Mr. Perez, that is still all I can say at the moment about your roommate."

Lorenzo thought, so why am I here?

"However, the consulate has been receiving many similar inquiries and a red flag has been raised. We have interviewed many other people with the same story concerning missing persons. It is painting a disturbing, grim picture, as you can imagine."

"Really? How many?"

"I don't want to alarm you, Mr. Perez, but since you ask, there are thirteen people that have been reported missing . . . including Felipe."

"Holy Mary Mother of God," Lorenzo said. He had begun to carry his rosary beads in his pants pocket since the crucifix incident. He reached a nervous hand to pat them through his pants being a little embarrassed not to take them out in front of strangers. "It's Mr. Crowley. I know it," he said with an ominous frown.

*   *   *

"I think I can stand now for a little while longer," Jorge said rubbing his full stomach, as the pair arrived back at their spot to look for work.

"Lunch has a way of improving your outlook about things," Armando observed. "Are you going to the dance Friday night with Rosalie?"

"Yes, but she said for me not to pick her up until ten."

"Ten? Why so late?"

"I don't know. I don't ask questions . . . keeps me out of trouble. I just do what I'm told. What do I care if we get to the dance late? So long as there's still time at the end of the night for fucking. I hope she's not having her period."

"I know. It'd be messy then. I wouldn't do it because I like eating it. But she's definitely worth the wait if she is. I like her. You did good for an ugly bastard."

"Fuck you, Armando. Hey, hey, here comes somebody. Look he's rolling his window down to talk."

Armando bent down to talk through the partly open truck window. "You need help, *senior?*"

*   *   *

Obviously surprised, Mr. Fuentes said, "You know who is responsible for these disappearances?"

"Yes. It's Mr. Crowley."

"Who's Mr. Crowley? How do you know this?"

Lorenzo felt a little embarrassed and strained as he shared his dream with José and his assistant. He covered all aspects of his revelations including the recent dust devil. When he finished the two consulate employees looked at each other in silence. José rubbed his receding chin. Jane massaged her beautifully proportioned forehead.

Jane was first to break the uneasy stillness. "Getting back to the reason why you're here Mr. Perez. We need more information about Felipe . . . his description so we can check the city morgues in the valley. You know, to see if there are, God forbid, any matches."

Lorenzo's hand began to pat the rosary beads with fervency. He began reciting silent prayers to himself and rocking in his seat. They were uncomfortably mixed with foreboding.

"We have already begun the process with the others," Mr. Fuentes said, his voice a little edgy. "But no matches have been found. I'm not sure that this is necessarily good news,

"*I need you . . .*" Tears ran from his eyes into his ears as the continuing lack of control foretold his doom. He concentrated on visualizing his mother's face.

Beside an autonomic, respiratory-system convulsion that heaved his chest and produced gurgling sounds in his neck, the only control left for Jorge to command in his entire body was his eyelid function. He knew he was about to die and he wanted to see his mother as he passed on. Her face always comforted him. The view, at this instant, entailed the garage ceiling, but what he saw held a gentle hand out to caress his cheek and wipe away his tears.

"I know, I know, it hurts, but I love you. Don't worry, my son," she said in her solace-laden voice. "I'm here and I love you."

His eyes remained open to behold salvation as he waited, desperate, gasping, bleeding. Life ebbed away.

*   *   *

Hearing the crash of glass inside, Armando ran from the backyard to the garage and fell to his knees at Jorge's side inspecting his friend, careless of the broken glass. Frantically, he considered what to do as he watched Jorge's open staring eyes. He momentarily looked first left and then right, inspecting the greater garage scene; nothing but chaos all around. He resumed focus on his friend and called to him in Spanish.

"Jorge! What the fuck happened, man? Are you okay? Can you talk?" Armando asked, hysterically.

At first, Armando thought Jorge somehow cut himself while working in the garage. All the broken glass around showed evidence of some sort of freak accident. But now panic began to settle in and Armando experienced inaction. *What should I do? Oh, Jorge, what do I do?*

Jorge continued to stare straight up to the ceiling, never glancing at Armando. His labored breathing seemed to change slightly trying to accommodate speech, but his attempt failed.

Armando reached his hand to Jorge's cut shirt and pulled it back revealing the gash in Jorge's upper torso. His fingers dipped into a pool of blood. Armando felt his face twist into an expressive grimace at the sight of the huge wound and the blood dripping down his fingers as he held his hand to examination.

"Oh, Jorge! What the fuck, man . . ." Armando exclaimed with a shiver. He looked directly into Jorge's fixated eyes. "I'll go get some help!"

At the last moment, before he left Jorge's side, Armando saw that Jorge's eyes not only grew larger, but shifted focus to a point just behind Armando. The fear of death visible in Jorge's eyes changed to stark terror in the focus shift from the ceiling to something that seemed to be looming right behind Armando.

Instinctively, Armando felt a presence behind him. A creepy, sickening feeling in his loins told him something bad was about to happen, and it was coming from behind.

Instantly, the terror transferred from Jorge's eyes, forcing Armando to raise his right forearm up in a defensive, protective posture as he prepared for some sort of assault. He cringed almost closing his eyes.

Armando's head turned toward the right in time to glimpse, out of the corner of his squinting eye, a flashing, metallic blur that swept into his right forearm carrying pain and suffering, like thousands of angry hornets descending down and stinging along the nerves of his forearm, swarming down to his hand and up to his shoulder.

"Ahhhhh!" Armando bellowed, as the machete made contact with his forearm at mid-blade where less speed had developed in the swing, but even so it hacked clean through the ulna bone only protected by a thin layer of skin. The radius, the second of the two forearm bones, stopped the force of the blow from continuing right through the arm, but at the cost of splintering in half. "Shiiiit!"

The force of the machete continued to push Armando's forearm toward his head where the tip of the blade nearly sliced off his right ear. It hung upside down from the side of his cheek by a small flap of skin at the lobe. He felt a sharp jabbing pain, short in duration; it reduced to a pulling pressure by the all-consuming pain in his arm.

The force of the blow shoved Armando from his kneeling position to his left. His injured arm fell dangling from mid-forearm as blood pumped freely. His good arm reached for the floor, in an automatic attempt to cushion the landing of his body and move away from the danger. His hand landed in a multitude of geometric-shaped, beveled-glass prisms where continued savagery assaulted his senses.

As Armando pulled his arm away from the retreating knife to a position behind himself, it bent like a limp wrist and swung, attached by one tendon, scant muscle tissue, and skin.

"You fucking bastard!" Armando roared as the hate of a thousand illegal Mexicans shot through his eyes. His head snapped back and forth between assessing his injury and viewing the assailant as he tried to escape.

He fell to his back cradling his nearly severed limb in his lap. Glass punctured through the back of his light shirt and heavy jeans, followed by dark growing stains of blood. "Shit, shit, shiiiit!"

Instinctively, he began to scramble backwards amidst profanity. He used his legs for propulsion in a desperate endeavor to avoid his assailant, but his feet slipped in blood and glass, unable to secure solid footing. The screaming, slipping, scrambling Mexican gained precious inches of escape across the garage floor.

*   *   *

Charlie exhaled a grunt as he delivered the blow, then bounced backward in a defensive posture. His arms recoiled and held the machete like a baseball player at the plate preparing for another swing at a fastball. Armando's screamed obscenities produced an auditory overload on Charlie's hearing. He scowled with each scream.

"Shut up you Mexican fuck!" Charlie demanded. "Shut up!"

Desperate to stop the howling and relieve the sensation overloading his hearing, Charlie rushed to the man in preparation for the final, silencing swing when his left foot landed on smeared blood. All his weight transferred to the slipping left foot causing him to drop to the floor in a cheerleader-like split. Caught off balance, Charlie fell on his butt.

Surprised, he sat in the blood watching Armando scamper backward clenching the injured arm in a semi-sitting position.

Before Charlie could rise, Armando scooped up broken pieces of glass with his left hand and pelted Charlie in a shower of red-stained razors. "*Pendejo, gringo hijo de puta!*" he yelled in a valiant effort at survival.

Charlie tried to block the incoming assault with his left hand and arm while he attempted to rise from the slippery floor. Pain cut into his buttocks and hand as he pushed off from the floor. His face and scalp suffered as some of the projectiles hit their mark. "I'm gonna kill you, you worthless piece of shit!"

He eventually accomplished the grueling task of standing under a shower of glass. He was bleeding from various parts of his body and his clothes were splattered with red spots and sweat. The relentless screams from Armando continued. "Shut up!" Charlie shouted as his senses reached critical mass.

Charlie felt blood mixed with sweat streak down his forehead and cheeks from cuts suffered in the glass shower. His eyes burned and blurred, so he rubbed his face on his shoulder in an attempt to regain sight.

He resumed a more balanced, regulated offense, hacking first Armando's feet held in defense, then legs, and finally silenced the Mexican with numerous fatal slashes to the body and head.

Armando and Jorge, friends to the end, died together in matching blood baths; one a mutilated pulp in the corner of the garage, the other lying on a bed of glass.

Charlie sat down on a clean portion of garage floor and, like a zombie, did nothing. Totally and physically spent, bleeding from his wounds, he waited. And twitched.

"Well, that was a disaster, Charles," his mother remarked with insolence. "The whole neighborhood will be knocking on our door now."

Charlie listened with his highly acute hearing ability getting more nervous by the minute. "Shush, Mom. They'll hear you. Be quiet."

"Don't shush your mother," his father snapped. "You have some explaining to do, young man."

Charlie reached into his pocket for his lighter and a cigarette. Once lit, he blew the smoke into the hot air of the garage observing the blood stains on the cigarette.

"I don't know what happened," Charlie whispered. "Somehow the guy knew I was coming. You saw it. Why do you think he raised his arm like that?"

No reply was offered.

"It was as if he had eyes in the back of his head. None of the others did a thing. In every case, they all just sat there moaning like cows over their friends' body." He blew more smoke into the air and wiped blood and sweat from his forehead. Blood was smeared on his arm. He looked at it unconcerned in thought.

"My system was always quiet and worked to perfection—efficient. But once that asshole raised his arm, the whole thing got out of control."

"Watch your mouth, young man," his mother warned.

"I'm sorry, Mom. I just can't . . . wait a minute. Everything was the same, except for the glass. The glass . . . that's it! That . . . guy could hear me coming because of the glass."

"But you were quiet, Son," his father said.

"I know," Charlie sighed, "but that had to be it. What else could it be?" He inhaled smoke from the cigarette then shook his head.

"If you say so," his mother agreed. "All I know is that we have some seriously unconcerned neighbors. I thought they would be pounding down the door by now."

"They all work during the day," Charlie explained. "Don't you remember? A bomb could go off around here and nobody would hear it. I guess we're lucky in that respect."

"You know, Son," his father said, "you're all cut up from that shower of glass you took. I think you need a break. Take some time off. Let yourself heal. The work can wait. Can't it, Hon?"

"Yes," his mother said. "We should not have you trying to do the work with your face and hands cut up. You will alert the strays to something amiss. Take a couple of weeks off and let your wounds heal. Maybe even trips to the store should be delayed to avoid questions. We have to be smart about this, Charles."

"Okay, guys. You're right. I'll stop until my wounds heal," Charlie said uneasily, crushing out the cigarette on the concrete floor. "But do you mind if I just go to bed for a while? I'm really tired."

"What about the cleanup?" his dad asked. "If you wait, the mess will be harder to clean and take longer, need scrubbing."

"My hands are all cut up, Dad," Charlie paused and then added, "and I don't really care right now."

"But—"

"Look, Dad," Charlie argued, "I'm too tired. I don't want to talk about it anymore." He stood up slowly putting his hands on his lower back, groaning. He surveyed the carnage and remarked, "Looks like they aren't going anywhere. Blood is way too far from the door to be of concern. I think the work can wait until tomorrow. Then, when it's done, I'll take my well earned vacation."

CHAPTER 26

COUNTER INTELLIGENCE

"Good morning, Mr. Perez," José Fuentes said, greeting Lorenzo with a hardy handshake and a power smile. "Would you like a cup of coffee?"

"Yes. Please," Lorenzo replied, sitting down on the cloth sofa in the small room at the Mexican Consulate clutching the rosary in his right pants pocket through the jeans. He sat in the same spot yesterday.

"Normally Jane would be taking care of this, but since she's not here yet, I'll get it for you."

Fuentes left the room. He returned quickly with a Styrofoam cup of black coffee, packets of sugar and cream, and a small straw stirrer. He set the coffee and condiments on the table in front of Lorenzo.

"You said over the phone your other two roommates have now gone missing. What happened?" asked Fuentes. He unbuttoned his pinstriped, blue suit jacket and sat on one of the chairs across from Lorenzo.

Lorenzo picked up the packets of sugar with trembling hands. "I . . . I know it's him . . . the demon . . . Mr. Crowley."

"Okay, Mr. Perez, calm down now. Take a deep breath and tell me what happened."

Lorenzo inhaled and exhaled slowly knowing that controlled breathing had helped him in times past when nerves got the best of him.

"Well, after I left here yesterday, I went back to work and finished the day as usual and then went home," he explained while tearing the packets and pouring the contents into the black liquid. Some of the white granules missed the cup. The controlled breathing didn't work as well as he hoped it would. A jittery hand reached out to clean the mess.

"Don't worry about that," Fuentes said, waving a hand.

"Okay," Lorenzo complied. "My roommates were not there when I arrived," he said, stirring his beverage. He placed the wet straw on the empty packets on the table in an effort to not add to the mess he already made. "But that's not unusual."

He looked up from his coffee to view Fuentes. "I wasn't concerned about it until around ten o'clock, just before I went to bed. They still had not come home and that was unusual. They've come and gone out again before, staying out late. But not coming back at all. No. That makes me think something has happened, something bad . . . the demon . . . especially because of . . ." he paused, thinking about the dream and decided not to go into the details about the demon, "the problems lately." Lorenzo reached his left hand to rub his forehead bowing slightly.

"Go on, Mr. Perez," Fuentes said.

Lorenzo yawned and tears came to the aid of his tired eyes. "Sorry. I had trouble sleeping again last night. And when I finally did . . . I had the dream about the woman in the desert again. She keeps telling me, 'It's Mr. Crowley.'"

"Woman in the desert?" Fuentes asked.

"Never mind," Lorenzo sighed, remembering Fuentes didn't believe his dreams or that the demon is responsible. "Anyway, this morning, when I got up for work, they were still missing. That's when I went to the pay phone down the street to call you . . . and my boss." Lorenzo paused to sip his java.

The door to the room opened and Jane entered carrying a large pile of folders that she placed on the corner of the table.

"Hello again, Mr. Perez," Ms. McDonald said. Her gentle blue eyes seemed to really welcome Lorenzo. He rose to shake her outstretched hand. Fuentes did not stand, but sent a look of distain her direction.

"Hello," Lorenzo said, awkwardly. He offered a tender smile.

"Mr. Perez was just explaining what happened yesterday and this morning, Jane," Fuentes said. His tone seemed contemptuous, probably due to her late arrival.

She sat down and placed the yellow pad on her lap to take notes. Lorenzo returned to his seat on the couch and sipped his coffee.

"Please, Mr. Perez, continue. What are your roommates names?" Fuentes asked. He nodded to Jane looking at her pad.

"Armando Gonzales and Jorge Salazar, both from Veracruz. They live at the same address you have for me. I met them through a mutual friend. I don't know anything about their families back home, but they are both twenty-two years old, single. Armando is around five foot six and weighs about 140 pounds. He has no facial hair. His hair is cut short, black . . . ah, brown eyes."

He paused to let Jane catch up with the writing.

"Jorge is taller, maybe five foot nine, weighs, I don't know, about 160 pounds, black medium length hair, brown eyes, has a moustache . . . ah . . ."

Lorenzo stopped. He ran out of readily available descriptions. He began to think harder about other facts concerning his roommates and felt the deepening of the pronounced wrinkle over his nose, which he hated to see in the mirror. It looked like a scar and he thought it made people think that he was always angry. He didn't like being thought of that way.

"Do you have any pictures, Mr. Perez?" Ms. McDonald asked.

Before Lorenzo could answer, Mr. Fuentes said, "Jane, do you really think he's got pictures?"

"I'm sorry Ms. McDonald, but I don't even own a camera," Lorenzo said in her defense.

"See?" Fuentes said to her. Looking at Lorenzo he continued, "So when you got home, they weren't there and today they're still missing. You became concerned and made phone calls," Fuentes offered.

This guy is a real jerk.

"Yes. I called you to set up this meeting and I called my boss to explain what happened. My boss knew about Felipe and our meeting yesterday. I asked him for extra time off this morning so I could meet with you. He suggested I take my two weeks of paid vacation. That I should take the time to find out what's going on with my friends."

"What do you intend to do with the time," Fuentes asked.

"Well," Lorenzo said, clutching the rosary through his jeans, "maybe take a more active role in the investigation, God willing." Feeling a bit bolder from holding the beads, Lorenzo asked, "What is being done? You ask all the questions, but I don't hear any answers."

With raised eyebrows, Fuentes said, "We have not accomplished much regarding Felipe yet. It's only been since yesterday we learned his vital information. We gave our local people as well as our Mexican contacts and authorities the information. We have yet to receive a response from the local morgues."

"We can tell you, though," Ms. McDonald offered, "in regard to the other missing people that have already been reported, no bodies have turned up yet. The local police have assigned a detective to investigate. But they're reporting difficulties in their efforts. They can't find witnesses or any people that will talk to them. People are scared of being deported, I imagine. The police want us to help in this regard, but we don't have the resources to commit."

Fuentes said, "Another problem they're having is that the underground workforce of day laborers have probably been warned. Now there's nobody at the stores where the

disappearances were thought to have occurred. Maybe they're looking for jobs in other locations. I'm not sure. Personally, I think the investigation is going poorly so far because they haven't allocated enough personnel and they need to go undercover. They're frustrated. They probably have a history of only dealing with witnesses that help and give information willingly. In this case, they're dealing with people who don't want to assist an investigation."

"Did you say they need to go undercover?" asked Lorenzo.

"Yes. It may be the only way to obtain the information they need," Fuentes said.

"Maybe I can help with this," Lorenzo suggested. "I'm Mexican. I can talk to the workers. Even look for work at the stores."

"You?" Fuentes asked, with a pitiful grin.

"Why not?" Lorenzo looked to Ms. McDonald not liking to talk to the idiot.

"Well," McDonald said, "you're not a detective and it could be dangerous."

"But he said the police can't do the job. Look, I'm personally involved already. I can't sleep. My friends are disappearing and you don't have enough manpower. So?"

"So, go out and get yourself killed?" McDonald asked sharply.

"What would you do, Mr. Fuentes?" Lorenzo expected some lame excuse suitable to an asshole as to why he wouldn't lift a finger to get involved.

Fuentes ignored the question.

"It's not a matter for us to directly get involved in," McDonald said.

Lorenzo asked, looking at Fuentes as he put his empty cup on the table, "Didn't you say that most of the people went missing while looking for work at Home Depot stores?"

The two consulate employees looked at each other with frustrated faces in silence.

"Look," Lorenzo said with a sigh. He paused trying to form a plan of action. Nothing was forthcoming. Finally, he snapped, "Something has to be done here." He held fists up in a non-threatening manner.

"Okay, okay, Mr. Perez. Calm down," Fuentes said shaking his head. "All the reported cases went missing from the streets near the Home Depot stores, except for Felipe. He was the only one who disappeared while working the streets as a panhandler."

Jane sifted through the stack of files, found a map, and spread it out on the table.

"I've compiled information based on reports provided from our sources as of June 30th," Jane announced. "I placed a red dot at each location where disappearances took place."

Lorenzo looked at Fuentes who in turn looked at Ms. McDonald with apparent surprise. Lorenzo shook his head in disgust with Mr. Fuentes and began studying the map.

Jane produced a file that indicated store locations; it had a list of victim's names and the dates the incidents took place, in chronological order.

"This is where the first disappearance, Felipe, took place, around 83rd Ave. and the freeway," she looked up at Lorenzo. "On June 16th, the second occurred here," she continued and pointed to the location. "The third location here. From this point forward in time, the disappearances become two people at a time here, here, here, here, and here. The facts seem to be indicating a pattern radiating outward further and further from a central point located in either Peoria or Glendale here," she stated, making a circular motion with her pen. She tapped the map in emphasis then looked again at Lorenzo.

"I see," nodded Lorenzo, still looking at the map. He shifted his gaze to the file listing the names of the stores, "And they all vanished from Home Depot stores?"

"Yes," both consulate employees said in unison.

"Well, not quite," Jane informed. "Day laborers are allowed to look for work on the streets *near* the stores. The stores won't allow solicitation to take place on their property and everybody looking for work is aware of this stipulation."

"This is very interesting, because Armando and Jorge also look for work near a Home Depot parking lot. The location is here," Lorenzo said, pointing to a location without a red dot.

They all looked up from the map together. Lorenzo thought of the inference.

"It fits a pattern," Fuentes said. "It seems the disappearances only occur once in each location and then move to another Home Depot store located elsewhere." His gaze shifted from McDonald to Lorenzo, then back to the map. She looked at Lorenzo bobbing her head with a knowing smile.

Fuentes rubbed his clean-shaven chin between his fingers, apparently deep in thought. After a few seconds, he broke the silence.

"Assuming that these disappearances are abductions or murders," he said, to the others, "and I just now thought of this; they seem to be the result of some lunatic afraid to abduct more than once at any location. If he continues the pattern of random abductions at this specific chain store . . . and only at stores he has not yet visited . . . then it stands to reason, based on the established pattern, that his next target would be workers at unvisited stores out or away from the center point. Right?" Lorenzo and McDonald shook their heads yes. "This guy must be stupid. He's demonstrating a definite pattern. Stupid or young, probably both."

"I'll go get my laptop," McDonald said standing. "Lets look up the next few store locations further out from the center."

Fuentes said pompously, "Yes, Jane, do that."

Jane left the room. A quiet contemplative stretch of time ensued while both men looked at the map. Lorenzo thought Fuentes a jerk and his assistant a much sharper knife in the drawer. There was undeniable friction going on here and Lorenzo knew why. He formed a whole new respect for her and distain for him.

McDonald reappeared with the laptop, already Googled to the store listings. She dropped blue ink and red ink pens on the table. Fuentes grabbed them.

"Tell me the location you said your roommates went looking for work," Fuentes demanded.

"Here," Lorenzo replied pointing to the corner of McDowell and 75th Ave.

Fuentes drew a red dot on the indicated spot. "The other stores, Jane," he commanded.

McDonald read off unsolicited locations one by one. Fuentes placed a blue circle on each location. When finished, they sat back in their chairs and examined their work.

Again, Fuentes was first to speak: "I will inform the police about *my* theory and direct their investigation accordingly."

Jane passed a disbelieving glance toward Fuentes.

"What will you have them do?" asked Lorenzo.

"Ultimately, they'll be in control," Mr. Fuentes remarked, "but I hope they listen to the logic of this established pattern. I'm surprised they didn't think of it. They should stake out these new store locations, observe the undocumented workers accepting jobs, and follow them . . . to make sure the employers are legitimate. They can check backgrounds of suspects, you know, police work . . . directed to specific spots for specific time frames. They need to commit to the job of finding the guy responsible, your Mr. Crowley."

"I'll contact the authorities in Veracruz," Jane said, standing.

Lorenzo and Fuentes stood as well. Jane held her hand out to Lorenzo.

"It was nice to see you again, Mr. Perez, but I'm sorry it's under such trying circumstances," she said shaking hands.

"My pleasure," Lorenzo admitted, looking at Jane with a tired smile. "Thanks for all your help."

Fuentes interrupted, "Thank you, Mr. Perez. Don't mention it. It's my job."

Lorenzo watched her pick up papers and files frowning at Fuentes as she left.

The apparent boss of the consulate took Lorenzo's hand. "I'll keep you in the loop about events on this end and hope you'll do the same."

Fuentes held the door open for Lorenzo and lead the way out with his extended arm.

As Lorenzo walked down the hallway to the lobby of the consulate, he wondered what "being in the loop" meant.

He opened the front door of the consulate already committed to his own personal involvement in the investigation for at least the next two weeks. He didn't care what that shit head thought. He knew the store locations to ask questions. He remembered the addresses of unsolicited stores. If he had to pretend looking for work to flush out Mr. Crowley, so be it. He'd be alert, ready for anything . . . maybe even bring a knife. God would protect him.

He brought out the rosary from his pocket and began fingering the beads as he walked through the parking lot, heading for the corner of McDowell and 75th Ave.

* * *

On July seventeenth, eleven days after Lorenzo's second meeting at the consulate, he called Fuentes from Efren's house to obtain an update on the investigation by phone.

"This is José Fuentes. Can I help you?"

"Mr. Fuentes, this is Lorenzo Perez."

"Hello, Mr. Perez. How are you?"

"Fine. I called to find out how the investigation is going. It's been a while since we talked and I thought we should—"

"Follow up on things?" Fuentes asked, interrupting Lorenzo in a most presumptuous manner so typical of the well-dressed, rotund Mexican man who seemed to be full of self-importance.

"Yes."

"Well, I can't say I wasn't expecting your call, Mr. Perez, but there's been nothing to report. I mean nothing . . . at all. Which is why I didn't call you," Fuentes said, his voice sounding slightly agitated, disturbed. "There hasn't been one disappearance since we talked. The police are pissed. And I'm surprised myself. I thought my plan was accurate. I mean, the way I saw things unfolding and playing out. I would've bet heavily on the certainty of the next disappearance happening at one of the circled store locations. Now, I've been embarrassed."

"What do you have to be embarrassed about?"

"I convinced the police detective in charge to dedicate a large team of personnel to assist in the investigation for one week. You know the previous disappearances were no more than three days apart. I told them to expect something to happen in the next three days, a week at the most. I gave them the list of stores to target with their surveillance. I got right out on a limb, Mr. Perez, and they agreed with me, at the time."

"But now they've changed their minds?"

"The limb I was on snapped when nothing happened in a week. I became the fall guy. That's what changed Mr. Perez. It's *very* shameful. The bottom line is that by the fourteenth, last Saturday, the authorities refused to continue to approve the funds for all the extra work and overtime. They think the investigation is getting too costly for a 'wild goose chase' and dropped the extra man-hours involved. Over time's very expensive. Now what is it? Um . . . eleven days later and still nothing. It's very frustrating for me and embarrassing."

"But this is not the end of the problem," Lorenzo said. "Maybe the guy is taking a break, on vacation or something. It's not going to stop here, Mr. Fuentes. I still have a bad feeling. I know the guy is out there. You do, too. I know you do."

"The threat exists. But the funds have been cut. They're back to a detective team that doesn't speak Spanish. They won't listen to me anymore. I have to leave it in their hands. Let the authorities do their job as best they can with a smaller work force. Maybe they'll get lucky. What else can I do?"

"I'm sorry to hear that," Lorenzo stated uneasily with a sigh. "Is there anything else?"

"Our investigations determined that none of your people went home, none of the missing returned. Nobody deported and no matches at the morgues either. Officially, all are listed as missing persons."

"Okay then. You're a busy man," Lorenzo said, sarcastically, knowing Fuentes would agree with his remark.

"Good-bye, Mr. Perez."

Lorenzo hung up the phone.

"Things aren't going so well in the search, eh Lorenzo?" Efren asked. He apparently heard the one-sided phone conversation from the comfort of his easy chair.

"No," Lorenzo muttered in agreement. "Nothing to report. No more people went missing, which is a good thing. But listening to that gay fuck, Fuentes, you'd think it was a bad thing because it didn't happen the way *he* said it would. I guess it's not so surprising though, Efren, when I've had nothing to report either. No laborers are showing up at the store on McDowell and 75th where Armando and Jorge worked, so I can't find any witnesses to talk to. Same thing with some of the other places I visited. At the Home Depot I picked to concentrate on, there are guys looking for work, but none witnessed anything. They weren't at the other stores. All had heard about the missing men, but none could offer any help."

"Don't loose heart, Lorenzo. You're doing a good thing, being responsible."

"I actually worked for two different homeowners in the last eleven days and made some good money, too. The work was hard and hot. Each time I left the parking lot with them though, I kept thinking, 'Maybe while I'm gone working for this guy, the real demon will show up at the store and drive away with somebody else.' I'd miss him and the opportunity would be lost. It's frustrating. I'm only one person. You know? I now realize how the police feel. It's not an easy job. I had hope at first, but now I don't know. I just don't know."

"How long will you continue your investigation, Lorenzo?"

"I only have two days left to my vacation time and then I'll have to go back to work at the printing plant. If nothing happens soon, Efren, I'll be forced to leave things in the hands of the

Wayne Patrick

authorities. The only time I'll be able to devote after my vacation is over would be on weekends. I'll be a part time private eye."

They both laughed, Lorenzo in frustration.

"The only good thing is that the abductions seemed to have stopped," Lorenzo continued, "But it won't be for long. Mr. Crowley's still out there. I can feel it. He'll surface again. You'll see. Dear God, I just want a chance to expose him."

Efren shrugged his shoulders and looked at Lorenzo with a searching gaze in silence.

"Regarding another subject, Efren," Lorenzo said, "have you found anyone else looking to rent for me? Money'll be getting tight if I don't get some new roommates. I hate to get new guys in the house in the hope that Felipe, Armando, and Jorge return. My money won't last much longer though. Any prospects?"

"There may be a couple of guys coming this weekend," Efren admitted, stroking his moustache in an offhand manner, "but the crossings have been unreliable lately. If I hear of any one else, I'll get in touch. You get a phone yet?"

"No. How could I with all this happening?"

Lorenzo rose from the couch he was sitting on and Efren got up from his comfortable chair.

"Thanks for letting me use your phone, Efren, and for everything else you do for me," Lorenzo said. He headed to the front door.

"What are friends for?"

"You're a good friend," Lorenzo paused, then added, "I owe you and one day I'll repay you."

Efren flushed a little, "Don't worry, Lorenzo, you owe me nothing. I was once in your position and a friend helped me out until I got established," he admitted. "Good deeds are forever passed down. You have enough to worry about without adding me to the list. It's what we do for each other here in the North. If we can't rely on friends, where would we be? When you find yourself in a secure position, pay the system back by helping someone else instead."

"Your reputation is well deserved, Efren. Be well."

"By the way, Lorenzo, you never told me what you intend to do if you find Mr. Crowley."

"I'll know him when I see him. My plan is just to find him. Then I'll report him to the consulate. Let them report him to the authorities."

"Don't you think this might be dangerous?"

"I'm prepared," Lorenzo said hauling out of his left pocket a small knife. "I'm always on guard and God is on my side," he said holding the rosary in his right hand. "I'll be protected."

CHAPTER 27

THE DREAM COMES ALIVE

Puffy cumulus clouds loomed all morning behind the mountains that surround and guard the Valley of the Sun from bad weather aggression. Within two hours, the thunderheads turned dark gray, and like an evil weather prison break, charged away from their rocky confinement.

Angry specters assaulted the arid valley below and swept into the Phoenix metro area. Late afternoon gales rose with reckless speed throwing a wall of dust into the air collected from the desert floor. The portentous brown mass of turmoil obscured the sun preceding the rain sure to come. Darkness ruled by four o'clock. The Monsoons were poised for another unwelcome attack.

Time was running late for Lorenzo this Wednesday afternoon, the eighteenth of July, as he stood near a Phoenix Home Depot store. He shook his head looking up at the wall of approaching dust in the southeastern sky. All hell was about to break loose in this alarming weather scene. His search to find his roommates' abductor had not produced any leads yet. By the look of the storm approaching, today would be no different. Although he felt the need to be directly involved in the unofficial investigation of his friend's disappearances, there was always tomorrow.

Lorenzo considered the short-term possibilities while watching the wall of dust approach. There was still one more day left of his vacation, one more chance to investigate while getting holiday pay. He would go back to work Friday, but the weekend afforded one or two more investigation days. After that, unfortunately, the search for Mr. Crowley would probably be left solely to the authorities.

Lorenzo didn't trust them. They didn't care about missing illegal aliens. "Those people shouldn't even be here," he could imagine them saying to Fuentes. He told himself he was doing all he could. His friends deserved his best effort. With a sigh he put his hands in his pockets feeling the knife in one and the rosary in the other. Both items provided comfort.

It seemed to him that Wednesdays were notoriously bad days for homeowner projects and standing in the Monsoon was crazy. With no prospects for work and the threatening storm literally minutes away, he decided to cancel the rest of the day's efforts looking for work.

Lorenzo decided to wait out the storm in the Home Depot store. The trip home would be impossible right now. The bad weather was coming so quickly and with such ferocity.

Lorenzo's pants flapped fiercely in the tempest as he left his post and stepped off the curb headed for the store entrance. He froze with the sound of screeching tires. His hands ripped out of his pockets in surprise offering protection from a swerving vehicle that slid past him. His squinting eyes witnessed a near death experience if not for a few inches. The rush of air from the vehicle and self-preservation forced Lorenzo back to the safety of the curb.

The small pickup truck stopped ten feet away. Break lights illuminated the blowing dust with an eerie, hazy glow. The driver rolled down the window.

"You . . . okay?" the driver shouted into the howling winds.

"*Si, senior,*" Lorenzo hollered back, shielding his eyes from the sand and wind. He headed back out into the parking lot entrance and walked around the truck to come along side the driver's open window. "I'm okay," he said.

"You stepped off the curb . . . didn't look. Almost hit you."

Lorenzo could see the man now standing two feet away from the window. The young man had a dark beard and wore equally somber sunglasses. Lorenzo bent over.

"*Si.* I was no looking. The dust . . . my fault, *senior*. Sorry. I will try to look better," Lorenzo explained, in his best Spanglish. Apology now given, he resumed his course for shelter.

The driver shouted after Lorenzo, "You . . . ah . . . need work?"

Lorenzo stopped and turned, "What? You say something, *senior*?"

"You looking . . . to work?"

"I was," Lorenzo said. "Now I go home. The storm, it is too *loco* to work now."

The driver's head tilted toward the sky, his face scowling, displaying perfectly aligned teeth. "For outside work maybe. I need help . . . for inside work. You interested?"

The small Toyota pickup with a camper shell edged further into the parking lot. Lorenzo followed. *This seems a little strange. I think only Mr. Crowley would be looking for labor in weather like this.* He felt for his knife through his pants as his heart began to pound a little faster.

"What kind of work, *senior*?" Lorenzo asked.

"Painting. You paint?"

"*Si.* I paint."

"I got . . . rooms to do," the young driver said. "Ten bucks an hour. Still interested?"

"*Si.*"

"Get in."

Lorenzo read the license plate heading around the truck to get in at the passenger door. While trying to remember it, an odd feeling gripped him. His stomach quivered. It felt like the time he was a teen and got into a fistfight with another guy over a girl they both had intensions to date. Anticipation. It wasn't so much the physical confrontation but the racing thoughts of what he would do, how he would react. Considering this might be the possibility for which he had been waiting, he opened the truck door with one hand while reaching for his knife with the other. All his senses heightened as he got in concealing the knife in his right hand..

"The car," Lorenzo said, "it is safe inside."

"Shelter, eh," the driver said, with a grin, "from the storm."

"*Si*," Lorenzo agreed, "shelter from the storm. As you say."

The driver rolled up his window and turned the truck around in the parking lot.

Lorenzo decided to make idle conversation and get a feel for the guy. The line of questioning would probe the subjects discussed at the consulate meetings. He would look for visual evidence of nervousness, maybe even signs of guilt, something emotional or a slip of the tongue, which would give away true intentions. When certain this was Mr. Crowley, he would ask to be dropped off. If the request not granted, he would bolt from the truck at a stoplight. He would use the knife as a last resort in self-defense. If this young man turned out not to be Mr. Crowley, he would paint for ten dollars an hour. Extra rent had to be paid.

"The bad storm, it ruin work for today, I thought," Lorenzo started making conversation. "It is good you came when you did. I was just going."

The driver said nothing as he turned left on McDowell Road and headed west.

The howling wind outside the truck reduced Lorenzo's ability to clearly hear the music playing on the stereo. It sounded like rock and roll, something Lorenzo didn't like anyway. Stale cigarette odor and smoke pervaded the cab. The driver, dressed in jeans and a black T-shirt with a white skull printed on the chest, lit a cigarette with the butt of his current smoke in a classic chain routine. He ground out the butt in the overflowing ashtray. Lorenzo was surprised it fit without knocking any others to the floor.

"Where do we go, *senior* . . . to your home?"

"Yes."

"Where is your home?"

"Glendale."

The answer fit one of the criteria Lorenzo remembered from the consulate meetings: The suspect would probably live either in Glendale or Peoria. Also, he seemed to be the right age, a younger man in his early twenties. It seemed strange to Lorenzo that someone from Glendale would look for labor help this far away in Phoenix. He knew from locations on the map that there were stores closer to Glendale than this one. He pursued this aspect of questioning.

"You live in Glendale, *senior*?"

"Just said so . . . didn't I?"

"*Si, si*, but why come to Phoenix for help to paint? Is there some place closer to look? No?"

The bearded man turned and with contempt in his voice said, "What?"

"You are far from home. No?"

"What does it matter to you . . . where I get help?"

"It is a long way to go in the bad storm for help, *senior*," Lorenzo maintained. He knew the young man's reply was an evasion. Pressing the issue would force the driver to explain his actions, if he could. Credible answers would be hard to justify if this were the man responsible for the abductions.

The driver stopped for a red light. The ensuing silence told Lorenzo that the driver had no ready answer or was trying to think of one. Lorenzo considered whether this constituted proof or maybe the guy was just a man of few words.

Uneasy quiet continued for the next mile as the storm worsened. Rain sprinkled slowly at first. Water streaked across the side windows in elongated dashes of liquid dots, small drops on the windshield. Then suddenly, huge drops came in a microburst downpour that made visibility impossible without windshield wipers. The driver turned the switch on high to see.

Water washed the streets. It accumulated at curbs and in potholes. The sound of thumping wipers joined that of water spraying into the wheel fenders. Lights from approaching cars cast glowing prisms on the windshield. They sprayed huge waves of water obscurity in passing. The sky became black as night. Gusts of wind buffeted and rocked the small truck. It lurched back and forth in the roadway. All drivers struggled to remain in their proper lanes.

Lorenzo decided to ask for the man's name. If he says Mr. Crowley . . . "What is your name, *senior?*"

"Can't you see I'm busy," came the young man's sharp reply, accompanied by deep lines kneading his brows. A contemptuous voice returned, "You ask . . . too many questions." He took a drag off of his cigarette and blew the smoke in Lorenzo's face.

I don't think I want to work for this mother fucker.

"Let me out at the next light," Lorenzo demanded.

Shit! I forgot the plate number. No matter. I'll get it when he drives off. If anyone fits the roll of kidnapper it's this asshole.

Sweat began to form on the hand holding the small knife.

The driver took his eyes off of the road, turned his head directly at Lorenzo, and said with a deliberate and slow voice, "You talk too much . . . *senior!*"

A horn sounded from a vehicle to the right as they drifted into the next lane. The bearded driver turned his attention back to the road, corrected his drift, and accelerated. The shrieking wind pushed the truck to the right again. And again, the other driver laid on the horn.

"Fucking bitch!" the driver yelled, flipping the other car off with his sweeping right hand. The cigarette he held passed inches from Lorenzo's face.

Lorenzo ducked to the right in delayed avoidance.

The crazy bastard brought his hand back to the wheel overcompensating to the left and the truck lurched. He accelerated fishtailing slightly.

"You hear that?" the driver said in a huff.

"What?"

"What? The horn you idiot. *That* was the signal. You heard it. Now they'll come . . . in droves . . . helicopters, cops everywhere!"

"Ahh, the horn . . . *si* . . . you almost hit him," Lorenzo snapped back in disbelief.

What signal?

"Shut up!" the driver screamed. "You don't know . . . we're being followed."

The driver's head swiveled, searching. He seemed to overreact to the slightest sound. He accelerated faster passing the vehicle on the right and cut in front.

"Fuck you!" he yelled, looking back through the camper shell.

Lorenzo didn't know what to think or say. His grip on the knife couldn't be tighter. He thought about moving it to his left hand for a closer defense. But it might be noticed. His left hand reached for the rosary. He gripped the beads through the material of his pants.

The driver ran a yellow light.

"*Senior*, maybe you take your glasses off. It is dark." Lorenzo's concern raised his voice a few octaves.

"I can see fine . . . better than you. So, shut the hell up! Okay? I'll lose them. Don't worry."

"Who? Who are you losing?"

"None of your business, beaner."

Another microburst poured down. High-speed wipers were no match in the battle against the rain. Lorenzo was temporarily blinded. Yet they drove faster.

The truck shuddered through rain swept streets. The driver gripped the wheel with both hands and his head poked forward, as if it would help him to see through the rain distorted windshield.

In vain, Lorenzo searched his mind for what to do. He began to pray for a red traffic light. He would bolt from the truck at the next red light. He would much rather be in the rain and wind getting soaked to the bone than stay in this truck.

The asshole seemed embroiled in a battle with not only slick roads, but phantoms as well. His face twitched. His head jerked. He seemed overwhelmed. And still the truck gained speed.

Lorenzo was becoming terrified.

At this speed, he couldn't jump out or even try to stop the idiot. The attempt would result in an accident. The jerk was constantly looking in the rear view mirror more concerned about traffic behind him than what was in front. Lorenzo was desperate to get out.

"Pull over, you *chinga tu madre!*" The words burst out of Lorenzo's mouth. "I no need work now."

The driver, once again, turned his head toward Lorenzo this time with a broad smile and bulging eyes. "Shut the fuck up!" he roared back.

"*Senior,*" Lorenzo pleaded, "*por favor,* look at the road. We go too fast not to see."

The driver turned his head to look behind them and drove even faster. He looked forward. "Look . . . look . . . they're still there," he shouted wagging his thumb toward the back. "Those bastards! Can't believe it. No matter what I do!"

He swerved to avoid another slow moving vehicle and changed lanes with reckless abandon. Then he cut in front of another car to the right. Again someone beeped. In the distance a police siren sounded. Lorenzo looked around but could not see flashing lights. They were not the cause. He wished they were.

"Oh shit!" the young man said, as he ran another light, this one red. "You hear that? This is your fault!"

"Me?"

"Yes, you, fucking beaner."

Rain on the windshield was blinding at the speed they were going. Wipers strained in the driving rain. Lorenzo craned his neck to see the speedometer. They were doing sixty.

"Stop the car!" Lorenzo shouted. His hand pulled out the rosary. He prayed to the Virgin of Guadalupe for intervention:

"Why are you allowing this to happen?" he asked in his prayer. "Please do something to save me." And for the first time in his life, he admitted, "I don't know what to do . . . help me." He was sweating, more from nerves and fear than the summer heat and humidity.

The truck blew through two large puddles of water. They seemed to be hydroplaning. Huge sprays of water were tossed from the street.

At sixty-five miles an hour, the jerky driver took another drag from his cigarette. He reached his hand back to the wheel just as the truck hit a huge pothole. His hand bounced on the wheel. The cigarette dislodged from between his fingers. Lorenzo followed the burning ember as it tumbled down and bounced from the driver's leg. It wedged between the *gringo* and the seat.

"Shit . . . Shit!" the driver yelled, swatting with his right hand and bouncing in the seat. He tried to flush out the lit cigarette without success. His feet pushed down lifting up his ass from the seat depressing the gas peddle fully.

The speeding pickup converged on the next intersection pushing seventy. The driver screamed as the cigarette burned his leg. His hand frantically mashed the hot ember scattering sparks around the seat.

Lorenzo looked up to see the approach of an intersection just ahead. A left turning vehicle was edging across their path. Immediate action was needed to avoid a head on crash.

"Look out!" Lorenzo yelled. He dropped the beads and knife reaching out with both hands to yank the wheel sharply to the right.

The truck fishtailed to the left and clipped the turning car's front bumper. Without restraint, Lorenzo flew into the driver and steering wheel on impact. The truck's path straightened after contact, but veered off to the right in a thirty-degree angle from the roadway.

They careened over the northwest curb of the intersection, bounced violently, and flew over a yard out of control.

CHAPTER 20

GUESS WHO'S COMING
TO DINNER

The Enricos prepared to eat an early dinner. The dining room table, charmingly set for two, displayed a cheerful flower centerpiece. The colors brightened the room on such a dark, gloomy, and rainy day.

They had moved to Arizona from Brooklyn following friends that led the way west to paradise years before. They sold their moving and storage business, retired, and relocated to the warmth of the sun. Today's rain reminded them of their old stomping grounds.

Julie carried a tray of salads, sauce, spaghetti, and meatballs down the hallway from the kitchen. She headed for the dining room where her husband of forty years, Lenny, sat at the dining table watching the television playing in the adjacent room. Judge Judy finished hearing testimony and was about to deliver a verdict.

In a raised Brooklyn accent from the hall, Julie said, "Did you bring the wine glasses like I asked, Lenny?" Her feet shuffled as she watched the food balancing on the tray.

"Yeah, yeah . . ." the retired old man said, "Shhhh . . . quiet, I want to hear the ruling."

Suddenly, the wall behind Lenny exploded inward with a tremendous roar of splintering wood, shattering glass, cracking sheetrock, and crumpling metal, drowning out the sound of the TV. The force of the implosion sent sharp fragments of windowpane and debris flying through the dining room, as if a misguided wrecking ball had demolished the outside wall in a cloud of white dust.

Julie dropped the tray of food in shock, but the sound of it crashing to the floor was unheard in the midst of calamity. A shrill cry, born in horror, reached out to her husband, as she watched the front end of a truck emerge through the haze of destruction. A crumpled front bumper loomed larger and larger forcing its way to her husband's chair. She watched in horror.

The truck thrust the remains of wall into the back of Lenny's seat at an angle, throwing him to the floor. After being vacated, the chair snapped in half against the table. Everything slid across the room in a trail of mud and shrubbery toward the china cabinet. Priceless heirlooms of glass and ceramic art, collections of a lifetime carefully packed and unpacked from the move across country, shattered into worthless rubbish joining the disintegrated mess littering the floor.

The base of the home was pushed off of its foundation by sheer force. The entire house shook. Pictures fell from walls in other rooms and keepsakes rocked on distant shelves. The disaster echoed throughout the neighborhood.

The front end of the small pickup truck finally crashed down to rest upon crushed chairs and the collapsed remains of the table. The battered Toyota chassis bounced in the middle of the room as blown tires nearly pinned the scrambling old man. The spray of shattered glass filled the room. A handful of shards found the soft spongy skin of Lenny's back. Dust attempted to cover the resulting red spots of blood forming through his shirt as he crawled on hands and knees to relative safety.

The motor sputtered to a grinding halt. Its metallic-ticking sound joined the patter of rain from outside and a commercial playing on the television in the other room. Julie reached out to the wall for support feeling like she was about to faint. The room was spinning and she was not sure if it was because of her light head or as a direct result of the accident. Out of the corner of her eye, she watched Lenny scramble to a far wall where he eased into semi consciousness.

The truck's back wheels rested on the sill that had moved inward from the foundation where the recently installed bay window once stood. The bashed in front end of the pickup dripped water together with leaking green radiator fluid on the littered oak flooring.

The windshield, smashed in a spidery web of cracks, lay on the dented hood of the vehicle. The passenger, having been thrown partially through it, seemed to be wearing an odd shaped splintery glass skirt. Blood dripped from multiple lacerations on his head and a foot long splinter of wood protruded from his neck. Pink rainwater pooled in depressions on the twisted sheet metal. The driver sat slumped behind the wheel bloody and unconscious. Nobody moved. Even Julie could not manage to run to Lenny's side. She waited for her head to clear. Feeling like she did, an attempt at moving would surely result in a fall.

Rain sprayed through the ten-foot gaping hole in the dining room wall as the wind howled. Judge Judy's show finally went off the air, the litigants bickering about the results of tough justice.

In shock, Julie watched through the gaping hole in the wall neighbors and witnesses gathering outside, some with umbrellas, most without. The police were most likely summoned. Darkness seemed to be crowding in on Julie as she let go of the wall.

Four police cruisers and two paramedic units were dispatched to the scene; their flashing lights reflected in the dark, slick streets and wet umbrellas. Yellow police tape, stretched across the yard, vibrated wildly in the wind and rain as the rescue and investigation of the accident commenced.

CHAPTER 29

SECOND ARTICLE

"You need to read this," Tammy Heart said to Ben Marshall as he entered his apartment late Friday afternoon. Ben heard a slight urgency in her voice.

"What is it?"

"Your father dropped it off an hour ago," she said handing a section of the newspaper to Ben. "It's a newspaper article."

"And? What's it about?"

"Read it. You'll find out," Ben's girlfriend said turning to head for the kitchen.

"Is it important?" Ben shouted after her. "I mean, do I need to read it now?" Ben didn't like reading, not even text messages.

"Yes! Right now!" her voice came from the kitchen.

"Can't ya tell me what it's about?" Ben made a last ditch effort at getting Tammy to tell him what the article said.

"It's about, Charlie, Ben. Read it, damn it!"

"Charlie?" Ben dropped his stuff on the coffee table and sat on the couch wiping sweat from his forehead. He held up The Arizona Republic already turned to page three of The West Phoenix section. It was dated Thursday, July 19, yesterday:

"CAR CRASHES INTO PHOENIX HOME"
One dead, two hurt
By Linda Goode
The Arizona Republic

Phoenix—One man died and two others were injured on Wednesday when the driver of a vehicle lost control on slippery roads, hit another vehicle at the intersection of McDowell Road and 67th Avenue, and crashed into a house around 5:00 pm.

Julie Enrico, 64, and her husband, Lenny, 66, were eating dinner when Charles McShane, 21, lost control of his 2001 Toyota pick up and crashed into the Enrico's dinning room.

"It was like a bomb went off," Julie said. "The whole house shook, things went flying everywhere." Mrs. Enrico fainted in the hallway unharmed. Lenny, who was seated at the dining room table, sustained severe lacerations and bruises mostly to his posterior from glass and wood debris. He was taken to Banner Estrella Medical Center, treated and released.

Authorities said the driver of the vehicle, who was unconscious when they arrived, was also taken to Banner for treatment of moderate injuries. A Mexican National passenger in the vehicle, Lorenzo Perez, 29, sustained fatal injuries and died at the scene. He was not wearing a seat belt.

The Toyota truck was mangled, officials said, and had to be towed. Its twisted front end sat in the Enrico's dining room. Inside, a china cabinet and furniture lay in ruins. A gaping hole in the wall of the house was later temporarily boarded up. Fire department officials on the scene estimated the property damage to the house and contents to be over $100,000.

Neighbors said people frequently run red lights at the intersection and have had numerous accidents near the Enrico residence, but none have previously left the street.

The driver of the other vehicle involved in the accident, Phil Piechocinski, 42, was unhurt with minimal damage to his Ford Tiempo. He said, "The Toyota was speeding and lost control in the rain."

"I'm sorry about what happened to the Mexican man," Mrs. Enrico said. "I'm just happy Lenny was not killed. But all my valuable ceramics and crystal were destroyed. Irreplacable collectibles and dishes of a lifetime, all gone."

With assistance from the Phoenix Fire Department and the Red Cross, the couple were put up in a nearby hotel after Mr. Enrico's release from the hospital. It will be at least twenty-four hours until they might be able to return home after the damage is temporarily fixed.

"It's a dinner we'll never forget," Mr. Enrico said. "I guess we'll just have to pick up the pieces and move on."

Ben, read through the article twice. When finished, he tossed the paper on the coffee table. After discussing it with Tammy, he made two phone calls.

The first was to Becka, Charlie's fiancée, to give her the news. Even though Tammy warned about Charlie's possible reaction to seeing Becka, Ben knew that she was still deeply in love with him, frustrated but not hopeless. They were all waiting for Charlie to emerge from his funk. Maybe this accident would soften Charlie's attitude toward her, toward everyone. For Becka, the crazy and violent turn Charlie had taken added to the bad-boy loner image she fell in love with from the start. The call represented another debt that Ben could collect and deposit in his rainy day credit account.

The second call was to Banner Estrella Medical Center. The hospital would not release any information due to HIPAA regulations governing privacy. It seemed a bit odd to Ben. He couldn't discover Charlie's condition or even if he was ever admitted. He finally left a message with the front desk operator that he called giving his name, why he called, and a contact number, in case anything changed in the future.

PART 4

THE FATES OF WAR

But the brilliance, the versatility of madness is akin to the resourcefulness of water seeping through, over and around a dike. It requires the united front of many people to work against it.

Tender Is The Night—F. Scott Fitzgerald, 1934

CHAPTER 30

THE AFTERMATH

The need to find the bathroom faded at the same time Charlie lost control of his bladder. He sat on the edge of his bed, emotionless, eyes closed, trying to contemplate options. Nothing he considered represented a desired choice. The muscles in his neck stretched as his head bent down to face his ostensibly dry lap. He had first hand knowledge though, of the soiled fabric beneath, a revolting thought. He felt it, originally warm, but cooling fast.

This understanding seemed similar to the knowledge he had about who turned the wheel at the last moment to cause the crash. Unlike this current urination problem that needed immediate attention and would be handled by hospital staff, the destiny of the crash information should never surface.

Why should it? An accident is an accident. Enough said.

Nobody should ever have to know what happened, why it happened, or how it happened, except his parents, of course, and they already knew. The argument he had with them when he woke in the hospital emergency room caused considerable embarrassment. He remembered frantic orderlies and nurses interrupting the conversation repeatedly.

They wouldn't leave him alone. He had to resort to physical violence to get his point across. And what did that get him? *You should know you dumb ass, a four-point restraint!*

Since then, the nurses wouldn't listen to anything Charlie said. Their attitudes seemed abusive and the care rough and unfeeling, if care is what you called it. Even the doctor seemed angry, untrusting. Charlie remembered him saying something about being moved, but because of the constant sedative injections he couldn't recall much more. About that time his parents had become very quiet. Charlie felt abandoned.

Puffy and sleep encrusted eyelids opened wide enough to allow observation of an elongated, swaying drop of saliva attached to his quivering lower lip. The overstretched drop snapped in half without provocation. It soaked his hospital-issued, pajama bottoms with a dark-blue wet spot. There were three such blemishes arranged on the light-blue material over the crotch area in a crooked line, like the stars in Orion's belt. He felt out of touch unaware of the creation of the first two.

Charlie raised his head with a great deal of effort. Lately, he moved at a snail's pace. Thoughts slithered across his mind like dying worms. Everything seemed in slow motion. The view from the perch on the edge of the bed challenged his recollection, but his mind balked at memory work. The scene included the plain room he occupied and a steel door that stood ajar revealing a hallway beyond. His lid-encumbered eyes made tedious progress as they shifted left and right, beholding green colored walls illuminated by a small florescent light. No windows. The survey, familiar but at the same time vague, forced a déjà vu experience. He became certain that he sat in this very same place before. As sure as a person sitting in his own piss and drooling into his lap could be.

Charlie heard voices in the hallway, but could not make out what was being said. The voices were definitely not coming from inside his room, or inside his head for that matter. His acute senses were no longer functioning at optimum levels. He wanted to strike the side of his head with his hand to clear things up a bit, but the strength to accomplish this was seriously lacking. The sign on the door to his energy reserves read, "be back tomorrow, maybe later."

As he considered his embarrassing problem, he looked into his lap and saw one big and irregular, dark-blue spot on his pajamas. Charlie couldn't remember if the large spot was created by drool or by his leaky plumbing. He couldn't tell if he had been sitting here for a few minutes or a few hours. Everything was so strange, so disconcerting. Finding the strength to lift his finger, he touched a thin wet line bisecting his smooth lower lip and wiped it dry.

This was so fucking typical of the way things had been going these last few days: Gaps of time passing without notice, uncontrolled events, surprising discoveries. It was as if he'd been lying asleep on the beach and suddenly awakened from his slumber to the roll of waves adrift, heading toward a dark and unsettling horizon, the beach nowhere in sight.

Charlie squinted as he considered the size of the spot in his lap. He was not happy. His emotion, with an absence of hate, felt more passive than in times past. Even though he sat in a sea of piss with a drool spot the size of Texas on his lap, he could not muster hatred. Instead, he decided to act calmly and search for assistance in the hallway. It was time for help.

On weak knees and holding the bed railing, he rose and shuffled toward the door. On the way, wet pajamas sent a cold chill throughout his body, evidence of the violation he endured yet helpless to avoid. He tried to push feelings of anger to the surface as he opened the door to the hall. The attempt was met with a violent interruption.

A screeching car slid to an abrupt stop in front of him. Danger flashed across his mind causing him to lean back out of the doorway in avoidance. If he'd not voided himself prior to this event, he surely would've done so at this time. Instead, he blinked and the vision vanished. The incident gave no real cause for alarm. The observation was all in his mind, but oh so familiar.

Was that my nightmare.. again? Oh no, the dreams are not going to start again are they?

Weaving in and out of the doorway with his hands on the jambs, he shook his head and peered down the hall. Strangers dressed in blue and white pajamas moved along the corridor in both directions, all with a dragging gait and most talking to no one in particular. One person sat on the floor, another motionless in a wheelchair parked in haphazard fashion along the wall. He shook his head again to make sure his eyes were not deceiving him, to make sure this was not the nightmare happening again.

From a distance down the hall, two large men dressed in white appeared. They came running toward Charlie greeting him at the door and with force lead him back into the room. Without words passing, his guides acted upon his immediate concerns.

*   *   *

"Mr, McShane ... Mr. McShane."

Charlie opened his eyes. A well groomed man with black hair and a precisely shaped beard, both speckled with gray flecks, wiped away evidence of drooling from Charlie's mouth and cheek with a tissue and tossed it into a trash can near the bed.

"Mr. McShane, wake up," the man said speaking with a slight Spanish accent.

Charlie felt a hand on his arm. His lazy eyes watched the smiling man who stood over him, dressed in a white lab coat, shirt, and tie.

"Mr. McShane, in case you've forgotten, I'm Dr. Hernandez," the slender Mexican said.

"How could I forget? You remind me every time you inconsiderately wake me up."

Charlie rubbed his eyes and brushed his hair back with his hand. "Where's my cigarettes? Can't you give me one, just one?

"No. I told you, they're forbidden."

"What do you want? Can't you ever leave me alone? I'm still not going to answer any of your stupid questions. I got nothing to say to you."

"I've contacted some friends of yours who would like to visit with you. Please, indulge me. I think you'll benefit greatly with a visit from friends. In order for this to happen, we must have your consent."

Charlie rolled over and with a monumental effort sat up in bed. The slumped over attitude demonstrating a new twist to poor posture.

"Here," the doctor said, shoving a clipboard containing the necessary papers for Charlie to sign under his inspection. "If you'll just sign here. Let me help you."

"I can do it." Charlie took the pen and autographed where the doctor indicated. "I know you think I'm nuts, but I'm not an invalid."

"Did you enjoy your nap?"

"Yeah, as if *you* care," Charlie said, but felt as if he did not sleep for days. "Who . . . who'd you say, wants to visit me?"

"Your friends. Specifically, Ben, Rebecca, and Terry."

"Oh. Okay. Ah . . . what day is this and what's the time?"

"Just about noon, I'd say," the doctor replied without looking at his Omega watch. "Saturday, July twenty-first. They'll be here soon. You need to wake up and put your robe on. Get yourself ready for a visit. Okay? Be on your best behavior."

Get a load of this fucking beaner telling me to be on my best behavior.

Charlie sat in silence while the doctor left to fetch something from the closet. This information represented a welcomed change from the usual hellish interrogations the past few days. Charlie actually found himself looking forward to seeing some familiar faces.

CHAPTER 31

THE DOCTOR IS IN

The sign on the door to the Acute Behavioral Care Ward at Thunderbird Medical Center read: "Welcome to the fifth floor waiting room—Please proceed to the desk for assistance. Thank you."

Ben held the door open for Tammy and Becka to pass. All three made their way around two-dozen empty waiting room chairs to the reception desk. The unattended desk stood between visitors and that which was hidden behind various doors. Four of the doors were numbered consultation rooms; the main double-doors, composed of stout steel, led to a hallway beyond, as seen through a small window. The restricted entrance read: "Authorized Personnel Only" and was accessible by keypad numbers.

Ben and the girls assumed the lack of assistance at the counter was due to lunch. They were early for the one o'clock appointment with Dr. Hernandez, so they settled into three chairs closest to the reception area. After mere seconds of sitting, Tammy popped up from her chair, announced her intention to visit the ladies room, and headed for relief.

"Don't ya got to go, too?" Ben said, to Becka, wagging a thumb in Tammy's general direction. He raised his eyebrows accompanied by a devious smile.

"No."

"Why not?" Ben asked, and pointed to the woman's bathroom door marked *"Bano."* "Can't ya read Spanish?" He laughed at his own joke. "Check out da silhouette of a woman in a dress. I guess that's for people who can't read at all. Don't women always go to the bathroom together?"

"We only go together when we want to talk *about* someone," Becka said with a frown, "and you aren't worthy of discussion. And how can you be so . . . happy? Joking at a time like this. Aren't you concerned about Charlie?"

"Sure I am, but I deal with my problems this way. Better to laugh than cry," Ben said, then changing the subject, "Pretty imposin' place, huh?" He indicated with a nod to the security dome on the ceiling. "I love da paint color selection, too. Light puke-green on top of dark puke-green, two-tone puke."

"I know, huh," Becka agreed, "I think it's called wainscot."

"Yeah, whatever."

"Ben, do you think Charlie is going to be okay?" Becka asked, concern written all over her face. "I mean this is the psych ward of the hospital. Do you think Charlie's crazy?"

He turned to look at the information desk. Still empty. "Ya know, Becka, I—"

A man in a white lab coat and tie entered the waiting area through the door marked number one followed by another man dressed in a suit jacket and bolo tie. The man following was huge, at least six feet eight, and had a bent nose that looked like it had been broken numerous times within the confines of the square ring. Ben stopped their conversation to see if it was Charlie's doctor coming out for the appointment.

"As I said," the man in the lab coat stated in a slight Spanish accent, "my patient needs absolute quiet and rest. He's been in an accident resulting in physical trauma along with other complications." The doctor turned to face the huge man.

"I understand, Doctor," the bent nosed man said closing the door behind him. "But you need to understand, I have a job to do." His voice inflected on the word *you* and his head bent down as sharply as the cascading bridge of his nose, towering over the doctor.

Becka seemed ready to say something and Ben held a hand up to silence her. Ben thought the conversation might concern Charlie and felt compelled to eavesdrop, possibly learn the nature and depth of his injuries.

"That job will have to wait until he can deal with the agitation your questions are sure to induce, detective," the doctor said with an authoritative tone most likely learned in a special medical-school course featuring counter-intimidation.

"When do you think the time will be right, your majesty?" the detective asked.

"I don't know just yet, but I do know, *you* need to exercise patience and respect."

"Humor me with an educated guess, doctor. With all your advanced degrees, I'm sure you can envision an acceptable time frame," the detective said, inflating his chest and stepping closer to the doctor with kneaded eyebrows.

Ben looked to Becka and smiled in expectation of some sort of physical confrontation. They both snickered, witnessing the heated argument.

"I'm a psychiatrist, not a prognosticator," he proclaimed looking up at the big man. "And I'm not in the habit of whipping out my crystal ball for the likes of you. Especially when it comes to the well being of my patients. When he's ready, you'll be informed, and not a minute sooner."

"All right. I'll question him later," the detective said backing down and away from the psychiatrist, "But you better call. This investigation covers more than just an accidental death. You have my card." Then in a lower tone of voice he continued, "You know, d*octor*, there are many people at the Mexican consulate looking forward to hearing about my discussion with him. You, of all people, should be interested in helping them get the answers they need in this investigation."

"In due time, detective," the doctor advanced to the door and twisted the knob, "In due time you'll hear from me." The doctor exited and the heavy door sighed shut ending the discussion.

Ben watched as the detective stormed across the waiting room and shoved his way through the door leading to the bank of elevators.

"Ya know, Becka," he said without turning toward her, "I'll bet your life they were talkin' about Charlie." Becka nodded her head in agreement.

"Can I help you?" asked a nicotine-riddled voice from behind the desk.

Ben and Becka turned to see who addressed them. They rose in unison from their seats heading for the desk.

"We're here to see Dr. Hernandez," said Ben. "We have a one o'clock appointment."

The hoarse voice belonged to a two hundred pound woman that seemed better suited to female wrestling or body building than helpful information desk work—maybe even as an armored guard.

"Just a moment, please," the dark-haired woman dressed in white said. "What is your name?"

"Ben Marshall."

"I'll see if he's available . . . one moment please." She picked up the nearby phone and dialed.

Tammy joined them at the counter.

"Hey, Hon," Ben said, to Tammy. "She's checkin' to see if da doctor's available."

"Don't you have an appointment?" Tammy asked Ben.

"Yeah, but you know how doctors are," Ben said with a chuckle, then in a whisper so the wrestler wouldn't hear, "your time's not as valuable as theirs is."

The desk attendant hung up the phone and said, "Please wait in consultation room two."

*   *   *

The barren walls of the eight-by-ten foot visitor consultation room provided a plain working environment containing only the necessary tools for visitor conferences. A blunt metal desk occupied one corner of the room next to a blank white board on an adjacent wall; colored markers lined the shelf under it. The desk supported a computer, phone, writing pads, and a green pull-chain lamp not in use. Florescent ceiling lights bathed the room in a brusque white glow. A black-leather executive chair completed the clinical ensemble. On opposite walls stood four gray stacking chairs matching the room color. A pair of metal crutches leaned against the corner wall and a wheeled, patient-serving tray held condiments for beverages in paper cups near the desk. A second door, controlled by a keypad locking system, stood across from the visitor entry.

"Security seems pretty tight," Ben said, looking at the keypad door as they settled into three of the four ass-numbing, visitor chairs. "Nobody's gettin' out of da ward unless da hospital approves it."

"Yeah," Tammy said, "scary . . . almost like prison."

Ben asked, "When were you ever in prison?"

"Never. But I imagine a prison would be like this."

"It is creepy," Becka agreed. "Poor Charlie, I feel so sorry for him. Did the doctor say he was sick, Ben?"

"Doctor didn't say. I told ya . . . all he said was that he wanted to talk and that we were to meet on da fifth floor," Ben clarified. "I didn't know da fifth floor was da nut ward."

The secured door opened with a click. A slender man with a full head of black hair and an architecturally shaped beard, both speckled with gray flecks, entered the room. They all stood to greet him. The man observed the visitors employing a discerning brown-eyed gaze in silence, then turned to Ben and held out his hand.

"I'm Dr. Hugo Hernandez," he said, shaking Ben's hand. "You must be Ben Marshall."

"Nice to meet ya doctor," Ben said.

"And who are these lovely young ladies?" asked the forty-something doctor, dressed in a knee-length white lab coat and tie. He glanced from Terry to Becka with an engaging smile and then transferred his attention to Ben, seeming to expect an introduction.

"Oh, ah . . . yeah, doctor," Ben stammered, "This is my fiancée, Tammy Heart."

"How do you do?" the doctor said, shaking hands.

"Hello, Dr. Hernandez."

"And this is Rebecca Grubb."

"Hello. It's a pleasure to meet you."

"Hi. I'm Charlie's . . . well, his fiancée . . . or ex-fiancée, depending on whether seeing him or not for the past six months matters," she said with a nervous smile.

"Please . . . sit down," the doctor said, gesturing with his hand toward the chairs. The doctor moved behind the desk and sat down.

"Rebecca, is it?" Dr. Hernandez asked.

"Yes, but my friends call me Becka."

"All right, Becka. You've just said you haven't seen Mr. McShane for quite some time," Dr. Hernandez said, shifting his attention to Ben. "Does that hold true for you, too?"

"I haven't seen Charlie for maybe two months," Ben said.

"And you—"

"I haven't seen him for over six months," Tammy said. "He's more a friend of Ben's."

The doctor took notes with a Cross pen obtained from his lab coat pocket.

After a short pause, he raised his head. "I was unable to discover if Mr. McShane has any living relatives. He has been . . . uncooperative, refusing to offer any information concerning his past. If you hadn't left that message with the hospital receptionist, Ben, I'm afraid I'd still be in the dark."

"I overheard da conversation ya had with da detective in da waiting room. Was it about Charlie?" Ben asked.

"How is he Dr. Hernandez?" Becka inquired with urgency, leaning forward in her chair. "Why is he here, in the behavioral unit? Is he sick?"

Tammy jumped in addressing her two friends with pleading hands, "Guys, calm down. Don't give him the third degree. Let him talk."

The doctor smiled at Tammy acknowledging her intervention. "I suppose I should back up a bit, fill in some history associated with Mr. McShane leading up to his current situation. It might answer some of your questions."

Their heads nodded approval and encouragement.

"You know he was in a vehicular accident." The doctor seemed to want recognition on this fact before he continued. Ben nodded. "It involved a fatality and considerable damage to someone's home. The detective was here because a person died. He wanted to interrogate Mr. McShane. It's standard procedure. The police must follow up when a death is involved."

"So ya sent him away 'cause Charlie can't handle it right now?" Ben asked.

"That's right. My immediate concern is for the welfare of my patients. That detective can wait, especially since he was so pushy."

"So that means Charlie isn't doing well, doctor?" Becka whimpered, tears welling in her eyes.

"Becka, will you let the doctor talk? Pull yourself together," Tammy cautioned.

"Mr. McShane was found unconscious behind the wheel at the scene," the doctor continued. "The Phoenix Fire Department originally transported him from the accident to Banner Estrella, down on West Thomas. It was the closest hospital to the accident site. He was treated there for injuries sustained in the accident, which included head trauma, a concussion, localized swelling, deep contusions of the chest.

He was given a sedative and held for observation, to make sure the injuries were not life threatening in nature, just a precaution you understand—standard procedure."

"So, why is he *here?*" Ben asked narrowing his eyes.

"The next day, when he woke, he became verbally abusive and violent. Another sedative was administered. When he returned to consciousness, he was violent, physically abusive, and paranoid. The nurses and aids on duty said that he was talking to imaginary people. They wrestled with Mr. McShane, mostly in self-defense."

Becka's hands covered her mouth. Her eyes widened. Even Tammy's eyebrows shot up and her mouth opened. Ben was listening intently.

"A considerable scene developed. Mr. McShane hit two nurses during his violent outburst."

The doctor paused, shifting in his chair as he watched the various reactions.

Becka shook her head and said, "Oh, my God."

"According to standard procedure, Mr. McShane was sedated again and physically restrained. Since his vital signs were strong, the doctor in charge determined the injuries unrelated to the abusive outbursts. He assumed the problem to be psychological in nature."

"Oh, shit. Sorry," Ben said apologizing for his crude language leaning back in his chair. "That's why he's here."

"Right. The two nurses involved in the fracas documented everything and petitioned the RBHA, I'm sorry, the Regional Behavioral Health Authority, to authorize psychological testing and evaluation—a forced visit with a psychiatrist. That would be me. I was on call at the time he arrived here."

"So Charlie's crazy?" Becka asked, her voice quivering and tears cascading down her cheeks. She began to nervously turn Charlie's engagement ring round and round on her finger.

"Becka," the doctor said, "they were concerned, and correctly so, not only for his own safety, but also for the safety of others around him. They were influenced in their decisions by the accident and the death. Since Estrella is not equipped or prepared for psychological behavioral cases, and because the RBHA approved the petition, Charlie was moved here, to Banner Thunderbird." He wrote an observation on his pad.

"We provide acute behavioral care here," the psychiatrist continued looking up. "Charlie has been under my care ever since. That brings us current. But Charlie's not well, I'm afraid."

"I know," Ben agreed. "We, I mean me and Becka, have run into some problems with Charlie's temper, too, in da past, and that's why we haven't seen him in a while."

"Yeah," Becka murmured. She stopped turning the ring to wipe tears from her flushed cheeks. The doctor handed her a box of tissues. After using a few tissues to dry her face, she finally said, "We got into a fight about my joking around with him and he suddenly snapped. He threw a coffee mug at me and basically kicked me out of his house the last time I saw him. It was scary seeing him that mad. He was never that mad before, but he was under a lot of stress. He really didn't mean it." She seemed to speak with a forced smile and then dropped her head holding a Kleenex to her runny nose.

"Take it easy, Sweetie," Tammy said, rubbing Becka's back.

"I've tried to talk to him since then," she went on, lifting her head, "but every time he pushed me away. God, it's so frustrating. I still love him though and don't care if he's sick. He's got nobody to care for him. It all makes sense to me now, but if he's not well?"

The doctor had no immediate comment. He was busy writing notes.

"Me too," Ben added. "I love him like a brother, man. He's my best friend. But I thought da last time I saw Charlie, we were going to come to blows. I thought it best to leave him alone. I felt it was da only way for our friendship to last. He was actin' really strange back then and I told him he should go see a doctor about it. You shoulda seen . . . he had pots n' pans piled against every window and door in his house. He was freakin' me out. Told me he was talkin' to his mother."

The doctor stopped writing and looked at Ben with surprise. "That's very interesting you should say that, Ben. Very interesting indeed." He stroked his chin hairs as a frown, manufactured by this declaration, formed on the doctor's face. "You've just confirmed my diagnosis. Charlie has a very serious condition. But before I explain, I would like to ask you—"

The desk phone rang. The doctor answered.

"Yes? Yes." Then a long pause, "Okay. I'll be right there."

The doctor placed the receiver back in the cradle.

"An emergency's come up," he informed. "I need to leave, but there's more we need to discuss. I'll be back."

*   *   *

"Okay, where were we?" Dr. Hernandez asked, looking at the expectant faces of Charlie's friends. He consulted his notes. "Oh, yes . . . Charlie's condition. But first, about Charlie's parents, what can you tell me about them? Would you say they were normal? Were there any . . . issues or problems you can think of?"

"As far as I know they were normal," Ben replied. "A little too strict with Charlie, but okay, I guess. Originally from back east somewhere, New York, I think. Been out here for like twenty years. Since Charlie was a baby."

"Yeah," Becka agreed, "they were way too strict. Charlie complained a lot about their control over him, but he loved them. They always made decisions for him, always pushed him to be successful. They were hard workers and probably wanted him to be the same. Charlie complained about their interference at times, but I think he really, deep down, liked the help."

"Some background is helpful," the doctor said. "I'll eventually obtain this information from Charlie, but as I said before, he isn't very cooperative right now."

Dr. Hernandez rested his elbows on the desk and steepled his hands, making a comfortable triangle shape with his arms, apparently deep in thought.

"Charlie's not talkin' to ya, huh?" Ben asked.

"He gets moody like that," Becka offered, "especially when he's mad. He either blows up or gets real quiet. So what's wrong with him? Why are you keeping him in the hospital?" The look of concern returned to her face.

"It's beyond a mood problem, Becka," the doctor said, clasping his hands. "To your knowledge, has Charlie ever taken drugs?"

"I can answer that doctor," Ben announced. "No. He doesn't take street drugs if that's what ya mean. He's not on any medications either. Hell, he's got a hard time drinkin' beers most of da time. If anything, I'd consider him a health nut, 'til recently. Last I saw him, though, it looked like he wasn't takin' care of himself too good. He'd been drinkin' a lot, for Charlie that is. I thought it was 'cause of his parents dyin' and stuff, loosin' his job. Ya know, depression."

"We thought he'd eventually get over it, grow out of his funk," Tammy said.

"Yeah," Becka agreed looking at the floor, "but it's taken longer than anyone imagined . . . or wanted."

Dr. Hernandez placed his hands flat on the desk. "It seems Charlie was acting like a jerk, depressed, and drinking too much for good reason. He's on the slow, long, slide into schizophrenia."

"What?" Becka almost shrieked. Her hand covered her open mouth again and shock drained her face into a pasty white.

"I knew it had to be somethin' like that," Ben said, "when he told me he was talkin' to his mom."

"When was this?" asked the doctor focusing on Ben.

"Oh, sh . . . crap," Ben said, correcting his slip of the tongue, "I mean, it was way back, da last time we played pool . . . maybe five, six months ago."

The doctor took notes.

"I told him he was crazy. Then with da pots piled in front of his doors and windows. I knew it! I knew it!" Ben said, bobbing his head and emphasizing with a clenched fist.

There was a quiet pause in the conversation as the doctor finished writing. The girls looked at Ben with creased foreheads and wide eyes.

"It's true," Ben assured them.

The doctor looked up, "When did the pots incident occur, Ben?"

"Don't know exactly . . . 'bout two months ago. Da last time I saw him."

"And what did Charlie say to you when you told him he was crazy?" the doctor asked, poised to write.

"Said he wasn't and then threatened me and shoved me out da door."

"You said he'd been drinking alcohol?"

"Yeah, there were empty beer cans all over his house. It was a mess. He looked like hell da last time I saw him."

"Alcohol, cigarettes, self-medication," Dr. Hernandez said, "all contribute to making a person with schizophrenia violent . . . that and failure to take anti-psychotic medication. Which is why I asked earlier if he took any drugs. Alcohol is a drug, so is nicotine."

"Oh, *that* kind of drug," acknowledged Ben. "He smokes, too . . . a lot."

"I've been busy with Charlie the last few days," the doctor continued, "performing an initial diagnostic workup, including lab tests and scans, in order to rule out other diseases that could be masquerading as schizophrenia. I had to be certain he doesn't have a brain tumor or encephalitis. According to test results, he doesn't. Schizophrenia, in its full-blown stages, isn't difficult to diagnose. Once I ruled out the other possibilities, I began treating him accordingly. You've confirmed that he was having auditory hallucinations, Ben—talking to his mother."

"Yeah, so he really talked to her?"

"No, not literally."

"I didn't think so," Ben said, a bit embarrassed. "Just testin' ya."

"As far as Charlie was concerned though, it was real. Delusional thinking and auditory hallucinations are among the most common symptoms. Most schizophrenics have one or the other. Various kinds of thinking disorders become evident, too."

An uneasy silence ensued. Becka broke the stillness with sobbing, which became louder despite her hand covering her mouth. Tammy reached over and pulled Becka close to her bosom. "Oh, Tammy," Becka said sniffling, her face blanched and strained, "what am I going to do?"

Tammy looked at Ben, as if to ask for help in answering the question, "Let's just take things one step at a time," she finally said, turning to Becka. "Listen to the doctor for now, okay?" Becka shrugged her shoulders.

"Schizophrenia," the doctor explained, accepting the lead from Tammy, "has a hereditary component—it runs in families—which is why I asked about his parents. In Charlie's case, I'm sure somewhere in his family tree we'd find someone with mental illness."

"Maybe that's why they moved out to Arizona from New York," Tammy said. "Maybe it was easier to leave than deal with mental illness problems."

"That happens often," said Dr. Hernandez. "Most people have little patience when it comes to mental illness. You yourselves stopped communicating with Charlie."

"That wasn't our decision," Ben said.

"I know," the doctor said, "but communication stops one way or another."

"So Charlie wasn't physically hurt from the accident?" asked Tammy.

"No, not seriously."

"So how are you going to help him?" Becka asked looking up with narrowed red eyes.

"Charlie will be treated with psychological counseling, drug therapy, and continued tests and monitoring. It's a condition caused by a chemical imbalance in the brain. I've had Charlie on a drug called Clozapine for the last two days. It's the most important treatment I can prescribe. Unfortunately, it only treats or controls the hallucinations of schizophrenia. It will not cure the disease."

"What's it called again?" Ben inquired.

"Clozapine. It's an anti-psychotic drug, a sort of tranquilizer. In my opinion, the only drug that's effective against the negative symptoms of the disease. About ten percent of patients show dramatic improvement without major negative side effects. It effectively treats delusions and aids in suppressing hostile and violent outbursts. While he's on the drug, he can't have caffeine. Caffeine will cause problematical chemical changes."

"You said there are side effects. What are they?" asked Becka.

"You may notice it causes excessive salivation, which is temporary. It has the effect of a sedative—drowsiness. It may cause a decrease in white blood cells and possible cardiac problems in the first month, both of which will have to be closely monitored. Seizures, urinary incontinence, weight gain, increased blood sugar all can be negative reactions to the drug. So, Charlie will be here in the hospital for at least two months."

"Two months!" Becka and Ben exclaimed, together.

"Oh, God! How long before he's well?" Becka asked, as tears again welled up in her eyes.

"Charlie will be ill for a long time to come. Schizophrenia is a chronic disorder. We can only treat the symptoms. Our present view is one of guarded optimism. Possibly twenty-five percent of all patients on medication recover enough to live relatively normal lives again with no symptoms. Maybe ten percent remain severely psychotic. The rest fluctuate between severe psychotic episodes and relative phases of recovery. If Charlie is lucky, he'll be in the recovered twenty-five percent."

Ben noticed the girls had shock etched into their faces. They did not appear to be considering the twenty-five-percentile group.

"Oh, no, no, no," Becka said. "This can't be happening." She leaned over to Tammy and in a low tone of voice said, "I . . . I can't deal with this. I'm so . . . confused. What am I supposed to do?"

"What do you mean?" Tammy asked in a matching low tone of voice.

"Tammy," Becka said, tears streaming down her cheeks, "I love him, but . . . but if he's going to be sick for the rest of his life . . . what kind of life will I have? I don't know if I can do this." Tammy had no answer.

An oppressive quiet prevailed. Ben looked at the doctor.

"After about five years," the doctor said, "the psychosis does not progress any further. Instead, it tends to reverse itself and improves over time. The disease, sort of matures."

"Oh, great," Becka said wiping her cheeks dry. Her voice became steady and bold. "Then I have a mature psychotic to deal with for the rest of my life! And what about children? 'It runs in families,' you said," she pointed to the doctor. "I might have to live with more than one if we have kids." Becka's face hardened as she tossed Tammy a piercing stare. "I . . . I can't do this Tammy."

Instead of answering Becka, Tammy asked the doctor, "What about it? Will Charlie be a major burden for her? Will she have kids that are also psychotic? Is there any hope?"

"Well," the doctor said after a long deliberation, "we hope he responds to the medication, begins to function normally again, and will be one of the lucky twenty-five-percent. At first, he'll go home under constant supervision, taking his meds, and slowly returning to society. This is where you," the doctor pointed his hand at Charlie's friends, "will be of great importance to him. Whether he will be a burden depends upon your attitude. As far as children are concerned, the possibility exists they may be affected, but it can skip generations. Many people lead happy lives full of love without having children. Again, it's a matter of attitude."

"Could he have relapses?" asked Ben.

"Only if he stops taking his meds. Sometimes patients think they're cured and no longer need the pills so they stop. In Charlie's case, as a paranoid schizophrenic, that would be dangerous because he could commit a crime he believes to be in self-defense."

"So, if he gets better and reacts okay to da drugs, when does he get to go home?" Ben asked.

"When I'm sure he's responding to the medication and it's working well, with no serious side effects and he's not a danger to himself or others. Back in the day, mental illness was cause for people to be locked up indefinitely and forgotten. Now, with insurance industry pressures and government regulations, it seems everyone has a right to be psychotic, so long as they're no threat to themselves or anyone else."

Becka asked with some hesitation, "Can we . . . see him doctor?" It seemed the hardness visible a few minutes ago had disappeared along with the tears.

"Yes," he answered, "but there are rules regarding visits: Only one person at a time per day for five minutes, plus, you'll be searched. Keep in mind; he has just begun drug therapy so he may be tired, but I think he should see a familiar face. I'm concerned about his emotional state right now and too many people at once might overload his senses."

They all waited for the doctor to continue.

He finally asked, "So who wants to go first?"

*   *   *

Becka stopped at the doorway, collecting herself in preparation for her initial meeting with Charlie. Months had passed since she last saw her boyfriend. Clammy fingers twisted the engagement ring. She was nervous, like the first time she went on a date with Charlie to see *King Kong* back in 2002. The movie was her idea;

Charlie picked the feature. She recalled her date back then as she made her way over to Charlie. The flowers he brought showed thoughtfulness, but the clothes he wore, shorts and a T-shirt, didn't match her sundress.

Some things haven't changed.

Today, she wore a full-length, flower print from Ross and Charlie sat slumped in a chair by a bed in pajamas covered by a white institutional robe, displaying bed-head hair. The beard took her by surprise. She had never seen him with a beard before. She thought it looked grubby. Charlie's sleepy eyes with a hint of concentration greeted her big, nervous smile.

"Hello, Charlie," she said, when she arrived at his chair. "How're you feeling?"

Becka stretched out her hand and began stroking his hair into a more familiar arrangement. Charlie reached out and touched Becka's waist. She turned toward the door to see if Dr. Hernandez was watching their meeting. The doctor flashed a thumb up and closed the door leaving them alone. She slid the empty chair closer to Charlie and sat down in front of him.

"Oh, Charlie," she said, with a searching gaze into his hazel eyes, "I've missed you so much." Tears began to well in her eyes. She lifted Charlie's limp hand in hers and rubbed his fingers. "What's happened to you, Honey? Are you okay?"

"Becka?" Charlie asked squinting then rubbing his eyes with his free hand. "Is it . . . really you? You're not a dream, are you?"

"Oh, yes, Charlie. It's me. It's me," she said and leaned forward to wrap him in a long embrace. Charlie raised his arms to hold her and she felt strength return to them the longer they embraced. The overwhelming joy she felt at that moment could no longer be contained. She began to cry. Her chest heaved as she wailed, tears of happiness shed in a torrent. Heat warmed her entire body as her love returned at last with increasing vitality. The more Charlie squeezed the more Becka, with loving intensity, returned it. She held him so tight she thought she might hurt him. His arms felt good around her. Maybe this problem was not as bad as she was lead to believe. What was that stupid doctor talking about anyway? He's not even drooling.

When her emotional upheaval finally subsided, she pulled back, her hands still holding him by the shoulders. Charlie seemed reluctant to release. Streams of tears ran down his cheeks. Witnessing this, her joy returned in a rush. Kisses followed. A once lost bond of love, sympathy, and unrestrained happiness returned, surrounded her, held her in ecstasy. She thought pleasure of this magnitude far exceeded anything she had ever felt before. Sexual passion and fantasies followed. She wished she could do him right now. She thought that would cure him of the disease, shake him mentally as well as physically. But they were being watched. The idea was pure imagination.

Time passed far too quickly for Becka. Near the end of the allotted five minutes, she said, "Charlie, I need to tell you something . . . something very important."

"I'm listening," Charlie said, with a hint of the weary but still interested student displayed on his face.

"You have a psychological disorder."

"What? No I d–"

"Stop it, Charlie. You do, schizophrenia," she said with authority and then, in a whisper so nobody but Charlie would hear, "It's why you're in here. And the doctor will keep you here as long as it takes for you to get your act together." She raised her voice to a normal speaking level, "So wake up and start acting right. You've got to get out of this hospital. If you don't get better, your spirit will die in here. Look at yourself. Stop acting like a jerk and get well. I need you. We all need you."

"But—"

"You need to fight this disease, Charlie. Twenty-five percent of the people that have your disorder get well. You can do it, Honey. The drug the doctor has you on will help you get back. Try to overcome the hallucinations and anger and . . . and, the delusions."

Charlie tried to turn his head away. Becka grabbed his chin and forced him to look at her. "Talk to the doctor and show him you're well. Do you hear me, Charlie? Show them you're well."

She waited for Charlie to respond. "Stop the silent treatment crap. Talk. Give them the information they need so they can help you. Then come back to me when you get out. Understand?" She hoped she was being forceful enough to get through, but not enough to have a negative effect.

So this is how his mother must have felt all those years. Good ole, Mrs. McShane. She felt like she was performing on the balance beam trying to get the judge's approval. She wondered if this was how it would be from now on: Work just to get through.

"I'll talk to the doctor . . . show him I'm well," Charlie finally said with confidence, as he sat up in his chair and took a deep breath.

Becka saw a distant but unmistakable twinkle in Charlie's eyes that she took to be determination. She hoped it was. A shiver of excitement ran up her spine as she watched a small smile appear on Charlie's face.

"Our time is almost up, Charlie. I've got to go now."

"Becka?"

"Yes, Charlie?"

"My doctor . . . what do you think of him?"

"He seems nice, Charlie. Why do you ask?"

"What's his name?"

"Hernandez. His name is Dr. Hugo Hernandez."

"He's Mexican. Isn't he?"

"Yes, Charlie, he's Mexican," Becka confirmed. "Even so, I think he'll take good care of you."

"Maybe," Charlie said. "You know, Becka, I'm happy to see you. I really am. And I'm sorry for . . . for not answering your calls. I was busy."

"Oh, Charlie, there's no need to apologize. I love you, Sweetie." She gave him one last hug and a passionate kiss, then wiped the lipstick from his lips, and said, "Remember, Charlie, show them you're well."

Charlie stared down to the floor.

"Charlie? Charlie!"

Charlie snapped to and said, "Yes, yes, Becka, I love you, too. Don't worry, I'll show him I'm well. You can count on it. 'Cause . . . ah . . ." a big grin grew across his face, "I really do need to get back to work."

The End

AUTHOR'S NOTES

Research for this book involved numerous works on two major subjects: Schizophrenia and illegal Mexican immigration. Two important works for each subject stood out as indispensable in the completion of *The Silent War*.

The first, concerning the subject of schizophrenia, was written by E. Fuller Torrey called *Surviving Schizophrenia*. It provided the entire spectrum of medical, clinical, and behavioral answers needed to delve into the mind of a psychotic. If this subject is of interest to you, I strongly point you in the direction of this book. It provides an unparalleled view into the inner world of madness.

The facts concerning schizophrenia and the affects upon society are as frightening to the layman as the disease is to the suffering individual. Well over two million Americans are affected by the disease or eight out of a thousand people in any given year. The sobering aspect of these numbers is the fact that forty percent of those suffering are *not* receiving treatment—that's roughly one million individuals. They are the homeless living on the streets and in shelters, those in jails and prisons who have committed crimes of violence, as well as those increasingly becoming the victim of crimes, and those who are sheepishly reported by embarrassed relatives to be on sabbatical, or have moved away to be with a distant aunt nobody seems to remember, or occupy a singularly ignored corner of a psych ward.

The problem is grossly underestimated and services for these sick individuals are inadequate. The problem in America is getting worse and expensive. The total direct and indirect costs of this disease in America in the year 2000 exceeded forty billion dollars—more than the budgets of the National Institutes of Health and the VA medical systems combined or 2% of the GNP. The cost to American taxpayers is recognized and felt as disability and social security payments, which contribute enormously to the increasing costs of medical insurance and health care.

The second valuable treatment of the subject of schizophrenia is *Schizophrenia: What It Means To The Family*. It represents a wealth of information about the disease brought down to the family level, describing how individuals within families are personally and emotionally moved. The book attempts to address the issue by encouraging a grass roots change beginning with affected families and making the case known to the general population by the media.

The disease is insidious and needs to be brought to light. Most react to those suffering schizophrenia with an attitude of embarrassment and attempted cover-up. The problem is swept under the carpet, like dirt. This is an ineffective method of dealing with the problem because the dirt is still there and nobody can effectively clean the mess if the mess is unseen. The book makes a case for major change in attitude at the family level.

Two books concerning illegal immigration whose pages were well worn from use are: *Coyotes* by Ted Conover and *The Devil's Highway—A True Story* by Luis Alberto Urrea. The first covers the subject from the author's own involvement in making the border crossing with Mexican immigrants. In a hands-on approach, he relates the experience of living conditions beginning in rural Mexico, then crosses the border and continues to travel with the illegal and undocumented Mexicans throughout this country documenting how American laws are broken.

The second book is more concerned with the U.S. border policy and the problems associated with the political boundary that manages to scramble the basic humanity of everyone associated and affected by it. The story follows the unfortunate incident of the so called "Yuma 14"—an ill fated illegal crossing that involved careless mistakes by coyotes and cost the lives of fourteen Mexicans who became lost in the crossing attempt following their inept guide who was to blame for the disaster.

These books describe the real stories behind the events—the motivations, the business, and the tragedy of the entire border calamity. Living in Arizona and dealing with some Mexican workers, I have had numerous opportunities to come into contact with illegal immigrants who are already here—working—not talking. It seemed to be a taboo subject when brought up and, suddenly, their command of the English language escapes them as they find ways to leave the interview by whatever means at their disposal. I had a growing desire, on a personal level of my own, to find out the answers to questions regarding the crossings. Books at the library were my only source for information on the subject that enabled me to write this book.